KU-498-557

Maggie
FORD
Affairs of the Heart

 CANELO

First published in Great Britain in 2001 by Severn House Publishers LTD

This edition published in the United Kingdom in 2022 by

Canelo
Unit 9, 5th Floor
Cargo Works, 1–2 Hatfields
London, SE1 9PG
United Kingdom

Copyright © Maggie Ford 2001

The moral right of Maggie Ford to be identified as the creator of this work has been asserted in accordance with the Copyright, Designs and Patents Act, 1988.

All rights reserved. No part of this publication may be reproduced or transmitted in any form or by any means, electronic or mechanical, including photocopy, recording, or any information storage and retrieval system, without permission in writing from the publisher.

A CIP catalogue record for this book is available from the British Library.

Print ISBN 978 1 80032 802 0
Ebook ISBN 978 1 80032 439 8

This book is a work of fiction. Names, characters, businesses, organizations, places and events are either the product of the author's imagination or are used fictitiously. Any resemblance to actual persons, living or dead, events or locales is entirely coincidental.

Originally published as *Autumn Skies* by Elizabeth Lord

Look for more great books at www.canelo.co

Printed and bound in Great Britain by Clays Ltd, Elcograf S.p.A.

For my daughter, Clare, who suggested the idea for this series

One

In the crowded pub, William Goodridge let his thoughts wander. Several days since his friend Henry Lett had passed peacefully away in his sleep. For a man who had achieved so much in life, perhaps a good way to go.

Now Goodridge sat across the pub table from the man's nephew, Edwin. He had been so engrossed telling the young man the history of Letts, once one of the best restaurants in London, that he wasn't quite sure what had been said aloud and what had been merely in his mind.

At the moment he was thinking of Mary, who'd married Geoffrey, the younger of the two Lett brothers. Everyone had loved her. He too. Over the years he'd come to admire her resilience despite all that the brothers had done to her – perhaps unwittingly, he gave them that much.

Geoffrey, the more wayward, had never stopped to think what his natural selfishness had done to her. As for Henry, he'd harboured the best of intentions towards her, yet in his way he had harmed her too – something of which to his dying day, Goodridge suspected, he also had not been aware. He couldn't condemn Henry any more than blame Geoffrey for his thoughtlessness.

But Mary had always reminded him of a butterfly at the mercy of the elements. When summer fades and autumn takes over, some butterflies will succumb to the cold. But others who can hibernate can rise again for all their apparent frailty. Mary had been one of those. He'd tried to protect her through the cold times, though he now wondered if that protection had been of any use, for it occurred to him in this pub, talking to Henry Lett's nephew, that she'd proved herself to be made of stronger stuff than he'd first believed – even though it had taken her years to recover from the death of Marianne.

He remembered Henry telling him of his grief when Mary's baby had died of diphtheria. Boxing Day 1924 – a long time ago. It was now 1953 and Henry himself was dead, heart attack, a few days back.

"Henry and your father Geoffrey were good men in their way," he said to young Edwin above the din of the lunchtime pub. "Over the years your uncle and I grew to be the best of friends. And Letts was his whole life. Even more so after your father was killed in that air raid."

He took a swig of his drink. It was going to be hard explaining how deep their association had really gone. Without it how could he get Edwin, with his considerable inheritance, to consider buying out his uncle's second wife? The restaurant had been in the Lett family for generations, yet Henry's widow, now holder of the majority share though with little interest in it other than what it would fetch by being sold to an interested restaurant chain, was busily persuading the family to sell their shares too, leaving her free to take her money and run, proving herself the grasping woman she was.

If he could entice Edwin to take on the restaurant, all that Henry Lett had worked for would remain. The man deserved that. Despite all that had happened between them in the past, Henry's death had hit Will hard.

"I'd like to see Letts continue, Edwin," he said, gazing into his half-empty glass on the polished pub table. "Your uncle and I were very close."

More than close. Indeed, Henry had taken him into his confidence far more than anyone. Not normally one to confide in people, he had shared his troubles openly with Will. And of course he would, there being so much more between them than mere friendship. Will's recollection of all Henry had entrusted to him was as clear today as if it had been yesterday. And he knew that the information Henry had shared with him was so confidential that he could never pass on much of it to the man's nephew, even to save Letts.

He remembered the way he would listen quietly as Henry let slip so many small personal details of his and the family's private lives, quite often without realising. Often it would be something deep and disturbing, other times little and ludicrous, such as his dislike of his family home. William's memory, as ever unimpaired, gauged that to have been told him around 1925...

–

To Henry, having spent so much of his time in London, Halstead Green was the Gobi Desert. So when his mother, having been alone for so long at Swift House since his father's death, entreated he make that his home after his marriage to Grace Chamberlain, his argument that he should remain in London to be near the business was a little desperate.

"And you're not alone, Mother. Victoria and Maud aren't all that far away." One sister lived within six miles of her, the other something like twenty miles away, and both then-husbands had cars.

"London's not Timbuktu," he went on. "I shall visit as I have always done – me and Grace together."

After all, she had plenty of local friends, church friends, her vicar, and Grace's parents still took her to church on Sundays. The church took up a large part of her time so she couldn't be that lonely. But she had a ready argument.

"There is no need for you to be so near the restaurant, Henry. Your brother is nearer to London and, wilful and thoughtless though he is, he is quite capable of keeping an eye on it and will merely have to toe the line a little more."

She would no longer mention Geoffrey by name if it could be helped, still disapproving of his marriage, behaving as if it had never been. She never spoke of Mary or referred to her in any way, vigorously turning her back if that name was spoken. She'd never forgiven Geoffrey his marriage to a "mere kitchen skivvy" who had eventually got herself promoted to the office, having proved herself good at figures.

4

Henry could see how the proud and stalwart matriarch, still full of old Victorian beliefs in good habits and respect for parents, felt. She had not been consulted or even pleaded with to be generous-hearted towards the woman with whom her son had fallen in love. As far as she was concerned he had married below himself and without her leave. That to Mother was near to sacrilege.

Geoffrey never came near the house these days, he in turn unable to forgive her, for even the death of his child hadn't dented the barrier she had put up between herself and him, making his loss all the more cruel and painful.

Henry too had almost broken with her over it and it had taken him a year to bring himself to speak to her with any filial love. Even now a small bitterness against her attitude would rise from time to time. He felt he would never truly forgive her her treatment of the grieving parents at a time they, especially her son, had most needed her comfort and understanding.

There had only been him to give Mary a shoulder to cry on, other than her husband, and Geoffrey had been too close to their shared loss to afford much comfort for anyone but himself, which was natural, Henry imagined. As for himself, he'd had to hide the love he felt for Mary and behave as a mere uncle, just far enough removed from the tragedy to see a little more clearly. That fact had maybe intensified his pain on their behalf, whereas they'd been in blessed shock, blessed in that the loss of a loved one will numb brain and body and for a while the more poignant sting of grief, that coming later as one is more able to cope – nature's way, he supposed. It had broken his heart hearing the way Mary had cried: long-drawn-out, shivering moans that drained her whole body as though crying had not been enough to fill the empty senselessness of Marianne's death. Yet in life, she had spent so much time away from her. Maybe it had been that awareness that had made her weeping so distraught.

Yes, there had been only him to put an arm about her and draw her to him, Geoffrey slumped in chairs, gazing at nothing, leaning forward at times to put his head in his hands, seldom an arm spared to put around her. Her old aunt had been no good. He had seen her at the funeral, chattering away as though it were a celebration of some sort, gone rather soft in the head – healthy enough but not seeing the world about her any more, still cared for by her neighbour who, needing to have someone to look after, he suspected, apparently found her no trouble. Everyone needed to have someone to care for and someone to care for them. Mother should have seen that but had closed her eyes to it. And now she wanted someone to care for her and Henry did not feel inclined to be that someone. He felt the old bitterness again, his heart going out to Mary every time he thought about her.

"It's often the done thing in good families," she had said, "to have a son and his bride taking up residence in a wing of the family mansion."

"This isn't a mansion, Mother," he'd pointed out as patiently as he could. "We don't have a separate *wing*." But he was talking to a brick wall.

"My dear, Swift House may not quite be a mansion but it is a sizeable home. If you're concerned that we might get under each other's feet, half the upper floor is totally self-contained. Your father had his offices there as you know. The attic has a perfectly spacious set of bright and airy rooms for a small family. I am rattling round in this place and not getting any younger. It would be nice to know you were at hand should I need you."

He hadn't really had an argument. His mother was a strong-willed woman, her stiff composure persuasive as any flood of tears from a weaker character, and he had finally given in with a heavy heart.

The problem with Swift House was that it lacked character, inspired him with no wish to live there. The grounds had once been lovely, but when Henry's father had died and the head gardener retired, his mother had lost all interest. An indifferent gardener now presided, and though he and his two assistants kept it tidy enough, they had no imagination.

The village was equally dull and uninspiring, the Norman church its only redeeming feature, the countryside drab, not even a low hill to break the flatness of the horizon, no babbling brooks to lose oneself by. The people were insular, unadventurous; a couple of fetes held each year, one by the tiny school and one by the church, a weekly social at the village hall to which the older generation went, the young taking the short bus ride into Halstead itself or the slightly longer one into Braintree for their enjoyment, dancing, swimming, sports. That was it.

Only two reasons had made him spend more time here than usual this last year, and the first was his mother's wish that he get to know Grace Chamberlain better – her father was a wealthy landowner and gentleman farmer who owned Dendle Hall, the other side of Halstead Green. The other was that he'd had to get Mary out of his mind and settle down. Marrying Grace was easier than being nagged by Mother, simpler than looking around for someone else.

Grace was beautiful, quiet, sedate, a fitting girl for a man of his type who'd never had any real longing for the endless round of pleasure Geoffrey enjoyed. She was suitable in every way. Very well, his heart didn't go pit-a-pat, but it was said that love built slowly out of respect for a person was far stronger and longer lasting than any of the wildly beating heart and pulsing blood kind of stuff. He hoped so and at least he felt comfortable with Grace.

Thus in the June of 1925 they became engaged, and in the autumn married in Halstead Green Church where his father lay, a huge reception following at Dendle Hall. Geoffrey and Mary didn't come, but sent a wedding present, a grandfather clock, assuming Henry and Grace would settle down to life in the country.

Henry had not settled. After honeymooning in Tuscany, he and Grace returned to Swift House. But he longed for London, felt stifled here. Though his mother didn't interfere, her presence cast an artificial light upon their married state, acted as a restriction to a free rein to run about should they fancy to, to laugh and play and act the fool – though Grace was a little too sedate to do much of that, taking what she saw as her wifely role rather too seriously. Even arguing (which they didn't, she being a placid soul) would mean being overheard by his mother and judged or even frowned upon.

Mother got on well with Grace. Two of a kind, apart from Grace being far more pliable, they shared an insistence on old-fashioned protocol and spent hours talking together, and though he knew Grace was in good hands – her own family were a mere step away so that she was never bored when he went to London once a week – he felt out of it, his longing for the bustling vitality of the place growing steadily deeper.

"I hate this travelling back and forth," he said to Grace as they lay side by side in the four-poster bed.

They'd made love, a restrained sort of love with Grace submitting herself quietly to his penetration of her – if that was what it could be called. She did not complain, merely submitted, not understanding that it was quite in order to participate in the joy of the thing even though he had told her she could let herself go if she wanted to. She had looked at him in bewilderment that first time.

"I don't know what you mean, darling."

"Well…" It had been awkward to describe. "The getting excited bit."

She had shaken her head, confused. "What do you want me to do?"

"Just – did you like it? Or did it upset you? I didn't hurt you, did I?"

"No." She had lain there afterwards, blinking at him. "Why should you have hurt me?"

9

He'd realised then that she hadn't brought her legs up to clasp him to her in order for him to go in deep; hadn't understood what was required of her, even that she should get the maximum enjoyment from it. With her legs flat on the bed, how could he have penetrated far enough to hurt her? He'd been gentle, resisted the temptation to take his fill of her, and she'd remained virtually virginal, her hymen broken only by degrees as he made love to her gradually over the following couple of weeks. No longer a virgin, the impression was nevertheless as if she remained untouched. To her this was a wifely duty to be given to the husband, his conjugal rights, and so long as she did that, she was fulfilling her duties, was content. She knew nothing, utterly innocent.

Had she been Mary… He could imagine Mary giving herself to him in ecstasy and abandonment—

Alarmed and ashamed by an uncontrollable hardening between his legs, he thrust the vision aside.

"Do you find it enjoyable?" he had asked. Grace's reply: "Well, it's what married couples are meant to do, isn't it – so that they can start a family?"

He'd given up. At least she didn't abandon herself for cries of joy to filter through the floor below to the disturbance of his mother. That was the trouble; Mother's presence curbed all that ought to come naturally.

"I detest leaving you to go into London," he said now, bringing his mind back to the matter in hand. "I've been wondering; if you came with me we could stay a few nights in the flat over the restaurant. Just us two."

"I've never lived in London," she mused, raising his hopes only to put them down again by adding, "I don't really think I would like it for too long. I prefer the country, the peace. London can be so noisy. I didn't enjoy it much when I was there two years ago as a débutante. I was presented at Buckingham Palace to Their Majesties, but the parties given for us were noisy and went on too late. The people all talked at once and no one listened. No one had any time for anyone but themselves, and I didn't understand half of what they said. Such absurd colloquialisms - 'utterly maddening, darling', or 'how too too divine', and 'simply marvellous', even stupid contradictions of speech – '*awfully* delightful' *or* '*awfully* nice'. It was so silly. I couldn't even begin to speak that way, Henry. I even heard some of the débutantes swearing out loud. Their behaviour was quite brittle. After seeing them so demure in their white gowns, curtsying to Their Majesties in that beautiful blue and gold Throne Room at Buckingham Palace, I can remember being quite shocked to see the way they behaved afterwards, at the parties held for them, and they supposedly hoping to attract a suitor."

Perhaps, Henry thought as he listened, her own attitude had been why *she* hadn't attracted a suitor, too prim and proper, frightening off any who approached her. There was a limit to demureness. But his purpose was to attract her to London. He needed so desperately to return there and never take up residence at Swift House ever again. Once he had Grace on his side it wouldn't be so hard to face Mother with his wish.

"If you come to London with me just for a day or two, my sweet?" he cajoled gently. "I miss you so much when I'm there alone. To please me?"

Pleasing him and making this a good marriage was her sole aim, and to his delight, he saw by the moonlight streaming in through the window her head move up and down on the pillow beside him in a nod of assent.

–

"Geoffrey, when can we start thinking of another baby?"

Geoffrey Lett threw Mary a peeved glance as he dressed for the party they were giving in honour of Mr Alan Cobham's spectacular first flight to and from the Cape in his seaplane. Any excuse for a party! But Alan Cobham had already been feted by several social climbers and Geoffrey Lett wasn't going to be missed out. It was important he kept in the swing of things, important socially and for business. The last thing he wanted at this moment was another fight with Mary over this baby question.

Lately all she ever did was mope and nag. Outside the flat none could be more lively. The "giddy flapper", the press were lately calling the young 1926 socialites, a term that had stuck. Mary's dresses were as short as any could be, revealing rouged knees and rolled-down stockings as she kicked up her heels. She seemed inexhaustible, the life and soul, drank cocktails until they came out of her ears, came home finally exhausted and tipsy to fall into bed. If he'd wanted to make love it would have been useless.

In private she had became a bore, constantly crying, constantly nagging, pleading.

He ignored this present plea and went on with his dressing. He would snap her out of it in a minute by getting her to help him tie his tie. She was practically ready except for a second touch of make-up, but looked about as keen for this important party as a murderer for the gallows.

Nearly eighteen months since they'd lost Marianne – yes, it was taking time to get over it for her, and for him. As her father, he had suffered the loss as much as anyone possibly could, and he knew how poignantly Mary had grieved. She had been like death for months afterwards until he'd grown fearful for her sanity. She had come out of it to some extent but was no longer the girl he'd married. He'd done his level best to help her over it, but one couldn't go on grieving forever. By now she should have put it behind her. But daily she spoke of the baby, any little thing bringing it to the fore again: any event, happy or sad, silly things – last April when Eros was removed during the construction of Piccadilly Circus Underground station: "It's like losing a baby, seeing it taken away." And when October brought the successful launch of an aeroplane from the powerful R33 airship: "Such great leaps and bounds in science – Marianne will never see it, will she?" In November, with the death of Queen Alexandra, the Queen Mother, Mary had stood with him watching her funeral through the snow-covered streets, sobbing openly and saying: "I know just what it's like to lose someone dear to one." No matter that Queen Alexandra was an old lady.

This year it had become worse. The Duchess of York's first child, due sometime in April, had brought on several fits of copious tears and renewed begging to have another baby. "I want us to be a family again, Geoffrey. If royalty can have babies, why can't we?"

They would have another baby. Mary wanted it soon, but he needed time. They'd had a good life together before Marianne had been born, and could have again. But he had come to realise the stress of being a parent and the way it changed a marriage. His brain could not get itself around the emotional upheaval of having another baby just yet, and constantly worrying about its survival after losing their first one. Mary was bad enough now. How would she be if it happened again? How would he cope?

In any case, when Marianne was alive Mary had been much more interested in her own pleasures than in her baby, so why this obsession for another one? Didn't she realise that it was spoiling their social life together and making his life a misery? He was getting tired of it.

She was putting on long pearl pendant earrings and a double row of natural pearls that dangled almost to her waist. He paused to watch her. She'd had her hair restyled in a shingle which made her look fashionably boyish but which otherwise was delightfully feminine. A wealth of bangles on her wrists and bare upper arms completed the silver and gold dress by Vionnet, those deep handkerchief points giving it a dramatically uneven hemline.

He emerged from the dressing-closet to stand behind her, his hands on her bare shoulders. "Are you nearly ready, darling?"

She looked up at him and smiled. "Nearly."

She didn't feel like smiling. She felt tired. At this very minute her one desire was to undress and go to bed to lie there and think of Marianne. Yet letting Geoffrey down was unthinkable. The party had cost so much to put on, how could she refuse to appear?

"Guests'll be arriving any minute."

All was ready in the reception room, a beautiful room done out in art deco style. They hadn't relied on their cook or the maid for this party, giving them the evening off and using an agency instead. More reliable, Geoffrey had said. He spared no expense in trying to make their social life exciting, like it had been before losing Marianne. Almost as though trying to pluck that loss from his mind.

Of course he felt the loss of their baby, deeply, though not as deeply as she did. She was a mother, it had devastated her, and despite what he told her it would take more than eighteen months to get over the loss of a child. It might take a lifetime and still never happen completely. And there was guilt too. If only she'd given more time to her when she was alive... But there had been so much excitement, Geoffrey bent on taking her here, there and everywhere, that she hadn't stopped to think of morbid things like Marianne's time on earth being so short. Why should she? Who could have predicted that a healthy, happy little girl would be suddenly plucked from her by diphtheria?

Geoffrey was trying his best to buck her up, but men didn't feel these things as a woman did. She couldn't blame him for his impatience towards her. But for him, she wouldn't be here getting ready for a fabulous party costing the earth, wouldn't be wearing a Vionnet dress and dripping with jewellery. He had married her because she had refused to get rid of his child. He had been selfless in that. He had flown in the face of his own mother's sense of class snobbery to marry her, a girl without a penny, because he had loved her. He still did, despite the fact that her continuing grief over Marianne must irk him sometimes. For the sake of their marriage she knew she must learn to face up to things, but it was so hard.

"You go on ahead, Geoffrey," she said, managing a stiff little smile which she hoped would convince him that she was all right. "I'll be there in a little while."

Geoffrey sighed and took his hands off her shoulders. It was hard on her, he knew. But it was hard on him too. He tried to ignore the small, cruel voice that echoed in his head, *Here we go again*, as Mary turned her face from him to peer once more in the mirror, at the same time picking up a smouldering cigarette in its holder from the cut-glass ashtray. She smoked far too much. Sign of a disturbed mind? Drank too much as well. Hiding a yearning for something other than what she had? But she had *everything*. An exciting social life, a wonderful lifestyle; she only had to ask and he provided

– clothes, perfume, parties, the theatre, holidays abroad. What more did she want? She wanted another baby. Well, he didn't. Maybe in time, but not yet. How would his reluctance to be a father affect another child? Were it to sense itself to be a barrier to his social life, it would surely end up bewildered and unhappy and not knowing why.

In this frame of mind it was best to ignore Mary's pleas for another child, at least for the time being.

"Don't be long, then," he told her sharply and went down to meet the first of his distinguished guests already being ushered in, and, as often happened, make apologies for Mary not being at his side to greet them.

–

The General Strike had clinched it. Unable to get to and from London repeatedly by car – the garages were without deliveries of petrol – and certainly not by train, Henry all but grabbed Grace by the hand and drove there with what he had in the tank. There they remained the full nine days of the national strike. It worked. By the twelfth of May things were back to normal despite the miners, in support of whom it had all been about and who were dragging it on alone, and Grace had become a little more used to London, happy to stay a little while longer.

"It's not so bad here," she remarked in the quietness of their sunlit sitting-room above the hubbub of Piccadilly traffic. "It's quite cosy too. It's not as large as I expected it to be. It really feels quite comfortable." Used to spacious rooms and echoing passages, it was still a novelty to her. "London doesn't seem the same as I remembered it."

Up here, secluded from the social excitement that had been her unfortunate initiation her first time round, she sank into the deep armchairs or put her feet up on to the sofa and would read fashion magazines while he spent his time in the restaurant taking up where he'd left off. He discovered that in all that time Geoffrey had put in few appearances, preferring his social lifestyle to keeping in touch with the administrative staff or discussing catering finances with the head chef and keeping in with their more important customers.

"The place has gone to pot," he accused Geoffrey during one of his rare appearances. "I find you've been taking time off without a word to anyone or making appropriate arrangements for those in charge to carry on."

"And what about you?" came the retort. "You haven't been in for weeks." But he was seething, seeing the state of the situation.

"I've been on honeymoon, and keeping Mother happy. I thought the place had been left in good hands. Apparently it hasn't. Though I see by the books that you're ready enough to help yourself to your share in the profits and, I suspect, already spending it living beyond your means, as always." No sooner had Geoffrey shown his face that day at the beginning of June than he was hinting of a need for a "small advance". Small? A couple of thousand — enough, he'd suggested, to keep his bank balance respectable and tide him over until the next quarter.

"How is your bank balance, then?" Henry challenged.

His brother gave an easy shrug. "Still have a few thou in it, but I've some bills to pay."

"Hefty no doubt."

"Slightly."

He would have like to say "hard luck", but despite Geoffrey's lack of supervision, Letts was thriving under the management of his senior staff, exquisite menus from Sampson, the stem supervision of his restaurant manager, and unerring dedication of station head waiters like Goodridge. He had chosen his staff well, even though his restaurant manager was ever full of moans and complaints.

With the word "slightly", Geoffrey's tone had become sharp and challenging and, loath to aggravate what threatened to turn into a heated moment, Henry changed the subject.

"How is Mary?" he asked inanely, leaning on the gleaming brass and dark oak railing of the balcony on which they both stood to gaze down over the dining area, the waiters already busy serving morning coffee.

In a way it was just as well that Mary hadn't come here with Geoffrey. "Being fitted for an outfit," he had said. "For Ascot. Can't be seen in any old thing. Fashions change so fast these days." *And no doubt costing you a fortune*, Henry had mused, but had put aside an urge to give tongue to the thought.

So long since he had seen her. The last time, several months after the loss of Marianne, she had looked so sad, as though she wore her sadness as a second coat over her finery. And so thin. Thinness was the fashion, some people swearing that girls were starving themselves, smoking too much and drinking alcohol, even taking drugs to keep themselves waiflike, that they would all end up consumptive. Mary had always been naturally thin, had hardly gained any weight since the first time she'd come to the kitchen door of the restaurant begging for work and had later been shown to him. It felt to him another life that day he'd seen her and been taken by such prettiness for all the pinched paleness of her cheeks. She had come a long way since then.

"She's fine," Geoffrey was saying, his reply betraying obvious relief that the awkard moment between them had passed.

Together the two brothers made their way down the narrow, curving stairs from the balcony to the dining area to be immediately greeted by customers whom they knew and who knew them. It made for good relations and ultimately for good business for the two brothers to be seen together.

"Don't see much of her these days," Henry remarked as, after greeting several people, they went up by the wider, more ornate stairs to the bar where tonight people would crowd on to the small circular dance floor to jazz the night away, without doubt taking in the new dance that was all the rage, the Charleston. Saturday night, a late night. Geoffrey was going on somewhere else with Mary. He himself would stay until midnight, then go upstairs to Grace and the peace she brought him. But he would have given anything to have set eyes on Mary, even though it would have destroyed his heart a little to see her. Just as well that he hadn't.

Two

Downstairs the party was still going on. Mr Noel Coward was entertaining guests, including several girls from Charles Cochrane's current revue – "Mr Cochrane's Young Ladies" as they were known. Crowded into Letts' cocktail bar at one in the morning, full of champagne, excited by jazz music and ogling young men, their behaviour was far from ladylike. Perched on bar stools, slim legs crossed at the knees with skirts up almost to their thighs, or leaning casually against them, handbags dangling limply from bangled wrists, hats rammed down over their ears so that not a single shingled hair of their head could be seen to say if they were dark or fair, they vied with the men in making themselves heard above the four-piece jazz band. Their conversation rapid, their laughter excitable, their wisecracks brittle, they squealed and smoked and drank Manhattans and Sidecars.

Henry yawned as he made his way up to his apartment, having finally said goodnight and left the party in the capable hands of his waiting staff, now weary, though none of them would dare show it lest they lose out on the generous tips that would inevitably be issued when the party eventually broke up. The kitchen staff had gone home long ago. Of course the longer the party went on the more money would be spent, but one could take only so much and he was tired too.

Geoffrey would have stayed on, keeping the money for drinks rolling in, but Geoffrey was in the South of France, he and Mary having fun in the casinos, probably losing most of that advance he'd wheedled out of him if Henry knew anything about Geoffrey. If he won, it would go just the same. There seemed no way to stop his spending, as though he saw Letts as a bottomless well. "Just a small advance," he'd pressured, not letting on that he planned to take Mary off to Monte Carlo with it.

Thinking back, Henry felt annoyed at not seeing through Geoffrey's look of having the world's debt on his back. Had he been more astute he'd have told him to take a running jump, but his thoughts had flown to Mary. How could he deny her? He still saw her as grieving for her daughter, for all it had been a year and a half since losing her. To his mind her need for high living was Mary's only way of smothering her grief.

Geoffrey had thanked him profusely, and gone happily off to enjoy himself. He took Letts too lightly, seeing in Henry's idea of expanding the business merely another source of more money for his own pleasure.

For a long time Henry had been playing with the idea of a second restaurant in London. Not so much to make more money as to bring more prestige to the business. A restaurant always full to capacity wasn't as good for business as one would think, with advance bookings having to be turned away. A second restaurant with the same high-class service and cuisine would compensate for that. But it needed careful thought. Finance.

Geoffrey was all for it, the bank and their accountant less so, pursing lips and cautiously announcing that though thriving, it was doubtful if the business could bear the cost of procuring second premises. In the manner of all financial people, they advised not to jump without a long, hard consideration of the consequence should the outlay fall short. It would take a long time to recoup, they predicted, even if the second restaurant was successful.

They spoke of hidden snags, unforseen circumstances, higher fees than expected from surveyors, decorators or possibly even builders of these as yet unfound premises, as well as a host of other pitfalls. It all sounded so negative. The other solution was to float a company to raise what was needed, but that too had its problems, stated the bank. It sounded fine when said fast. But who was going to sink their cash into a premises not even up and running? It needed great faith on an investor's part. No, it wouldn't be wise to go in with both feet at this moment in time.

Then there was Mother, with the controlling share of the business. Mother hadn't been happy.

"Go public? You mean float shares on the stock market? Have it go out of the family, on a whim? I cannot allow you to take such chances with what your father has built up so carefully." She had spoken as though his father still held sway over it all. "He and your grandfather were quite happy with what they had, Henry. Why can't you be?"

His argument that the first of the family to have started Letts had possessed foresight and imagination and courage enough to turn a stall into an oyster bar and then a thriving restaurant, and that all he wanted was to carry it that one step further, moved her not one inch.

"It's that brother of yours pushing you on this. It sounds like him - wanting to be provided with a few more pounds to fritter away. If he had his way he would already have his hands in the trust your father left for both of you and your sisters. I wonder he hasn't suggested you using that for this ridiculous proposition."

He had felt annoyed. Even Geoffrey with his need of money would not cast an avid eye on that. One hundred and fifty thousand pounds, their nest egg, not to be squandered on some madcap expansion idea that might prove unsuccessful, as the bank had intimated it very well could. If Letts ever failed, though he couldn't imagine that happening, that trust would be the family's insurance against total bankruptcy; would help to start up the business anew. No, that must never be touched and Mother should have had better sense than even refer to it.

"Money flows through his fingers like water," she'd added. "No doubt all going on that woman – that gold digger – alienating him against me. As to your idea of another restaurant, Henry, too much ambition is not good for one and I would prefer you to let it lie. For my sake. I feel I am too old to be worried by so much ambition." The two of them, mother and son, had put forth their opinions – one all for it, the other against, each of them for the wrong reasons. Thus for the time being he had shelved it, to Mother's relief and Geoffrey's disappointment.

No point dwelling on it now and getting upset. He let himself quietly into his apartment, and after a stiff nightcap just as quietly let himself into the bedroom.

Grace stirred as he closed the door gently, almost no sound of the revelry below penetrating the flat. They could have been buried away in the country for what sounds of London filtered up to them beyond a faint buzz.

"Sorry, my sweet," he whispered as though she were asleep still. "Did I disturb you?"

"What's the time?"

"Around one o'clock."

She rolled over and opened her eyes to look at him. "I do wish you wouldn't stay at those parties so late. I've been waiting such a long time for you to come up."

A small twinge of irritation took hold of him. "I can't just leave, my dear. I need to be seen. Customers look for me. It's part of the business."

"Geoffrey ought to be doing much more," she complained. "He leaves so much of it to you most of the time."

"Yes, I know." He tried not to make his tone sharp, but reference to Geoffrey skiving off always made him so. "But he's away."

She sat up slowly, sleepily. "Yes… again. It would be so nice if we could get away occasionally. He and Mary are always off somewhere."

Henry gave a brittle laugh as he struggled out of his evening jacket and undid his bow tie. "Someone has to stay and earn the money."

"Yes. Well, why always you, darling? I feel so tense left up here all on my own. Why can't *we* have a holiday where we could relax?"

Tense. The word hit him. Yes, she was tense, had been from the first day of their marriage. Here in the peace of this apartment she had unwound for a while. Their love life had improved. But just lately tension had crept back into their sexual relationship. Maybe it was his having to keep late nights. Geoffrey would have to pull his weight a little more if this marriage was to succeed. She spoke of missing the country, complained, if mildly, at these late nights he had to spend working. If they could have a little holiday… It came to him that this was what she needed, what they both needed. France, maybe – the Loire Valley would be nice, its gentle rolling vistas with the quiet Loire running softly through it just right for her. Perhaps there she would relax.

–

The Loire Valley did more for them both than he had hoped. It was while they were in the Loire Valley that Grace conceived.

"Henry, I think I might be pregnant." Her face was so filled with brightness, lighting up the dull October midday as though the sun had suddenly broken through, that for a moment he looked at her, stunned. Then, galvanised into action, he dropped the jacket he was putting on and bounded across the room to clasp her to him in joy, swinging her around.

Just as suddenly, realising her delicate condition, he let her feet back down on to the Indian carpet, and held her away from him, his face working with consternation of what harm he might have done her. Grace laughed.

"Darling, I'm not fragile. I'm only having a baby." Her blue eyes grew dreamy, loving, adoring. "Your baby, my darling. Our baby."

His heart beating heavily and rapidly with the joy of her news, he felt a little sick, but it wasn't unpleasant. There were little knots in his stomach but they too were not uncomfortable. He had a wild impulse to rush down to the restaurant, which at lunchtime would be overflowing with customers, and scare the life out of everyone by bellowing that he was to be a father.

He did go down, but with a little more decorum, after he and Grace had broken open a bottle of champagne which he had ordered be brought up. He announced the news to the Milton sisters, Dilys and Dolly, the beautiful singing twins who, along with having voices like angels on stage, had the gift of the gab off it. Two pairs of light grey eyes sparkled beneath the plucked eyebrows and deep cloche hats. Like wildfire, his news went from table to table. Before he knew it he was standing at one end of the restaurant, the entire staff on duty, from the *maitre d'* to the youngest *commis*, the *chef de cuisine* to humblest scullery boy, seeming to come out of the woodwork to gather in a half-circle behind him, the whole restaurant on its feet, wine glasses raised in his direction, while the walls and mirrors echoed to the clink of cutlery against crockery in salute, finally in one voice singing, "For he's a jolly good fellow…"

Henry felt there could never be a man more proud than he at that moment. Though that wasn't quite correct. When the baby arrived next May he'd be even prouder. No one and nothing would be able to touch him. He'd make Letts the most visited, the most talked about, the most envied place in London – the place to be and be seen at. He would seriously consider that second restaurant, or else make this one larger. Which of the two he wasn't sure, but one thing was certain; his child, his son, would have the very best that money could afford and that meant enlarging the business. Meantime he would be content, put behind him that one thing he had once hankered after, the woman he could not have, and concentrate on quiet, placid Grace, the mother of his child.

This he stubbornly told himself, resolve melting only when Mary put in an appearance. Then he would admonish himself for such immaturity even though acquitting himself with the excuse that probably all men had these weaknesses near a pretty woman.

But there was something of Astarte about Mary, the goddess not only of love but of war. A merest glimpse of her – and he had many, she being his sister-in-law and often here with Geoffrey – would set up conflict in his own breast. Conflict and an aching love.

These same feelings would also surface whenever restaurant matters brought him close to William Goodridge, whom he'd recently promoted from station head waiter to head waiter. William never spoke of Mary, but there was about him a lonely aspect as he went about his work, dedicated to a point of obsession, even desperation, a constant reminder that William had once been Mary's fiancé. In its way his attitude always got to Henry. If he could learn to conquer his love for her, why couldn't Goodridge?

"I doubt if I'll ever marry," William had recently said quite out of the blue when Henry had come to discuss something or other with him. Exactly what, he couldn't recall, but Goodridge digging up his bachelor state had reminded him how they both suffered. Were the man to find himself a young woman and get married, then that would perhaps go some way to ending his own discomfort.

"You're too wrapped up in your work, William," he'd told him tersely. Henry could predict with certainty that the loyal Goodridge, who apparently had no intention of taking his talents elsewhere, would end up as *maitre d'hôtel* of this restaurant. Over the years they'd become good friends and he found himself confiding in William far more than in his present manager – a miserable-natured if gifted man, always ready to see the worst side of things whenever Henry consulted him.

He'd have liked to have got rid of his manager but, with no reason to be dissatisfied with his work itself, it wouldn't have been fair. If and when a second restaurant came into being, William would be a good candidate to manage it. Henry knew one thing, that Geoffrey would hardly welcome such responsibility, happy only to reap the rewards. Yes, William Goodridge would be his first and perfect choice. But he thought it best not to say so just yet.

–

Things hadn't changed, though to everyone else they appeared to have done. This past year Mary had heard from others that she was becoming a pace-setter, but no one knew it stemmed solely from a need to submerge this longing inside her that was all but whittling her away.

Women remarked with ill-concealed envy on her fashionable thinness, men with overt admiration. Yes, she was thin, painfully thin, what everyone admired in a girl, but it was not due to the way she nibbled her food without enjoying it: caviar, hot lobster, crepe suzette, tasteless as plain bread to her. Rather it was due to this awful hollow yearning that daily grew more acute. In feverish need to alleviate it, she coaxed Geoffrey into more and more activity, excitement: holidays in Monte Carlo, Le Touquet, Venice; night-clubs adding to the spice of life, with the danger of police raids not only on the sleazy backstreets of Soho but on fashionable Bond Street; the brittle gaiety of it all – partying with famous names – Tallulah Bankhead, Olga Lynn, the Cole Porters, the Sitwells; seen in *Tatler* beside such as Lady Mendl,

Prince and Princess Jean de Faucigny Lucinge; ever on the move, though Geoffrey hardly needed coaxing, viewing her excessive energy and vitality with pride.

The reckoning came in the March of 1927, at the house rented by Elsa Maxwell in Berkeley Square, she giving what she called a Baby Party. She and her host of sparkling guests, even to the servants, were dressed in infant gear, from little girl's frocks and frilly knickers to boys' short trousers and caps to babies' diapers, lace bonnets and feeding bottles. Milk, laced with alcohol of course, ran freely from an enormous plaster bosom. "An absolute scream", as a woman with hardly any bosoms at all remarked in high excitable tones as she passed Mary, a little unsteadily, half-empty cocktail glass askew in her hand.

Mary, standing beside the buffet table loaded with jellies and blancmange, pink iced cake, and soft drinks spiced with whisky, brandy, rum or whatever potent stuff could be thought up so that few would end up steady on their feet by midnight, couldn't bring herself to raise a smile.

It was her "time of the month". Apart from inconvenience, it told yet again that nothing had come of Geoffrey's last love-making. Well, it wouldn't, he always insisting on wearing something and little she could do about that but sulk or refuse him altogether. Mostly she sulked. It would cause rows. He wanted sex but not children who would cramp his style. Lately, though, even love-making wasn't as often as it used to be. No wonder she felt down, smothering the threat of moodiness with shows of high spirits to allay being looked upon as a wet blanket.

She had felt down for a long time. More so since the death of Rudolph Valentino last August. To her it had been like losing Marianne all over again. Utterly foolish, but so real.

She'd met Valentino staying as a guest of Scott and Zelda Fitzgerald at the Grand Hotel du Cap at Cap d'Antibes in 1925, she and Geoffrey there at the same time. She and he had become good friends while he was there, those languorous dark looks overwhelming her the time he had put an arm about her shoulders. Even today she could feel the warmth of those hands on her bare flesh (most of her dresses had been sleeveless in order to combat the heat of Provence in high summer) after they, the Fitzgeralds and the Murphys, Gerald and Sara, had done gallivanting about the Plage de la Garoupe removing an influx of seaweed, laughing and squealing like children, until finally exposing white sand enough to call it a beach.

Now he was dead. To her it had been like losing a friend, or another child. She'd been inconsolable for days, Geoffrey saying she was as bad as those hysterical women admirers who had practically thrown themselves on the coffin at Valentino's funeral in the USA, one even said to have shot herself. For months Mary had wept silently and secretly at odd times, the untimely death carrying echoes of that of her own precious daughter and, worse, manifesting itself as a renewed longing to replace her own little lost being. But Geoffrey, enjoying his life, did not stop even to consider how she felt, becoming ever more irritated by her constant yearning. She tried not to speak of it, but it would out the moment they were alone. "For God's sake!" he would burst out, turning abruptly away, and she would go quiet.

Tonight she could hardly bear it. All around her the high screams of laughter, the incessant chortling from the men, the frantic, brittle gabble of tipsy conversation seemed to press in upon her like an ever-shrinking cage.

People shouldered by in the tightly packed throng of merrymakers, voices close to her ear sounded deafening, faces close to hers breathed alcholic fumes into her nostrils even though she, having drunk so much herself, should have been immune. Jostled, cuddled, swivelled this way and that, dragged off to dance – she obliged with an energy she hadn't thought herself capable of – the room swirled about her, the heat bearing down on all sides, yet she managed to remain upright.

"I'm giving an absolutely splendid party – don't you think?" blared the American twang of Elsa Maxwell in her ear, the fashionable clipped way of speaking superceding the suave drawl of only last year.

"Yes," Mary obliged as she kicked up her heels with a man she had never set eyes on before. "Lovely…"

Elsa passed on by without listening, the large hand on the end of her long arm raised to someone across the room as she made off.

Mary felt suddenly giddy. What was she doing here? Who was she? Or rather who did she think she was?

Questions bombarded her in time to the frantic beat of the jazz band crackling out a Charleston. The Mary she knew should be at home nursing a baby, proud and calm, not this gyrating thing with raised arms waving and knees twisting at unnatural angles.

She heard someone crying. Stiff, stifled, sobs that seemed to wrack her own chest. Who was it? She didn't realise it was herself even as she slid to the floor, the sobbing rising to screeching hysteria.

Through it she could hear a high voice: "What's the matter with her? She seemed OK a moment ago. Oh, how frightful! Someone do something!"

Someone was bending over her. Something slapped her face, hard. The involuntary screaming stopped abruptly. Her whole being racked now with deep sobs, she found herself sitting on the floor surrounded by people and for a moment with no idea how she could have got there. With slow realisation came embarrassment as she got to her feet, no longer the lively exciting pace-setter, the centre of attraction, the envy of other women and the lure of the trendy male, more the fraud exposed.

"Take me home, Geoffrey," she managed to whisper after being helped to a chair like useless extra baggage, people immediately losing interest in her.

His chagrin showed on his face, even as he said with forced concern, "Do you think you'll be all right if you sit here a little longer?"

Perhaps she would, but suddenly she wanted no more of this party with its brittle gaiety, its lack of feeling toward the underdog. So long as she was the life and soul she remained up there with them all. Now, having revealed a weakness in her bright and shining exterior, she wasn't worthy of a second glance. She felt foolish and exposed, wanted only to get away from here. "Take me home, Geoffrey," she repeated sharply enough to raise a few eyebrows in her direction. "Geoffrey, please," she hissed.

His lips were tight as he got her coat and she pulled on her hat with a viciousness that told of her anxiety to be out of the eye of these people. In silence he conducted her from the mansions of Berkeley Square and almost roughly took her arm to help her into the taxi he'd called. They sat in silence in the back and without speaking she waited while he paid the cab driver and then let him conduct her up the steps to their flat. She felt drained.

–

"Geoffrey, I don't want to go." The half-strangled sound of her words made him look up from tying his shoelaces, his eyebrows raised in surprise.

"What do you mean, you don't want to go? Why?"

She could offer no explanation. Since the exhibition she'd made of herself at Elsa Maxwell's party last month, she'd been battling with an ever-growing need to hide away from everyone. Her efforts to smile, to force herself to be as she had once been, shrieked pretence until it had become all too obvious by the way people looked sideways at her that they were not fooled, that they were talking about her behind her back, speculating as to what it was that had changed the vivacious Mary Lett – something terribly wrong, no doubt. They had no idea about Marianne.

That was Geoffrey's doing, wanting to keep her existence a secret from their social circle. So no one except the family was ever aware of her. He had told his mother, eventually, but she'd never acknowledged the child, hadn't even attended the small funeral. Mary felt she would never forgive her that. But for Geoffrey to insist they tell none of their friends about their having a child – ludicrous. She had argued with him but he'd remained firm.

"None of our friends have kids," he'd said. "I don't see why we should go around bragging about a family. It's none of their business."

So she respected his wishes though it had been hard avoiding making little references to Marianne's most recent and amazing action or saying. At times it was as if she didn't exist.

There lingered a sneaking feeling as to why Geoffrey had acted as he had. Marianne's existence would have explained why he, with all his money, had married a mere working girl, and their friends would have seen the explanation as a pretty sordid one. Maybe they were unfair thoughts, but she'd been foolish in going along with his request, though perhaps it had been that she too had felt the stigma of his having to marry her – which was what it had boiled down to, she pregnant with his child at the time. Perhaps he had been right. They had avoided the awkward questions and what people didn't know couldn't harm them.

Now, however, she didn't care how they speculated, except that she had lost the impetus to go out as if a blanket had come down over her social life since making a spectacle of herself that night.

Her voice was sharp with self-defence. "I just don't, that's all."

"You must know why?"

She tried to ignore the way he was looking at her. She shook her head. "I don't know why."

"You used to love going out, going places."

"I can't any more. I've had enough."

He got up from the edge of the bed where he'd been perching to do up his shoes. He was angry. "I don't understand you. Why the sudden change? I know you've been a bit edgy since Elsa Maxwell's party, but you were all right there – until you made a damned fool of yourself."

His tone shocked her. His behaviour towards her bordered on cruelty – there could be no other word for it. He'd never been this harsh before. He might often have been irritated by her prolonged grieving, but he'd never been deliberately hurtful, cruel. It was as though something inside him had snapped suddenly. Maybe it was his submerged grief coming out, but to her it was as though she were seeing a different man.

"I couldn't help that. I wasn't well. I had my usuals and I didn't feel up to it."

"Bursting into tears like that," he went on. "Passing out on the floor."

"I didn't pass out on the floor. I just didn't feel well."

"You were sozzled."

"I wasn't sozzled."

He gave a sceptical laugh and sat down on the bed again to start on the other shoelace. "Well, you're OK now. Just keep off the booze."

It was unkind. She never got that drunk. She gazed at her reflection in the dressing-table mirror. Despite the make-up she looked drawn. "I'm sorry, Geoffrey," she persisted. "I don't want to go out."

He sat up straight, his lips forming a thin line. "We're expected. We can't let them down. What the hell's the matter with you?"

"I don't know."

"For heaven's sake, Mary." He got up and came towards her, putting his hands on her shoulders to gaze at her in the mirror. "This is crazy. I always thought you enjoyed going out and about. I only do it for you."

"You don't. You do it for yourself."

His face grew bleak, stupidly bleak. "That's bloody unfair, darling."

"I just want a rest from it. Just to stay at home for a while."

From that silly look of bewilderment his expression changed to a darkly discerning one. "You don't just want to stay at home – you want to have a baby. That's it, isn't it?"

When she didn't reply, his lip curled sardonically. Their rows were only ever about that. Usually he became tetchy, changing the subject before she could get going on it.

Never did he react as she was seeing him now, with this dark and horrid mockery.

"That's it, isn't it?" he repeated. "You want a baby and you will do anything to get one."

"Geoffrey…" She looked appealingly at him. "If you'd only stop and see how I feel. Darling, every woman wants a baby."

"Not every woman, *darling*. Not the women we see."

She fought to ignore the horrid way he had addressed her. "I don't want to be like them."

"You could've fooled me, the way you caper when you've had a few."

"You used to love me being the life and soul of a party. I have to do *something* to hide from everyone how I really feel."

"And you think having a baby will cure it? Well, it takes two, and I don't want kids getting in the way of the life we lead. You having a baby will put an end to all that, and you know it. You won't ever want to go out again."

"I did last time," she cried, near to tears now.

"And keep on telling me at every turn that you've suffered over it ever since." He let go her shoulders and swung away from her, turning round to berate her again. "All this blasted guilt you keep feeling – I'm sick of it, Mary. It wasn't our fault Marianne died. We gave her all we could."

"Except ourselves," she countered, standing her ground.

"She had a damned good nanny who did everything for her."

"But *we* didn't, Geoffrey. We just went on enjoying life."

"For God's sake! We only have one life. I want to enjoy it."

"Yes, I know," she shot at him. "But I told you, I'm sick of it all."

He glared at her, coming to a decision and lowering his tone in a way that sounded menacing. "Well, if you're sick of it all, Mary, and want to stay at home, then I'll go on my own – whenever."

Anger had already dried the threatening tears. How dare he present ultimatums! "You do that, *darling*!" she blazed at him. "Go if you want. But don't try blackmailing me into being with you. You can go on your own!"

"I will!"

Silence came down like a solid curtain between them. In silence she watched him finish getting ready. She sat stolidly at her mirror as he went into the lounge. She heard him pour himself a drink, the heavy decanter being slammed back on to the drinks tray, moments later the tumbler too being banged down. In the mirror she could see through to the open lounge door, see him moving back and forth across the room. Then, without a backward look in her direction, he went to the hall door to yank it open, closing it with as much of a bang as the expensive carpet allowed.

Somehow she knew as she returned her eyes to her own reflection that this was the start of something that was to go on and on. But she felt so drained by it all that at this moment it wasn't truly registering with her.

Three

For hours the woman's birth pains had torn apart the ever-lasting night. Now, with the first grey wash of predawn relieving the stygian darkness, the cries had subsided to a weak moan telling of a dire urgency to get the child into the world – one way or another.

"We shall have to do a Caesarean section," Doctor Griffith informed the father, whose bleak, fearful eyes took in the other's professional gaze with something like desperate trust.

"Can you save her?"

"If we get her to hospital as soon as possible, yes. Should have been sent there from the very start. Pelvic girdle's far too small for such a large baby. Typical of these gently brought up young women, especially with this new fad for starving themselves slim."

Grace had never needed to starve herself slim, she was naturally so, but Henry had no interest in the man's views on fads and fashions. He had no wish to know that cutting her was the only solution now, and that it should have been done earlier except that he had not wanted to see his wife cut about. He didn't want that guilt sitting on his shoulders. But it appeared it would have to, and all he felt was crass fear for her. Grace could always have another child but she had only one life. It was for her that he felt at this moment, rather than fear that he might have to live on without her. That much desperate love he had never known for her. His wish for her to live was purely for her sake. He nodded as yet another moan floated out into the darkened garden from the upstairs room.

They had come to Swift House for Grace's confinement. Mother had insisted – compensation, he wondered, for her youngest son's child having been born estranged from her? Even now, she hadn't truly forgiven Geoffrey for marrying Mary the way he had. Still refusing to recognise her, she had therefore been unable, without losing face, to acknowledge little Marianne even after the child had been taken. How she felt about that, Henry had no idea; Mother kept her thoughts strictly to herself. Instead she had gone out of her way to have Grace here.

"She needs a chance to relax in the peace of the country. London is no place for an expectant mother to be."

They had been here four weeks. The baby should have arrived ten days ago but had remained stubbornly in the womb. Grace, distended and ponderous, worn down by the weight she carried, had only been able to sit, day in, day out, in a deckchair in the garden in the warm May sunshine with Mother and the staff doing everything for her. It was just as well they had come to stay at Swift House, especially now. Grace had been in labour for the best part of two days, her strength finally threatening to give out with the baby as yet unborn.

The father's permission given, Doctor Griffith returned to the house to make his arrangements. These people, especially the senior Mrs Lett, with their outdated ideas that the family seat must be the hub of their lives, that nothing worthwhile should take place outside it, had all but jeopardised the mother's life, he thought, exasperated.

–

Geoffrey lay beside Mary. She'd tried to cuddle up to him but he had eased her away just as he had done these several weeks. The last thing he wanted was sex with her. She'd been bewildered at first, then angry, finally falling into fits of weeping every night, culminating in furious rows. He was sick of it. Of course, all she was after was a baby, more so this evening after having been told on the telephone of Grace and Henry's happy news. But a baby, especially now, was the last thing Geoffrey wanted.

The night he had left the flat, furious at Mary, determined to go on to the party without her, he'd steeled himself to face the inevitable enquiries as to where she was. He had said she wasn't well, had promised to take back everyone's wish for her quick recovery and their disappointment at missing her vivacious company that evening. To avoid more questions, he had kept as far away as possible from everyone, longing to escape the jollifications, the loud music, the constant noise, yet not wanting to return home, perhaps to more rows.

A young woman, who said her name was Pamela, had come up to him uninvited, had been sympathetic when she discovered why he was alone. (Why he had told her the truth when he'd lied through his teeth to everyone else, he had no idea.) She had linked her arm in his and said she knew just how he felt; said a little tearfully that she had just broken up with her boyfriend, who had his eyes on another girl. "It's over," she had sighed when, putting his own troubles aside, he'd said perhaps they'd get back together again.

"No," she had sniffed. "It's over. I won't play second fiddle and that's that." She'd given another sniff, leaning against him as if for comfort.

Two like souls, they had kept each other company the whole evening, cheering each other up. It had ended with a kiss, and eventually they had made love, both been very much in need of the comfort it brought.

For days afterwards, he'd been unable to get her out of his head. He had been with her on three occasions since, each time heady, wonderful. He had been with her again this evening, coming home late, forcing himself to lie beside Mary, unable even to touch her though she'd pleaded with him to at least kiss her goodnight. He had turned his back, saying testily that it was late, that he was tired, that the restaurant – his alibi – had taken toll of his verve.

He now lay awake while she slumbered, too excited to sleep, his mind filled with the slim dark beauty of Pamela Fielding, his flesh still feeling hers cool against him, his loins tightening with the ecstatic recollection of her legs wrapped about his waist, their power pulling him in further to savour the moist warmth of her all the better. Suddenly life was pleasurable again, full again, filled with promise.

–

Her hand held gently in his, Grace smiled up at her husband. Beside her their perfect son, twenty-four hours old, lay asleep in his hospital cot. At peace with herself, she spoke quietly. "What shall we call him?"

Henry thought for a moment, tenderly caressing her hand. She had hoped all along for a girl, happily making a list of names and stubbornly refusing to believe a girl was only a fifty-fifty chance. A little disappointed to find she'd had a boy, she had soon settled for a son, quite happy at the perfection she'd brought into the world, with the timely help of the hospital of course.

For her benefit Henry began reciting what boys' names came to mind, commencing with existing family ones, to all of which Grace shook her head.

"I want something different. Something special."

"Hmm!" He thought again, enjoying the peace of this private ward, the tranquillity on his wife's face, the innocence of the infant, his son, in his cot.

"Dominic? Aubin?" He glanced at the golden down just visible on his son's head. Aubin meant "fair". But Grace, propped up on her pillows, shook her head, her nose wrinkling.

He let out a long contemplative sigh. "Edwin?" He liked the name of Edwin, but there was no response to that either. "Hugh," he offered and saw her smile.

"That's nice. I like Hugh."

"Hugh, then." he grinned at her and pressed her hand a little more firmly. "Hugh, Robert – after your father – Adair, after my third name, Lett. How does that sound, my sweet?"

"Just wonderful," she sighed, suddenly growing weary after her battle of the day before and the day before that. She closed her eyes.

Seeing it, he let her hand slip from his, leaned forward and kissed her tenderly on one cool cheek. Her eyes remained closed but he felt her flinch very slightly at his touch – or was it merely his imagination? Whichever, the comers of her lips quirked into a tiny smile, and after dropping a kiss on his new son's head, he left the two of them sleeping and crept from the ward, his heart full with pride.

–

William Goodridge glanced up as Henry Lett moved between the tables, hardly pausing to acknowledge those customers he knew well. The man had grown terse with almost everyone these past few months, William himself included to a certain extent even though Henry favoured him most out of all his staff. Though why that should be, William had no idea. But he was not concerned for himself, only that Mr Henry should not be behaving this way with valued customers. It wasn't good for business.

He had the business very much in mind since Henry Lett had spoken of a second restaurant in which he, William, could very well be in charge. It would be a marvellous step up, if ever it came about. William knew his talents. He got on naturally well with customers, they often addressing him in the familiar, an honour few waiting staff below the *maitre d'* himself could boast. "So what d'you recommend, William?" they would ask, and he would advise, aware of the restaurant manager's eyes on him as he bent obligingly over the customer to suggest something, his expert recommendations nearly always readily accepted.

That Mr Henry was wont to confide in him more than he ever did his restaurant manager, he accepted as a mysterious bond that had grown between them. He had never courted it. But lately Mr Henry had become as short with him as with everyone. He was growing a little rotund these days. It was supposed to reveal a sign of contentment, yet Henry's brow seemed lined with what William could only assume was worry, perhaps from most of the time having to bear the weight of the business and all its problems on his own shoulders, especially those concerning expansion. Mr Geoffrey was hardly ever around and Henry intimated that his mother was more a sleeping partner, yet these three were the sole directors. One would never have believed it, seeing the hours Henry put in.

The problem had to be something to do with this dilemma whether to enlarge the existing premises or consider the opening of a second one.

"If I do, William," Henry had mentioned on that one occasion, "I might toy with the idea of you as restaurant manager, but of course that's all up in the air at the moment."

William had been excited but it hadn't been mentioned again. Most likely it had all come to nothing, the way Mr Henry had looked of late.

Mr Henry's direction was taking him towards William. Pausing, he smiled a little wearily and asked if all was going smoothly and well in his area.

Assuring him that all was fine, William ventured a sociable enquiry: "Are your wife and baby well?"

He was aware that Mr Henry granted him the privilege of his friendship and would not have dreamed of abusing it. But the baby was now four months old, a fine sturdy youngster, his father fond of parading him proudly before everyone. Thus enquiring after the welfare of the child and his mother was far from abusing that special relationship built up between employee and employer. Yet Henry's voice came sharply, though admittedly the tone seemed directed more towards himself than William. "The baby's fine."

No mention of Mrs Lett. "Is Mrs Lett unwell?" William asked, alarmed. Maybe worry over an ailing wife was the cause of the terse reply.

"It's Mrs Lett…" Henry paused, then, needing to find a common ground on which to lay his heart, added,

"Grace." There was a trace of trembling in his voice. "She... well, we... we haven't been as man and wife since the birth of our son, if you see what I mean."

William was beginning to feel a hot awkwardness at being witness to such a confidence. He wished the man wouldn't be so frank about his private problems – this was too much – yet he knew he must decently hear him out, whether embarrassed or not.

Henry Lett was speaking more easily, glad at last to lighten himself of what had burdened him for so long.

"Grace appears terrified of my going anywhere near her. No sooner do I touch her arm than she shies away. As for... well, William, you know what I'm getting at. As for that, there is nothing. I'm frustrated. It seems having had such a bad time having the child, she's terrified of... well, the *deed*. I understand women can feel sensitive in certain parts, and reluctant after giving birth, but I thought by this time she would have got over that, been normal again."

The voice trailed off leaving William uncomfortably hot, perspiring with the discomfort of being privy to this man's private life. It just wasn't right. Not knowing what to say, he said nothing, and eventually Henry Lett straightened up and, taking his upper arm again, put pressure into the grip.

"William, I'm so very sorry to have burdened you with such a delicate matter but truly I am desperate. I know I should have confided in a doctor, for aren't they the people we all need to confide in? But even with him I cannot speak as I have with you, my dear friend. I feel a little better now."

William nodded slowly, and again the words that remained unsaid spoke of loyalty to this honoured confidence more than anything that might have been uttered. He could have wept for him as he stood bleakly watching Henry Lett walk away.

—

Geoffrey was at his wits' end. Several months ago Pamela had told him she was pregnant with his child. By her reckoning, it had occurred the second time they had been together. "I always suspected I was quite outrageously fertile," she'd laughed in a way that was intended to belie her fear. "It makes it due next February, or could be late January – I've not consulted anyone."

It was time to tell Mary, to speak of an ending to their marriage. For his part there was no longer any love for her. He was sick of her carping and he was frantically in love with Pamela. She was all he now knew he had ever wanted in a woman: good family, money of her own, vivacious, optimistic for all her condition had begun to show, having got over her first fears that he would desert her. He adored her attitude of what-the-hell-I-can't-hide-it-so-let-them-all-see and he wanted to marry her, his view of the world the same as hers. This time, it wouldn't matter that he was having an affair. She already part of the society set, all that would happen would be people saying what a hell of a chap he was and when was he thinking of getting divorced. With 1928 fast approaching, a decade almost over, young people had grown wildly abandoned. Nothing was too outrageous for them, and divorce was becoming quite fashionable. Yes, they would look at Pamela and her new lover almost with envy. Mary of the shrouded, debatable past would be forgotten.

He'd see Mary all right of course; make sure she'd want for nothing – in fact she could keep the flat and everything in it: her clothes, her jewellery, everything. But he had truly had enough.

He told her that September, leaving time enough for a judge to decree that the divorce must go through quickly owing to the child being born illegitimate if the guilty parties could not marry in time. Mary had gone potty, tearing at him with her claws, sobbing and shrieking until he thought she would go completely insane. There was nothing she could do but comply to a divorce for adultery.

At the end of January, he and Pamela were married – not a sly little registry-office marriage but a full-blown society one with a huge reception at the Cafe Royal. Though he'd heard rumours of it having financial difficulties, nevertheless it did three hundred guests proud, not one waving an eyebrow at the bride's condition. Her parents set them up in a spacious Bayswater address, their wedding present to the happy couple. Two weeks later Pamela gave birth to a son whom they called Edwin, Henry having mentioned the name when his own son had been born and Geoffrey having rather taken to it.

–

"I just want to finish it all, Henry. I don't want to go on living."

It was said without any trace of emotion. Sitting beside her in the lonely flat, Henry started. "For God's sake, Mary, you mustn't talk like that!"

It wasn't so much what she said as the way she had said it, her tone hollow, her eyes empty and staring into space. She had lost weight, was mere skin and bone. During the months he had visited her regularly once a week, so deeply sorry for her, he had seen what little flesh she had fall away. She no longer took care of her appearance. The flat was a mess. There had been a woman come in three times a week, but Mary had dismissed her, said she didn't want anyone around looking at her, seeing her misery. Neglecting herself, hardly eating, refusing his invitation to leave this place and stay with him and Grace, she sat alone day after day.

His first idea had been that she would be a tonic for Grace who since the birth of little Hugh had herself become insular, housebound, wanting only to bestow all her love upon her son and still cringing away from him if he so much as laid a hand on her arm. Of marital pleasure he had none. It would have been good to have another person in the flat and he thought it might have got Grace out of herself, but Mary constantly refused. Alarmed by her condition, he could only come and visit her. But it was hard going trying to converse with someone who hardly ever spoke in return. Harder still that his heart raced each time he saw her, for all her fast degenerating appearance.

It was April now, and he was becoming genuinely fearful for her health, her life.

He ventured an arm about her shoulders, the first time he had ever dared, her stiff composure seeming hitherto to forbid it, and was relieved that she didn't flinch away as Grace would have done. In fact she leaned against him, the warmth of her thin body penetrating his shirt and waistcoat, he having taken off his jacket in a room hot from her only effort at comfort, the fire in the hearth carelessly stoked up to almost danger height.

"Listen, Mary," he coaxed. "You mustn't go thinking things like that. Time will pass and you'll settle down. Maybe in time you'll find someone who will be a comfort to you."

For a moment his thoughts flew to William Goodridge who had once been her fiancé, maybe could be again. Old flames could be reawakened. Then he knew he didn't want Goodridge to be anything to her. The person he wanted to be something to her was sitting here right beside her. He felt a pumping in his chest, a pumping that was transferring itself to the lower half of his body. Wild imaginings were beginning to consume him and hastily he took his arm away from her. It was then she flinched, as if something dear had been snatched from her. She looked at him, her grey eyes wide.

"Don't let go of me, Henry. I'm afraid. Don't leave me alone."

What could he do but replace his arm about her? His face was close to hers as he whispered. "I would never let any harm come to you, Mary. I shall always be here for you."

Suddenly his lips were on hers and she didn't draw away. There was an amazing warmth in those lips. It flowed through his body like treacle. He hardly knew exactly when he pressed her down on the sofa, fumbling at her; hardly knew when she, gasping and sobbing but far from pushing him away, had drawn him into her.

Four

Alone in her flat, no one but Henry calling on her, Mary had felt as the dead might feel, if they could feel. She recalled little of what went on in the outside world, did not read the newspapers or listen to the wireless. The end of 1927 and the early months of 1928 passed her by unrecorded, events of consequence to others seeming incapable of penetrating her brain: London's worst flood in living memory — fourteen people drowned in their basements as the Embankment gave way at Westminster; Prince Edward, the Prince of Wales — Dickie, as she and Geoffrey had once come familiarly to know him — appointed master of the Merchant Navy. He had thrown an informal party but of course she hadn't been invited. Geoffrey and his new wife had. She did indeed feel dead.

She had smoked incessantly, no longer using the long elegant cigarette holders she had once used during her carefree society days — they reminded her too much of that time — but straight from the packet, one after another sometimes when she really felt at her lowest. Brandy helped too, but being drunk instead of blanking out her situation only heightened it and made her cry until her nose became blocked, her eyes swollen and her head aching.

It was all gone: the trips to Monte Carlo, tea at the Cafe de Paris surrounded by wealthy friends, and then the Casino; Le Touquet, aboard somebody's luxury yacht; Paris, lunching at the Ritz, dining at Maxim's; the races at Longchamps, the motor racing at Le Mans, and shopping, always shopping. Even here, there would be no more of that life: the exciting and often seamy night-clubs; the wild and outrageous parties that went on until daylight; the mad trips to the south coast in open limousines; circuit race meetings at Brooklands; the exclusive hats at Ascot. No more Coco Chanel suits, Patou bathing and beach-wear, Paquin cocktail dresses, Reboux hats. Her furs, the silver fox stoles, her fine coats with deep cuffs and collars of fox fur, hung unused in her wardrobe; the gold bangles and pearl necklaces lay untouched in her jewellery box.

But the year had moved on, and that first time Henry had come and made love to her in April had been for her a turning point. Yes, gone was the wild round of continuous fun, but she was beginning to feel less and less regret, and all due to Henry. Six months ago, she had been out of her mind, and later there had been that deadness. Now she had Henry and her life had begun taking a new turn. It wasn't that she was in love with him in the same way she had been in love with Geoffrey – first love could never be repeated – but his caresses were what her benumbed mind had needed and his love-making what her body craved, and it didn't seem wrong.

Yes, she was sorry for Grace. She'd reminded him of his wife that first time he made love to her, taking them both by surprise and frightening her even as she clung to him in the need to fill that awful emptiness Geoffrey's adultery and desertion had left her with. It had brought her close to wanting to destroy herself – the only way she could think of being rid of all that pain of rejection and the knowledge of there being nothing to live for.

Henry had changed all that. Afterwards, instead of expressing regret at what he had done, he had said how he'd loved her since before Geoffrey married her. He'd said how he had tried to push her from his mind by his marrying Grace, but that none of it had worked; said that he had only ever wanted her. He had pushed aside her arguments that he hadn't been fair to Grace by allowing what had happened, that they must never let it happen again. Yet she had wanted it to happen, a desire inside her equally as strong as that she once had for Geoffrey, and when he had visited her again and again made love to her, Mary knew that she couldn't help herself any more. Grace was, after all, refusing to allow Henry anywhere near her and only had herself to blame, and in that case she wasn't being harmed by it. Also, Mary asked herself as Henry's visits grew more frequent, why should she deny such a kind, lovely and gentle-natured man as he that which he so needed?

But sin reaps its own reward as her aunt had often said. She had died last year. A fatal stroke. Mary had gone to the funeral, Geoffrey off with his mistress though she hadn't realised it then but had begun to wonder. She had gone alone. She had wept – for the past when she had been young; for the woman for whom she had cared for so many years; for herself that Geoffrey no longer seemed to want to make love to her and was hardly ever at home.

Now, as Mary's "monthlies" failed, her aunt's words came back like a blow to the forehead. In a fever of anxiety, Mary waited for the next month. Again nothing. Nor during the third month. Her small breasts began to enlarge and grow tender as they had when she'd been pregnant with Marianne. A visit to her doctor confirmed her fears. When Henry visited that day, instead of rushing eagerly to greet him, she sat waiting, and as he came and kissed her on the cheek, mystified by her attitude, she blurted it all out to him.

"What are we going to do?" Her voice was high and frantic as he sat beside her on the sofa.

This time there'd be no timely marriage as there had been with Geoffrey. Henry was already married. She was caught. This time there could be no backing out of some surgeon's private back room.

Sitting so close to her, Henry must have read her mind, for he said suddenly, "One thing I am not going to do is sanction any idea you may have of getting rid of it – not unless you yourself decide you really have to. I realise that I cannot begin to know how you feel, but to me it's taking the life of an innocent being. We both enjoyed what we had without regard for any consequence. Now, when something comes of it, it's too easy to be rid of our responsibilities by taking the life our lack of caution created. Yet I've no right to say what you must do, my dearest. I want so much to protect you, Mary. What can I say?"

Such high-flown ideas were no ease to the knowledge that she was carrying an illegitimate child. The stigma would be upon it for the rest of its life, the brief birth certificate always there to condemn it into adult life and onwards, to be visited upon marriage and children yet unborn.

Sins of the fathers — and the mothers, in equal guilt. Yet sitting gloomily on the sofa, her hand in his, she knew deep in her heart that she could never destroy this life inside her. It wasn't in her to do so.

"How is Grace these days?" she asked inanely. He shook his head.

"Same as ever." His tone, like hers, was dull and lifeless. "She dotes on Hugh and has no time for me. I haven't touched her for eighteen months. It'll never be any different between us — not now."

A spark of hope flickered in Mary's breast. "If she doesn't love you, Henry, maybe your marriage isn't working."

"I don't know. We seem together only from habit. She pecks my cheek when I leave but never lets me peck hers in return. All she ever cares about is the boy. He's her life. So long as they are together, I don't count."

"She doesn't deserve you, Henry."

For a moment it was as though he hadn't heard her. "The first time I tried to approach her, and that was a full three months after the baby was born, it ended in a row and her in tears. She refused to let me near her. I felt sure I had given her long enough to readjust to our marital relationship. Grace isn't one to row and finally she let me touch her, but she lay there like a board, and when I tried, she let out a terrific scream and said that I was hurting her. She never let me even kiss her again, frightened that it might lead to other things. We ended up having separate beds and now she sleeps in the spare room with the boy."

It was then that the significance of what Mary had said began to register with him. He looked at her. "What did you mean, darling, what you said a moment ago?"

In Mary's mind her question had taken precedence over everything else. Now she said slowly, "I meant would you consider going on with your marriage under those circumstances, Henry?"

"You mean divorce?"

"Darling, it's not a marriage, is it? You have adequate grounds for a divorce, surely."

She didn't add that, divorced, he could marry her, give the baby his name. Such a suggestion had the flavour of a callous and calculating mind, and she didn't want him to think that of her. As it was, he was looking at her, aghast.

"I couldn't do that – not to her."

Suddenly all the tension of three months burst out of Mary. It came out cruelly. "But you could do this to me!"

For a moment longer he regarded her, pain dark in his sombre eyes, then slowly he got up from the sofa, gazing down at her face, now white and stunned from her own thoughtless words.

"It took two of us, my dear, if you recall."

She threw aside the fear that began to grip her, that he would walk out and not come back, the blood of his brother lurking there within him.

"Henry... darling." She found herself gasping, tears of terror misting her vision of him. "I know it's my fault too. I didn't mean to say it like that. It's that I'm so frightened. I don't know what to do. I don't want to destroy our baby. I couldn't. But what am I going to do? I'm all alone and I'm so frightened."

Abruptly he sat down again beside her, took her in his arms, held her close as she sobbed desolately against his chest. His voice crooned brokenly above her. "I can't divorce Grace. It has nothing to do with what society will think or what people will say. It's just – I couldn't do that to her, as much as I couldn't hurt her by telling her what we are to each other. But I shall find a way. I promise you, Mary. I will find a way."

The room around them lay silent as Mary's sobs subsided in defeat. There was no fire in the grate this time of year to crackle away the stillness. Only the small clock ticking rapidly on the tiled mantelshelf made any sound while outside, the hushed roar of passing traffic diminished the quiet in the room even more.

Suddenly Henry was kissing her damp cheeks, her eyes, her mouth. Continuing to kiss her, he bore her back upon the sofa, his hands feeling for her breasts. "I love you, Mary. I love you more than anything else in this world. I'll never stop loving you. I could never leave you."

She could feel the heat of him against her bared legs, a hard throbbing heat, the feel of which she had hitherto loved so much. Now it startled her, as though she were being abused. She shot upright, pushing him viciously away from her.

"No!"

He was looking stupidly at her. "What's the matter?"

"What's the matter?" Her voice rose to a shriek. "You mean you have to ask? I'm sick with worry and all you can do is… this!"

"I love you, darling."

"I want your help, not this. Is this supposed to solve our problem? Go and find your wife, Henry. I don't want you, this way. Go home to Grace. You can even tell her what you've been up to."

She said much more but was no longer hearing her own words, merely her screaming, seeing him backing away. It was as though what love she'd had for him had flown like a caged bird, suddenly released, finding an open window. The caged bird, knowing only the safety of its earlier confinement, would fly headlong into danger, not understanding it, only vaguely aware of it, and it would die. She would die. But she would not be caged by the name of mistress, harlot, kept woman. Nor would she give Henry the comfort of being released from his part in guilt by apathetically sitting back while she made her own decision about abortion. She would keep her child and make her own way in the world, and to hell with him. To hell with all bloody men!

She watched as he left. She couldn't see her own expression but it felt ghastly, and the look on his face confirmed it.

"I still love you, Mary," he said at the door. "I will always love you. And I promise I shall find a way."

–

His baby was due in April. Already it was early 1929. He hadn't seen Mary since late October, she so stiff and cold when he had last called on her that he had left feeling as if he had been thrown out. On one occasion he had sent her a cheque with some vague idea of helping her with the coming baby. She didn't reply; it was never cashed. He realised that it had been a stupid gesture. She didn't need his money. Geoffrey had left her secure, with the flat and a generous allowance, for all she no longer played a part in his life, he and his new wife enjoying themselves, at present in Egypt, the fashionable place for society people to holiday. But her refusal of Henry's help brought it starkly home to him that she saw it as no more than conscience money. There was nothing he could do. To take his mind off Mary and their present problems he concentrated on the business. In fact, the year coming to its close, business became an overriding obsession which he recognised as the only way of putting her out of his mind. The old idea of making Letts bigger began to cost him sleepless nights during which all he could see was the profits a second restaurant might have made slipping through his fingers. They even became the focus of his dreams, coins and banknotes being tossed in some capricious breeze just beyond arm's reach.

"We have to grow," he argued with his mother. "It's the only way forward. Things these days die if they aren't moved forward, don't you see? It's become a competitive world."

Geoffrey, of course, seeing only the extra shekels rolling in without a shrug of the shoulders at what it was going to cost before they did, was all for it, while Mother merely continued to miss the point that so many people were forced to book so far ahead it was reaching a ridiculous state of affairs.

"Why can't you be contented with things as they are?" she resisted. "Your dear father was. We have always had a fine enough living. I know you and Geoffrey are both ambitious, but at my age I don't want all the worry."

"You have to leave the worrying to us, Mother," he persisted, ignoring those lifted eyebrows. "Can't you see that people will start going elsewhere out of sheer frustration? We'll lose custom rather than stay as we are. That's how it works. More and more people are pouring into London" – its better theatres and huge new cinemas, now showing nothing but talkies, were drawing in the crowds – "and they need places to dine afterwards. We can't accommodate those hoping to dine at Letts with only our present number of covers. If we don't expand, we'll slowly go under. You wouldn't want my father's hard-won business to do that, would you, Mother?"

He'd hit the nail on the head. He could see that point starting to win her over, but she was still not entirely convinced.

"And where do you expect to find the money for all this?"

She had asked this before, had pointed out that his father's trust was not to be used willy-nilly, but patiently he again explained that the bank would advance funds if he presented them with proper statistics. He did not of course speak of the prospect of floating the company on the stock market if all else failed. Even so, she still pulled a face, much as she'd done before.

"I don't care for this borrowing, Henry. It's a very dangerous habit."

"Everyone borrows these days. It's part of finance."

"I still don't like it, Henry. I am getting old and cannot face change. But I suppose you and Geoffrey must look to the future. I pray you young people know and understand the modem ways of the world enough to know what you are doing. But then, tomorrow belongs to you, Henry. I can only see yesterday. Perhaps you know best."

Hardly able to believe that his mother had in fact capitulated, though admittedly without actually having said yes, Henry told Geoffrey as soon as he and Pamela returned home from Egypt.

"Let's get on with it straight away before Mother changes her mind," Geoffrey enthused and now it was Henry who held back.

"Don't start jumping the gun. There's a lot to go into first, all the book work, meeting with the accountant, getting estimates, all sorts of things." But enthusiasm was taking him over too. It was in his voice when he spoke of it to William even though the words of caution he'd given to Geoffrey still dominated. "Of course, there is a good deal to consider before it ever begins to get off the ground." Yet for all his excitement about new premises, always at the back of his mind was Mary. Even as he told William of his plans for expansion, juggling with which might be best, enlarging the present restaurant or going for second premises, Mary and what he was to do with her hovered there in his head. Impossible to ignore it, leave her to bring up an illegitimate child alone, his bastard, yet he was scared witless that Grace might find out and of the consequences that could evoke. Then, as he talked to William of all his plans for the restaurant, an idea began to form in his head.

What if he were to procure other premises and make concrete his promise of putting William Goodridge in as restaurant manager on a salary he couldn't refuse, but on one condition – that he make overtures to Mary and offer her marriage, offer to become father to the child she carried? Surely she would jump at the chance, seeing no other way out, and surely William would not let slip this opportunity of a lifetime, of security, high standing, money? All that would be required of him would be to marry the very girl for whom he still carried love in his heart after all these years. He had already seen excitement shining in the man's eyes at the prospect of this marvellous promotion. Surely the man would readily accept that other tantalising offer.

"William." Henry brought his voice down low. "There is one thing I have to mention. You can say no if you wish. Please don't think this is…" He hesitated over the word "bribery", feeling suddenly on level with a back-street tout. "There is one thing I might ask of you, a favour, in regard to the promotion I'm offering you." There was no way he could put it that would be as delicate as he would have liked. "I really am at a loss as to how to put this to you, William. Listen, let's have dinner together. I'll explain."

Intrigued, William sat opposite Henry over dinner at the Ritz – a most needless expense as William saw it – listening to the ways and means of drumming up cash, the possible need to persuade accountants, find financiers, entice investors, convince the banks, and wondered what all this had to do with him that Henry Lett needed to have dinner with him.

"So you see," Henry was saying as he touched a spoon to his sweet, a light Charlotte Russe, having eaten little of his first or main course, "it will all take a lot of thinking out, careful planning. It is a risk, a huge risk. I only hope we are doing the right thing."

"We?" William, toying with his own sweet, felt instantly cautious. Was Henry Lett expecting him to put his small savings into this venture? Was this the favour he was being asked of in return for being made restaurant manager? But by the sound of it, the new Letts would cost thousands – six figures, probably. His paltry savings book showed barely six hundred.

"We – my brother and I," Henry enlightened, pushing away his sweet plate and sitting back. "And, of course, if we do have to float the company, investors will obviously reap good benefits once it's up and running."

William pushed back his plate also, but didn't sit back. He was too tense. "Are you asking me to invest my savings in this business?"

"Not unless you wished." A light dawned in Henry's eyes on seeing the other's look. "Oh, no, I've not asked you here to take your money, William. No, I…" He broke off, and William saw him catch at his lower lip with his teeth. "If you did, of course, you stand to make yourself a tidy little sum. Once we're off the ground and our creditors off our backs, this business will rock the whole of London. I'm certain of that. And…"

Again he broke off. He took a deep breath as though steeling himself for something and sat forward on his seat.

"William, what I wish to ask of you is far more serious than anything to do with business. It's something about which I am going to have to swear you to secrecy, and if you say no, swear never to reveal to another soul what I'm about to say. And please, I would take it kindly if you try not to look upon me as a swine, for these things happen and are often beyond our control."

The man was looking positively sick, and by the time he had unfolded his story William too felt sickness in the pit of his stomach. How could poor Mary have been so treated? With all that had happened to her these past years, it was a wonder she hadn't indeed ended her life as Henry had told him at one point she had come near to doing.

He hadn't set eyes on Mary since Geoffrey had left her, there no longer being any need for her to come near the restaurant. He had thought her absence would have got her out of his mind, but time after time he'd think of her, wonder how and where she was. Geoffrey had appeared with his new wife and the baby they called Edwin. The new wife was tall, strikingly attractive, very much the society woman. Mary clearly hadn't been able to compete. William had always been as courteous to Geoffrey Lett as he was to Henry, but it had taken all his effort to face him calmly. Inside he had seethed knowing how Mary had been cast off. Typical of the attitudes of the wealthy towards ordinary people. He hated Geoffrey Lett. He had looked on the older brother as above all that sort of thing, loyal to his wife who, as he'd said that day many months ago, would have nothing to do with him. To realise how Henry had taken advantage of Mary, how he had got her pregnant and how, unwilling to ruin his own marriage in order to see her right, he was now asking this of him – to get himself out of a fix… William's immediate impulse had been to say, "Go to hell!" But what about Mary? All he could do was dismally nod his agreement.

He heard the sigh of immense relief that seem to fill the hushed air of the carpeted Ritz restaurant. "You won't regret it, William. I shall see you more than all right over this. I'll even bring you into the firm, buy your shares for you. That's how deeply grateful I feel."

"I'm not doing it for you." William heard his voice stiff and harsh. "I'm doing it for her. If she'll have me."

"I'm sure she will." William's hard tone had left Henry completely unruffled, so relieved had he been. "And I will keep my word, William. I will see you and she never want for anything. I'll not only make you restaurant manager but I will bring you into the company. I promise."

William stood up abruptly. "No need, Mr Lett. I'll marry her for you." Without looking at the man he turned and left the restaurant.

Five

The neighbours were giving her sidelong glances; she knew they were whispering: "Divorced, you know. Expecting, you know." Counting up on their fingers. "Why, my dear, you can see it! Who do you think the father can be? Not her ex-husband." Hands to their lips. "My dear, how absolutely dreadful."

It wasn't done, to be seen standing in the street gossiping like fishwives. Rather they met in tea-rooms over dainty sandwiches or tiny iced cakes and spoke in whispers as her name and her condition crept into the conversation.

In the past she too had shared in such conversations, sitting across a small table listening to an acquaintance picking someone else to pieces. A customary pastime among the upper classes, whiling away a morning or afternoon as a variation to shopping. Now it was she who was the point of discussion, no longer invited to join anyone for morning coffee or afternoon tea.

She'd been asked once, just after Geoffrey had left her. But they had only wanted to find out more about it all, drooling over it, hoping to gain a little information from her that could be passed on to other friends. She had refused the invitation, not too kindly, being in no mood for company, much less prying company. It had been her downfall. Had she accepted, cried on that person's shoulder, confessed all, she'd have been the centre of attention of the There-but-for-the-Grace-of-God-go-I brigade; have been sympathised with, found company for, given advice to, coveted, accepted. But she had spurned the invitation, and they in turn spurned her.

She seldom went out, would telephone to have her few groceries delivered, able to afford such service, the money Geoffrey had given her adequate for her needs still and accruing regular interest. Living frugally, for she ate little and no longer needed clothes to be seen in, the money would last her a long time yet. The baby when it arrived would cost little. She would feed it herself, and beyond nappies, which she would wash herself, and a few baby clothes, there'd be no need for any expensive outlay.

Abortion out of the question as far as she was concerned, for a long time she had toyed with adoption, but as her abdomen swelled and the life inside her began to move about, it became hers and the slightest thought of giving her baby to someone else just broke her heart as though she had already given it away.

The baby was due in six weeks' time. That Sunday morning Mary sat gazing out of the window at the trees lining the road, their as yet skeleton branches being tossed back and forth by a damp and blustery March wind. Not a soul in the street. Still lingering in their beds, no doubt, this time of the morning.

Nibbling the sandwich she had made herself, not really enjoying it but knowing she must eat for the baby's sake, she glanced at the blazing fire filling the room with heat. Even so, the strength of the wind was pushing tiny puffs of smoke back into the room. She could smell the sooty stink of it. She would have to get a chimney sweep out some time in the week.

A knock at the door made her jump a little. Few knocked at her door these days unless they were tradesmen, and no tradesmen were out on a Sunday.

Getting up and putting her sandwich back on the plate, Mary made her way to the door. "Who is it?"

The voice came muffled. "Mary? It's Will – William Goodridge. Do you remember me, Mary? I need to see you."

Mary felt her heart stop for one split second as old memories chased one another like butterflies through her mind, the very next second to be replaced by consternation. Bad news? Henry? Geoffrey? What? Hurriedly she opened the door. "What's the matter? What's happened?"

He smiled slowly, shook his head. "Nothing's the matter. I just took it on myself to call on you. I hope you didn't mind. Is it all right to come in?"

She could only open the door wider and step back to allow him into the flat, the state of it flashing through her mind. "I'm in a little bit of a pickle at the moment," she excused, leading the way to the lounge, already seeing it as he must see it: the dust, the bits lying around not put away. Snatching up a pile of undies awaiting ironing, she dropped them behind the sofa.

75

"You're the last person I expected to see." She made her voice sound bright and casual, put on a smile, but nothing could hide the bulge of her stomach and the way she waddled. What must he be thinking? She saw herself through his eyes, as a harlot who must have been made pregnant during some casual one-night stand. Did he even see her as a prostitute, supposing that she must have sunk so low?

Mortified, she bade him sit down, frantically clearing the small pile of magazines for him to sit. "Would you like some tea?"

For some reason the offer seemed to make her position all the more cheap, but he nodded affably, and she hurried thankfully to the kitchen to put on the kettle and collect herself, to control the sick feeling in her stomach, her thumping heart compounding it. Coming back with the small tray of two cups, milk, sugar and teapot, she found him still sitting there, tall and straight – she might have said tense, as tense as she herself.

"To what do I owe this call?" she began, again forcing brightness and, with an effort not to look too clumsy, easing herself into an armchair, glad at least that the furnishings were elegant, a legacy from the days of Geoffrey.

William took a sip of his tea then put it down on the occasional table beside him. "It's that I've been thinking about you a lot since your divorce. Several times it went through my mind to find out how you were but I didn't think you would want to bother with the likes of me.

When Mr Henry told me about how things have gone, it all seemed so very unfortunate. Sad."

Relief that she wasn't being seen as a harlot was almost painful. She sat silent as he continued.

"It's been on my mind ever since he explained to me how things happened between you and Mr Geoffrey that I had to see you. In all these years I've never forgotten you, Mary. I often wished we'd... that things had been different."

"I'm sorry," she said and immediately regretted what sounded like yet another rejection of him, though why he should see it that way she couldn't begin to imagine. Thankfully he didn't.

"No need to be sorry. That's how it happens. Of course, now..." He shifted uncomfortably on his seat. "You have nobody now. What I mean is, I still feel as I once did for you. After all these years, I still do." He leaned towards her suddenly. "Mary, the purpose of my visit, if you'll forgive me, is to ask you – you being all alone in the world in your condition, and myself still a bachelor with never an intention of marrying anyone unless it's you – what I mean is, I've come to ask if you would do me the honour of thinking about you and me – us – getting married. I could give the baby my name."

"Will..." Disbelief enfolded her brain, unable to take in exactly what he was saying. "I couldn't."

"If you don't want to, I do understand that. I just thought I'd ask."

"You can't want to marry me. I've behaved atrociously. Who'd want to marry me? Especially you."

"I wanted you to be my wife all those years ago. I still do. I'd rather not have sprung it on you this way, without giving you time even for me to come courting you again, but there is no time. Your baby will need a father. I can be that father. Mary, please, won't you think about it? Time is short."

He broke off, running out of words to coax her with. She sat staring at him, mouth open, heart racing, stunned, confused and sick from the suddenness of it all. Taking her silence as a refusal, Will looked away and, glancing down, picked up his hat which he had taken off on entering and put beside him on the sofa.

"I didn't mean to upset you," he said, standing up slowly. "It was a stupid idea."

"No!" She was on her feet, incredibly lithe for one so lumbered by her condition. "No, Will, wait! Sit down. I just need time to think. This has knocked me for six," she added as he sat down again, and went on, "Please, drink your tea — it's getting cold."

The most inane thing to say, yet he complied, picking up the cup and swallowing the tepid liquid in one gulp, replacing the cup in the saucer with great care as though he feared anything remotely more forceful might have shattered the porcelain.

Silence fell between them while she debated with herself, her eyes lowered. Finally she looked up, arriving at a decision, her words hesitant.

"William — it was kind of you to come and offer to do this. It was a big thing to do and I'm very grateful, but

I feel it's taking advantage of your good heart for me to jump at such a generous proposal. I did love you, William, all that time ago. But it *was* a long time ago, and, well, I need you to understand that I don't feel about you that way I once did. Too much has gone by. I know you realise that I'm in a desperate situation and I don't want you to think that I'm taking advantage of you. It's just that I can see no other way out. I don't mean for myself but for the baby's sake."

He was staring at her. "Are you accepting my offer?" he asked.

She nodded, turning her eyes away as he stood up and came over to her.

"Mary, I am so——"

"It'll have to be soon," she cut in, unable to look up at him. "The baby is due in six weeks."

It sounded so formal, so cheap in every sense of the word; a contract; she a market bride. She felt as ashamed as anyone could possibly be. There had been no embrace. He had stood over her for a while and when she finally looked up at him, he had nodded, gone back for his trilby, picked it up and, moving the brim round and round between his fingers, said, "Well then, I'll start things rolling, make arrangements."

"Yes," she had mouthed.

"I'll get it all done and finished in a couple of weeks. Has to be registry office, of course."

"Yes," she had whispered again, her whole being utterly numb.

"Well, I'll say cheerio then. I'll come for you when it's all arranged."

She had nodded and he let himself out of the flat, leaving her sitting there stunned, hardly realising what had transpired, unable even to feel relief. That came later and when it did, it was *only* relief, no joy attached at all. She realised too that not once had either of them referred to the father.

—

Two weeks later, as promised, Mary stood before the registrar, William next to her, she in a loose coat that hid as much as possible of her shape, he in his best suit. There were two witnesses whom they did not know but no one else and she was reminded of that other registry office wedding. She had been pregnant at that one too, had wondered if the man beside her really loved her or was just making an effort to give the coming child a father.

She could hardly recall how Geoffrey had been. She knew he'd made wonderful love to her on their wedding night. That was where this one would differ; William wouldn't do that, she was certain. If ever there was a marriage of convenience this felt it – her convenience, his sacrifice, or so it appeared.

"Sorry there's no honeymoon," William said as they left, bending their heads under an extended April shower, she thanking God for cloche hats that could be rammed down over heads so that no accompanying puffs of wind could dislodge them.

His tone was cheerful. "Can hardly go on honeymoon, you in your condition."

Mary laughed. It was a long time since she had laughed. The laugh was filled with sudden knowledge of her immense relief. She was married. That was all that counted. Her baby was safe.

"How about spending it going to the pictures?" he suggested. "We could go to a really good picture palace in Leicester Square. There's *The Last of Mrs Cheyney* showing somewhere — several stars from the silent days — Basil Rathbone, Norma Shearer, Hedda Hopper. I'm dying to hear them talk. They say loads of silent stars didn't make it when the talkies came in last year. Have you seen that Mickey Mouse cartoon?" As if she'd been able to in her condition! "First of its kind. We'll have a good laugh — at least we'll *hear* what's being said instead of watching Felix or Mutt and Jeff in silence."

He chattered on, finally pausing to enquire, "What d'you think, then? I admit it's not much of a honey-moon…"

She smiled up at him. "I think it will be a lovely honeymoon." And she meant it.

–

The main film hadn't been that exciting. None of the dramatic gestures of the old silent movies or the huge scenes many of them had portrayed, giving such marvel-lous entertainment; more like a play, set like one, a little boring. It was the audience now who were silent. The

81

chatter, the catcalls, the audible sighs of sympathy with the mute heroine, the rustle of sweet paper, the crackle of peanuts were all silenced in an effort to catch what the actors were saying, their American accents unfamiliar and hard to understand.

By contrast, *Steamboat Willie*, the Mickey Mouse film by Walt Disney – the first of its kind, as William had said – had the place in waves of laugher and more than made up for *Mrs Cheyney*. Unlike the stick-thin, stilted Felix, that goggle-eyed black cat stalking across the screen with his hands forever behind his back, soundless but for a pianist finking in the orchestra pit, this noisy "Mickey" with his high American voice and cheery lopsided grin, his believably funny remarks putting Mary in stitches, was rounded and almost touchable.

But halfway through it, she stopped laughing, gripped William's arm.

"Oh dear!"

William looked down at her. "What's the matter?"

"Will. I think we're going to have to leave. I've such a pain come on. It could be all this laughing, but I think the baby's started."

He was on his feet instantly, upsetting the person next to them. To the annoyance of all those around them, he began, in the height of the best joke from Mickey, helping Mary up. The two of them shuffled awkwardly sideways between the seats, her protruding stomach catching the back of the heads of people in front as she trod on the toes of the people behind her in trying to get past, several of whom were far from pleased.

"Cor! Mind 'ow yer go, missus! I ain't made of cement! Ain't used to 'avin' bloody elephants tramplin' all over me feet in pitcher palaces."

She mumbled "sorry" as came another's angry remark, "The moments some blessed people choose!" Stoically battling her way onward, she wished she had been given a seat at the end of the aisle in readiness for such a likely exit. But the place was crowded – had been when they'd entered.

Bundling on past another irate gentleman who had already had one dose of these two barging past him earlier to get to their seats, and more or less echoing the same sentiments as his neighbour about untimely exits, Mary looked only to get to the end of the row, and out of the place.

Even the lady at the end who had obligingly swung her feet into the aisle had one helpful foot trodden on by William. She let out a polite little squeak of pain but said nothing as, losing his balance a little, he put a heavy hand on her shoulder to stop himself falling.

Muttering an apology, he regained equilibrium and, with one hand under Mary's arm, assisted her up the sloping aisle to the exit while the ongoing antics of Mickey Mouse continued to send gales of laughter around the cinema. Out in the fresh, damp if sooty-smelling air of Leicester Square, another twinge of pain bent Mary over.

"Will, I'm sorry," she gasped. Straightening up carefully as it passed, she gave him a warning smile.

"If this is anything like my last one, it could pop out at any minute. I had Marianne early and very quickly –

no trouble at all. This one could be early too, and just as quick."

Speaking Marianne's name no longer brought the heartache she'd always felt before. There was a new baby to think of now. "Come on, Will, we must get home!"

"Home" was a flat Henry had found a week earlier, above a men's attire shop in Angel Court quite near the restaurant. Henry had arranged to pay the rent, saying it could be written off as a business expense. Business expense? For a head waiter? But Will seemed happy enough with it. Maybe Henry had said it was a tax dodge, with Will ready to go along with that.

Anyway, why shouldn't Henry pay? It was his child she was having. He could count himself fortunate in William's timely intervention. An added gesture of his gratitude had been to promise to put William in as manager when his proposed second restaurant was finalised, Henry as excited about the venture as a cat with two tails. The flat and his promise to William were indeed handsome. He could easily have shirked responsibility and let her get on her own way. It must have been a great relief to him when William had visited her and, seeing her condition, had proposed to her. A timely get-out for both her and Henry it seemed, and she would never cease to be grateful to William.

It was only a step from Leicester Square to the flat but they took a taxi. Just as well. There was barely time before she went into labour properly. But rather than the baby shooting out as had her previous one, it went on for nearly forty-eight hours, the attendant midwife calling in the doctor, saying the child was too big to pass easily. Mary was exhausted by the time the baby, an unexpectedly large but beautiful girl, finally thought fit to enter the world.

Her brow still damp with sweat, Mary looked fondly at the result then turned her gaze to William who, the moment he was allowed, had hurried in to kneel beside her, taking one of her hands in his.

"Are you all right, Mary my love?"

She nodded wearily. "I never want to go through that again." If it was said that once the baby arrived, the mother forgot all the pain and strain of bringing it into the world, Mary no longer believed it, maybe because she'd expected as easy a birth as her last.

William had hardly looked at the child. But then, it wasn't his, was it? She thought of how Henry would feel when he knew. He'd feel something – regret, maybe, that he could never tell anyone. She harboured no bitterness against him, merely sadness for him and a little for herself. She had Will to care for her. Dear William. If only she loved him all would be so wonderful, complete. She'd loved him once, years ago; she might again.

Hearing her sigh, he got to his feet. "You're worn out, dearest. I'll leave you to rest." To which she nodded and closed her eyes.

–

Things were going exceedingly well. At last they had got their feet off the ground, with Mother not well enough to argue. In August she'd had a small stroke and, though only slight, it had put her in a frame of mind to not find it in herself to care any further how the business did. The bank was being a little awkward still, needing to delve into the firm's books again and again, making Geoffrey fret and fume at each delay as further reservations were expressed. But banks will be banks. And Geoffrey was forced to be patient.

By early September 1929 the bank finally seemed ready to allow a sizeable loan. Not before time, though not as much as they'd hoped for. Jumping the gun a little, Henry had secured premises near Marble Arch as early as April, at no small cost. Though a little old fashioned, they lay in an ideal position. But now added on were architects' fees for redesigning both frontage and interior, surveyors' charges, insurance payments, working expenses, overheads and endless other costs to be taken into account. But the place was desirable enough to be worth all the outlay he could see lying on the horizon.

"We're going to have to bump the money up somehow," Henry had told Geoffrey at the time. "Going to have to find a financier or two."

Since then they'd spoken with several worthy investors who had expressed provisional interest. For all the huge costings it was looking rosy.

"By next year we'll be up and running." Geoffrey nodded hopefully to Henry's prediction, cash as always a problem with him, all the more with Pamela's natural bent for spending.

She knew how to spend, going through money like a knife through warm butter, unlike Mary who for all her penchant for shopping had at times expressed at least a little guilt about spending too much and now and again had pulled in her horns just to please him. Pamela, having brought a good bit of her own family's money into the marriage, deemed herself entitled to spend as she pleased, and not just on clothes but on diamonds, stables, hunting, exorbitant parties at the lovely big house her parents had given them in Epping. Now she was worrying him for a yacht – not just a nice little coastal yacht but one big enough for an army of guests and capable of cruising the Bahamas, not merely the Med. Either way it meant paying a crew, he being no yachtsman. With just one restaurant it was well nigh impossible keeping up with her. So he looked forward to 1930 with great anticipation, after what Henry had said. But more cash was needed if they were to even get off the ground.

Full of optimism, they sought a city house, a gilt-edged firm. But there the rosy dreams began to fade as one after another financier turned them down, seeing only a premises too in need of refurbishment to reap them rewards as quickly as they'd have liked. It was a financial friend of Geoffrey who recommended one of his firm's partners as a likely investor.

"The gentleman in question is Mr Clarence Hatry. In my books he's a financial wizard."

A board meeting arranged, they sat while the pale-faced, unsmiling man with a trim moustache, heavy-lidded eyes and a cold, blue, calculating stare under a receding hairline — every inch a financier and a little awesome in his manner — scanned balance sheets, profit and loss accounts and gross and net profits, the results of years of good management, which Henry laid before him.

Holding their breath expectantly, they watched the man's index finger trace firmly and swiftly down page after page, column after column, but when he finally looked up, his words, terse and to the point: "I regret, gentlemen, the proposition does not interest me," stunned them rigid.

That was all. Lost for words, they sat silent as he gathered his briefcase and left the room with not so much as a "Good day to you, gentlemen".

Angry but undeterred, they sought others. And after a few weeks a sprinkling of less astute investors, beguiled by Geoffrey's winning ways and suave tongue painting a marvellous picture for them, promised to give thought to the venture.

Seeing sufficient cash about to roll in at last, Henry went on laying out to surveyors and architects, borrowing from the bank at a percentage that rather took his breath away. But it was a good venture. A couple of years of hard graft getting it going until it began paying its way, then in would come the profits, hand over fist, for all the years to come. And who knows, this might be followed by yet another premises — even a chain of restaurants across the whole of England, one in all the large cities. And then the rude and arrogant Mr Clarence Hatry would be forced to laugh on the other side of his face.

Six

Bounding into the office three weeks after Clarence Hatry had turned them down, Geoffrey thrust the *Daily Mail* under his brother's nose.

"You seen this, Henry?"

Hardly giving Henry, who had been studying some figures, time to look up, he continued, "That bloody Hatry chap – gone down – crashed – under arrest."

"He's what?"

"Under arrest."

Henry glanced at his goggle-eyed office staff and hustled Geoffrey to one side, out of their hearing. "What d'you mean, under arrest?"

"Shady dealings, calculated swindles, making out false prospectuses. They say hundreds who've been involved in his enterprises have come a cropper. Cheeky swine – he knew he didn't have the money to invest in our project, yet he seemed so cool. We could've been caught up in that."

Geoffrey's mien was animated as Henry took the newspaper from him and read. He had to admit it was difficult to keep a twinge of delight and triumph from invading his own breast. Hatry had got what he deserved, the ignorant bastard! It was tinged with a tiny bit of disappointment, however. He had made a promise to himself that Hatry would be forced to laugh on the other side of his face one day, but he had wanted it to be because of their own success proving the man wrong, not from his own private doings. Still, it was triumph of a sort.

"That's what I call a damned narrow squeak," Geoffrey said, breathing sighs of relief. "Could have got our own damned fingers well and truly burnt."

But there was a backlash which in the excitement of the moment they hadn't seen. With the fingers of so many financiers actually burnt, those who'd been giving thought to investing money in Letts' second restaurant promptly pulled out, scared. Like most of these things, it would blow over, Henry said.

"But not soon enough to get us out of difficulties," reminded Geoffrey.

Nor was the bank as friendly as it had been, sensing their difficulties.

"I hope," Mr Bryant, the stony-faced manager, said when Henry came to see him, "that your finances remain sound, Mr Lett. Architects' fees, workmen's wages, surveyors' fees, et cetera, et cetera, all need to be promptly paid. Should any of them begin to doubt your worth, they will call in their money without a qualm. They won't wait around, especially with this Hatry scandal fresh in all minds. Everyone on edge. From the figures you've given us, the present bank loan will not in itself be adequate to cover everything."

"I must admit," Henry obliged hopefully, "the building fund's a wee bit low for my liking. But we'll manage if we go careful. Perhaps the bank might be willing to enlarge the advance we already have."

The manager leaned forward, forearms flat on the leather desktop, hands expectantly clasped before him, his granite features wearing down sufficiently to beam as far as they could. "I believe you've a trust fund. A hundred and fifty thousand pounds, I think? With that in mind, the bank would be willing to advance a further sum provided that your company would be willing to match it with the amount of that trust fund."

Henry blinked, his head already juggling with how any larger sum would be repaid within the time limit the bank would undoubtedly set. But the family trust fund?

"I think that would not be possible," he heard himself saying in a terse tone. It was almost with relief that he saw the manager shake his head and spread his hands apologetically. The loan they already had was frighteningly large, and all the while money going out. Great chunks of the original bank loan of £150,000 had been eaten into by various expenses: the purchase itself, insurance, professional fees, materials, workmen's wages, as well as unforeseen expenses such as delays, disputes, the collapse of some scaffolding two months ago, and all this before the new premises had hardly taken shape. It would be months, perhaps another year before it could open and start drawing back some of the money spent on it. By that time...

As he came away from the bank, Henry put his mind to attracting investors from wherever he could and with all his might. Hopefully the Hatry scandal would die more quickly than expected. There had to be financiers out there not scared witless by it. Henry hoped so, crossed his fingers and prepared to face the future without calling on the bank for more help. The family trust fund had to remain intact, no matter what.

–

Six weeks after the Hatry business, the man arrested but so far not brought to trial – and thank God for it, with financial houses again looking less hard-faced – Henry answered the private telephone in his bedroom.

Geoffrey's agitated voice sounded in his ear. "Henry, you seen the paper?"

"Not yet." Thursday's *Financial Times* had been delayed yet again. Henry made a mental note to have a word about it with the lad who usually brought it.

"Then turn your wireless set on to the BBC News," came Geoffrey's voice, high with panic. "Do it now. I'm coming round. Be there as soon as I can."

The phone going dead, Henry placed the receiver back on its hook and as advised went into the lounge and turned the on-knob of the wireless, twiddling the dial until the smooth voice of the daily news announcer became audible and clear.

"... panic this morning on the New York Stock Exchange with prices falling catastrophically. Much of the cause of panic is being blamed on ticker-tape machines lagging behind dealings, but near-hysteria selling is abundant everywhere. With orders to sell at any price and salesmen seeking non-existent buyers, stocks are being dumped overboard at whatever price they will bring."

By mid-morning Henry was smoking like a chimney, still taking in the accounts of near riots in Wall Street, the New York police riot squad having been called out and several ruined speculators having already thrown themselves off high buildings. He opened the door to Geoffrey's ring, he having sped from his country place in Epping in his high-powered Vauxhall in well under an hour.

Together they listened as finally the bottom dropped out of the market and the certainty of the collapse sent shock waves around the financial world.

"It can't concern us," Henry said to Geoffrey's worried expression.

"It could. Don't you see? We're looking to float a company, people to invest. Can you see them clamouring at our door now? First Hatry, now this. Where next? No one will take chances now. And we thought we were hard done by a few months ago when the Savoy offered to buy fifty-one shares in Letts. You said, not on your life! But who's going to bale us out now? The bank won't. Investors won't. Soon the bank'll want to be repaid. They're as scared as any of us. Before long we'll see every one of our creditors hanging on our necks, refusing to do another thing for us until they see the colour of our money. We can't pay 'em all. All right so long as bills come drifting in, but if they start coming in a deluge, what do we do? There'll only be the trust left to fall back on."

Henry turned on him savagely, the wireless voice forgotten. "We're not touching that. I told the bank that."

"I know you did. But what happens when they start calling in their loan? Where do we turn? We could go bankrupt."

"We don't touch the trust."

Grace came out from her bedroom, dressed for the street in a cream outfit and matching cream cloche hat, gloves and shoes. "Is something wrong? Why are you both shouting?" she enquired.

"Business, my sweet," Henry told her. "Where are you off to?"

"Hairdressers," she said blithely, picking up her handbag, also cream. "I'm having my hair Marcel-waved. It will be ready for the rather longer hairstyles coming in." Just about presenting her cheek for him to peck and say "toodle-oo" to her, she gave him a smile. "I'll be a couple of hours, dear."

When she had gone, Henry turned back to his brother, the disembodied voice of the wireless droning on unattended. While his wife had been talking about her hair, his mind had been winding itself around the inevitable. Now he gave despondent tongue to it, his heart having plummeted as low as had the Wall Street share prices, knowing how those men must have felt who had flung themselves to their death from high windows.

"The truth is, Geoffrey, we haven't enough money to see us through this, and that's it."

"Then what do you suggest?" Geoffrey's enquiring tone was hot and argumentative, the impact of what his brother had said not yet registering.

"I suggest…" It was hard to say this. "I suggest we call it a day."

"Call what a day?" The tone was still heated.

"The other place. The whole project. We can't go on with it, Geoffrey. We dare not start throwing good money after bad. The bank won't fork out any more. We won't find any decent investors now. We don't exactly owe money except to the bank, but soon we will. Our profits from here won't cover it. I was doing my sums while I was listening to that." He jerked his chin at the still chattering wireless. "After paying for this month's workmen's wages and materials, and with the insurance rising with every improvement we make to that place, we'll be down to rock bottom in no time at all as regards any more outgoings. If we call a halt now and resell the place, we can at least salvage something to pay back the bank with. Otherwise—"

"You mean, let it all go?" The look on Geoffrey's face told of his seeing all that high living to come fading away, and how Pamela would react to that. "We can't, Henry. We've spent so much, staked all we had on it. Let's wait a while. The market's sure to pick up again. People will come back. I'm sure of it."

No more did Henry want to see all those dreams going under, all the money they'd spent out go for nothing. At this stage it was nigh sacrilege.

True, by close of business as they sat tied to the wireless set taking in every last word of the news between the other programmes the BBC cheerfully put on, the market was reported to have recovered to some extent, thanks to reassuring statements by the big American bankers. But Henry's foreseeing eye told him that the time of the over-confident bull market had gone, and with it thousands of small investors, now in ruins, millions of dollars wiped out in one morning of frantic fruitless efforts to find buyers, countless small and large companies having lost everything, finding themselves bankrupt with the sudden-ness of an earthquake. Henceforth a dark and cautious bear market would rule for unforeseeable ages.

Common sense told him that they must pull out. And the matter did not end there. People would have to be paid off. The bank must wait a while, hopefully be a little clement. With investors they could have done it. But there were no longer any willing investors. Henry had never felt so sick in all his life and he knew Geoffrey was feeling exactly the same.

Four days later, the shares of the London Stock Exchange, lying in the direct path of the first shock waves from Wall Street, fell sharply, confirming the end of not only the Lett brothers' hopes, but the hope of the whole country. By early 1930, world economic slumps following the Wall Street crash, the country's unemployed would already top one and a half million – five hundred thousand more since Labour had come into power, the blame laid at its feet even though the United States and Germany too had several times that many out of work. Across the world ordinary people in despair blamed their governments. And the idle rich continued unaffected, their wealth safe in property, land, jewellery and art treasures.

Only those like Henry and Geoffrey Lett, who'd stuck their necks out at the wrong time, felt its weight. Doing his utmost to find a buyer for the half-completed restaurant while Geoffrey sulked; never having been faced with any such crisis before, and wishing he had taken Mother's wise words about his father being content enough, Henry hardly noticed the profits still being reaped by their one establishment, a mere drop in the ocean to what they owed the bank.

He stood now on a dismal Sunday morning in November 1929, gazing at the outside of his dream, the road behind him Sunday quiet, the place itself hushed and forlorn amid the debris of discarded tools and rubble within the fencing, upon which hung a huge red and white hoarding announcing "PLOT AND BUILDINGS FOR SALE" with more information in smaller letters as to where to apply.

The times he had stood amid the chaos and noise of reconstruction, his mind's eye visualising the end result, the bright interior, his mind's ear hearing the buzz of conversation from happy diners, the music to which they would eat and dance... It had all come to nothing, the heartache all the worse for having had the dream in the first place. And to add insult to injury, there was the money that had been thrown away on it, and money still owed to the bank with nothing to see for it. Dead. Not only that, but Mother had had another stroke, terminal the doctor was afraid, her left side useless, she only able to croak a few words. The fates seemed against them all this year.

–

They gathered around the bedside, the whole family, Henry hardly able to keep from glowering at his sister Victoria.

Having mentioned his thoughts on the family trust fund to her, he had sworn her to secrecy when she'd told him how appalled she was by his even considering it be thrown away merely to pay back the bank, his and Geoffrey's having been debts incurred by themselves alone. She had forgotten that her husband and Maud's had at one time been all for coming in on it – at a later date, of course, when the second restaurant had proved itself. Ignoring his wishes, she had relayed to Mother what he had said and Henry was sure this shock alone had brought on the second stroke, evident by her croaked words as she lay with her left side totally powerless: "Not… to be touched… your father's will – nest egg… for his children."

Invested in gilt-edged shares, there was a clause that it was not to be used for any expansion of the family business except with agreement by all. It was his seeking that agreement which had led to Mother's condition and for that he blamed himself as much as Victoria, though she had been wrong in not keeping it to herself, knowing Mother's condition.

He had already upset their mother with his suggestion early last year of floating the company on the Stock Exchange.

"I do not want that," Mother had sighed from her bed where she had taken herself for most of the day despite her doctor's advice that she could and should keep herself mobile. "Go public? No, Henry."

But he had tried to go public. As far as he could see it had been the only way. He remembered a conversation with William Goodridge. "I'm starting to lose my nerve a bit over all this," he'd admitted to him as financial teeth began to bite. "Sometimes I wish I'd never started it. But my brother's snapping at my heels. As fast as I make money, he's going to spend it."

"Can't you curtail him somehow?" William had suggested boldly, in a position of late to speak his mind.

Henry had shrugged. "He's a director. It's not easy."

He remembered the scene so well: standing on the brass-railed balcony above the diners, William surveying the crowded restaurant below, the lively chatter and the clash of cutlery on crockery echoing up to them. At mezzanine level, the small circular dance floor was filled with couples, a four-piece dance band striking up a one-step. Colourful, noisy, lively music and shrill laughter added its own share of echoes, the fabric-covered pillars doing little to allay the fault after all, yet somehow it increased the buzz of the place where a hushed atmosphere might have been daunting. People felt able to express themselves in loud talk, and that was its allure. Henry recalled wondering if the second restaurant when it was completed would be able to create this same atmosphere. Oddly he remembered not being sure. Even then doubts had crept in, doubts he had thrust aside hardly noting them. Now he did. This Letts was unique, could never be duplicated, and there had been a feeling in his bones even then that he was doing the wrong thing in pursuing the path of a second restaurant which might not only prove a white elephant but might even diminish this place. At that point William had blurted out: "Mr Henry, do you think you're doing the right thing – this new restaurant?"

Henry had looked at him as though he had blasphemed. "Right thing?"

"Pouring all this money into it. Trying to entice investors. None of them keen to take a chance, most of them only out for themselves."

Henry had been offended. "Because they've not seen the finished product. Once we convince them how great this second place will be, how it will pay, they'll be all for it. I see it paying for itself within a year of opening."

"Maybe," William had said stoically. "But at the expense of this place, taking custom away from here. Might you not be spreading the butter a bit too thinly, two lots of staff to pay, two lots of overheads, double insurance… ?" He had broken off as Henry glared at him. "It's only my opinion, Mr Henry. I'm not a financier, but… I only see it from an ordinary man's view…"

"Damnation, Will!" The explosion had burst from him. "Yes, you're an ordinary man, not a financier, and have no business telling me—" He'd pulled himself up sharply, recalling the sacrifice William had made over the business of Mary, a sacrifice that could never be repaid. Moderating his tone, he had apologised, adding, "But we can't go back now. We've spent too much, owe money in all directions. We have to go ahead, you see."

William had nodded and, leaving him, had made his way down to the restaurant, passing the crowded dance floor.

Then had come the Hatry business. He should have known then. He should have listened to William Goodridge. Now his mother lay dying and he was virtually broke in that they owed the bank thousands. But with Mother gone the house would come to him. If he sold that… Seconds later he was wishing himself dead for the thought that had smote him.

Half an hour later his mother passed quietly away. And he wept.

Seven

A vast change had come over Henry Lett these last six months. Not that he allowed it to show before his customers; he was the same with them as he had ever been; smiling, friendly, accessible and sociable, ever attentive to their little confidences, ready with a laugh and a witty aside. They still loved him.

With his staff he was a different man: sharp, carping – often over the smallest of errors – harassed and grim. At their home – Grace preferring Swift House these days to the hubbub of London and wanting to be near her own family – he was sulky and easily irritated. Unable to cope with his changes of mood, she turned even more toward Hugh, now a handsome toddler already displaying the spirited wilfulness of his Uncle Geoffrey, difficult to handle except by his mother whom he adored and whose gentle nature he could twist around his littlest finger.

Unable to cope with the excuses Grace made for him, Henry spent nearly all his time in his old flat over the restaurant or harassing his staff as he brooded on what might have been and on the repercussions from his failed venture. The bank leaned ever more hard upon him as the months progressed, tired of his palming them off with meagre amounts from the profits the original restaurant brought in, now seeking repayment in full of their loan.

Troubled, he'd had a blazing row, all over some little thing, with his head chef, Sampson who, having had a better offer from P & O Shipping Line, quit to perform his considerable skills aboard one of their liners. His replacement was as skilled but not as flamboyant and his dishes were to Henry's mind not as imaginative as Sampson's – another pinprick to add to all the rest in his side.

He was still unable to come to terms with his bitter disappointment, unable to share it with anyone. After half a year of bearing it all alone, it was to William that he spoke, in sheer desperation needing to lighten his mind, though even William could not possibly help materially.

"I don't know for how long this place is going to go on," he told him dismally, standing with him in the spot where they usually exchanged the odd comment, the balcony, in a way finding it more convenient to discuss matters of the restaurant gazing down at it rather than in the office. Odd how easily he could confide in this man, almost as an equal, a man who'd listened to so many confidences from him and in his way had quietly and unobtrusively solved many of them.

What Henry Lett didn't know was the fear his words had brought to the other man, who was presently seeing the great restaurant folding and he himself being thrown on to the dole queue. After all he had achieved, all he had worked for. In that moment his anxieties were every bit as great as those of his employer.

"The bank is climbing on my back," Henry continued. "I've managed to stall them so far, but all I seem to be paying back is the interest on what's owed. I can't keep up. Nearly all the profits from this place go to pay back the loan, yet it still isn't enough. Now they're clamouring for it to be paid up in full or else. I'll have to find thefrom somewhere. But where from, I don't know." He gave a sigh, preparing to move away, his chest for the moment lightened by the confession.

It struck William, in the midst of his shock, that Henry Lett never referred to the management as "we". As if his brother – and partner – did not exist.

"What does Mr Geoffrey say to all this?" he ventured in vain hope that perhaps Mr Geoffrey who, it was said, spent money as though it were no object, might have the answer if consulted.

Henry paused in taking his leave, gave a despondent, if slightly whimsical shrug. "Little point talking to him. He insists it'll all come right in the end. I've told him that the bank will be quite within its rights to foreclose on us if things go on too long. Had the other restaurant been going, they'd have been paid back well before now." There was another great sigh and this time his shoulders drooped. As if to support himself, Henry put his hands on the gleaming brass rail of the balcony, letting them support his body. "They're saying if I don't come up with at least half of what is owing within one calendar month, they'll call in the whole lot. I know what that will mean. I'm at my wits' end."

Trepidation flooded an even greater deluge through William's breast. "You mean you could lose the restaurant?"

Henry smiled wanly, gazing down at the place he loved. "Ironic, isn't it? A going concern. And they're willing to destroy it all – for their pound of flesh."

"Can't you still float the company on the stock market?"

"The only offers with the size of that bank loan looming are the big men looking for a majority share. My father would never have allowed that. The business going out of the family – Mother would turn in her grave."

"Isn't it better that than losing it altogether?"

Will felt he could ask questions such as this. After all, this was his own livelihood at stake. His standing had risen several months ago with his being promoted to restaurant manager, Henry having got rid of his sour-faced predecessor.

William had felt for the man as he left, one more to add to the dole queues, now topping the two million mark. It had clouded his joy somewhat but these days, with the depression biting ever harder, it was every man for himself. With the other man pushed down low enough the opportunity was there to step on his back and keep the mind averted from such luxuries as sensations of guilt.

"Doesn't Mr Geoffrey realise how deep in the both of you are?"

Henry spread his hands. "I don't know what he realises. At this very minute he's in the Mediterranean somewhere, he and Pamela whooping it up on someone's yacht I believe. His only complaint when I tried to talk to him before he left was that lack of funds had put paid to the yacht of his own he's always wanted, only temporarily he hoped, but that Pamela was in a sulk over it." He gave a small but sharply bitter laugh. "A yacht? I ask you! I only hope they never have any worse worries. Upset over a bloody boat! With all that's going on..."

He spread his hands wider as though to embrace the world rather than his own present predicament, then dropped them limply at his side.

"What I need is an injection of money from some-where, anywhere — some miraculous windfall from heaven." Again the bitter laugh, sobering sharply. "I could work a few shady deals. In this business you get to meet a good few dubious characters. Odd, the underworld rubbing shoulders with such as members of parliament. Yes, I know a lot of 'em. And they know me."

He seemed to be talking for the sake of it, as though to stop would recall the predicament he was in. "You know 'em too. Decent blokes, most of 'em, among themselves. They'd swing a deal if I asked. Trouble is, you're in their clutches forever more. No telling where it'd lead. But other than that, as I said, I'm at my wits' end where to turn. I can't lose this place, William. I can't."

William could see a glistening in those eyes of unshed tears. Henry took a deep, shuddering breath. "I've even toyed with the idea of mortgaging Swift House. Or selling it. But that's part of the trust fund, and without the agree-ment of my sisters I can't touch it. They keep saying things'll blow over in time and that if I touch the house or the trust fund, it will be ransacking their inheritance. What do they know, or care, about the state I'm in? Their husbands have their own businesses. They're all right. As for Geoffrey – he's got his wife's money to fall back on. Wonder she doesn't buy a bloody yacht herself and have done with it! I thought of asking him if her family would... But I'm not about to humble myself that far."

He fell suddenly quiet, then, as if William wasn't there, turned and walked off. William watched him go slowly down the carpeted gilt stairs to the restaurant below, noisy with lunchtime customers, then saw his back straighten, his head lift and his face become wreathed in smiles. The show must go on, William thought, watching the display, he alone privy to the true depths of the sorrow behind the bright facade Henry Lett presented to his world.

–

All this William had related to Mary. She had listened, said nothing and he, no doubt assuming she was filled with worry that he might be in danger of losing his job, went despondently to bed.

They'd said little to each other as he prepared to leave the next morning, and now, after a whole day with just herself and little Helen – who so filled her days that she wanted little else – she sat at her dressing-table after having put Helen to bed waiting for Will to come home.

Saturday. He would be kept there into the early hours until the last supper-goer had left, attending the wishes of the happy, over-stuffed, self-indulgent wealthy who popped into Letts after the theatre to round off their evening with supper and champers. Henry would be there too, showing them his untroubled face as Will had described, sharing a joke with them, spinning a tale for them or listening to any tale they had to spin. He would move among them – "mine host" – though he was perhaps not as sought after as Geoffrey, had the diners been fortunate enough to find him there. Geoffrey had always been one for making a party go with a swing.

She too, at one time, she remembered. There was no bitterness in that memory; in fact it brought a small shudder as though seeing someone else. The playing of a role, imagining she was keeping up with him while all the time ever vaguely aware of being left miles behind, shining only in his light. She knew that now.

Everyone still flocked after Geoffrey Lett. They never ever saw that empty side to him. That empty side that cared for no one but himself. Even now, in his absence, they basked in his distant sunlight. Little had changed.

It angered her, Henry practically killing himself to keep that place going while Geoffrey swanned off, spending as he pleased – more likely with his wife's money these days, and serve her right – yet continued to reap all the accolades.

Perhaps he did have something that Henry lacked, but Mary knew who was better of the two, the thought bringing echoes of the times when she and Henry had made love together.

But there was William now. All any girl should want: sweet-natured, understanding, kindly, patient. He needed to be patient, for she was aware that the love she gave him was merely the residue of that which she'd given Henry during their all too brief affair. She now understood behaviour of the woman she'd so lightly blamed for driving Henry into her own arms. But unlike Grace, Mary did allow William to make love to her, if feeling guilty at doing little more than obliging him, faking the joy, all the while lying, hating her own dishonesty.

"But how can I tell him the truth?" she challenged the mirror. "And see him hurt?"

He was too good a man to be hurt, a man whose heart would bruise easily. How she must have broken that heart all those years ago by running off to marry Geoffrey. William might not set her heart aflame, but he was the most reliable, the most honest of all three of the men she'd known.

He'd be moving among the tables tonight enquiring if this party was being taken care of and if that party required anything further. Friendly but not servile, as respected as Henry, and unflustered by affluent customers.

Mary didn't envy any of them their wealth and situation. She too had enjoyed money, married to Geoffrey, had lived life to the full, often regardless of the not so fortunate. Nowadays wealth had become degraded before the queues of shabby unemployed, shuffling drawn-faced and sunken-eyed towards the dark aperture of some building for a pittance to be thrust into a hand that had once done honest manual work. Unemployment was no respecter of skills – clerk, shop assistant, insurance salesman, manager too drew their insulting benefit, they too with a family to feed and rent to pay and no job. World depression, after that brief tumble in share prices on one day last year had sent countless businesses to the wall, had put millions out of work. Mary found herself thanking God for the wealthy still around to keep places like Letts going and those like William in work.

What riled her was how they patronised the less fortunate poor, the fine ladies who made a great do of gathering together to run soup kitchens. It was commendable, charitable, but for the wrong reasons – to get a kick out of it. Last week William had come home with the story of one middle-aged, well-cushioned woman with a capacious appetite for Chateaubriand feeding bits of especially ordered chicken chasseur to her Pekinese while remarking to a companion: "Awful seeing people lining up for a hand-out. So dreadfully embarrassing, my dear, having to pass by. I do hate the poor!"

Pushing her thoughts away, Mary turned her mind to the jewellery laid out on the dressing-table, every last piece of which she'd had taken out of the bank vault this morning, all that was left of her marriage to Geoffrey.

Dreamily picking up the huge solitaire engagement ring he'd bought her, the memory of that day came flooding back. She'd gasped at its size – not only in amazement but fear. A girl who had nothing – with such a ring.

"Geoffrey, I can't wear that. People will say I've stolen it. They'll start asking questions. I'd be so embarrassed having to tell them. They'd think I'm a gold digger. They'd wonder what I had to do to get it. No, I can't!"

But he had reassured her, told her to wear it around her neck if she were that particular about what people thought of her. She had at first, her association with Geoffrey a secret.

Then he'd married her and it all became so different, she accepting jewellery as if it were her right.

But before that, in Paris, he'd bought her this necklace with earrings to match. Diamonds. She picked the set up from the dressing-table, held them aloft, the glow of the table lamp catching each stone with blinding sparkles of reflected light. She and Geoffrey had stood outside the exclusive little jewellers in the Rue de la Paix, she still flushed by all his attention of her, bewildered by the immensity of her first trip abroad. He'd dragged her in and had not asked but told her what he was going to buy for her. She'd not said a word, had been unable to, stunned by the cost of the set. Now she looked at them with the memory of their purchase embittering her.

So many beautiful things he had showered on her and now she could only look on them in bitterness, eager to be rid of them: the waist-length string of natural pearls; the earrings; a sapphire and diamond anklet; another in gold set with tiny rubies; a diamond wristwatch; gold and silver slave bangles; several shoulder and corsage brooches, their designs set out in coloured gems – nothing less than real, nothing less than the best.

Each time Geoffrey had presented her with such a gift, he'd murmur, "I love you, my darling, with all my heart. Nothing is too good for you."

Then suddenly he had tired of her, had spoken of divorce, another woman; had said she could keep everything he'd bought for her, that this other woman was above accepting second-hand goods. The way he'd said it had pierced her heart more keenly than any dagger.

Mary stared at the rings she had gathered to one side of the dressing-table. Each held a memory: the cluster of diamonds about a huge central emerald, bought at Tiffany's in New York; another with an ox-blood ruby. That one had slipped off her finger on the first evening she had worn it. They'd both scrabbled about on the pavement in the rain in electric-lit Times Square, laughing like kids, to find it again. Others had been bought to console her after Marianne had died. Mary pushed them hastily away, her eyes filling with tears. Memories, happy and sad – too many of them sad, it felt now, crowding out the happier ones.

She gathered the pile into a sparkling mound. How much would it all bring? Each piece had been exorbitantly expensive at the time, but were now second hand, as Geoffrey had so delicately put it. Even so they would still fetch quite a bit.

Snuggled among it all was the heavy brooch that had once belonged to his mother. An ugly thing, but made of gold encrusted with emeralds in an old-fashioned design and looking as if it could be worth a good deal of money.

Geoffrey's mother had given it to him to hand to the woman she had expected him to marry one day. When he went off and married a girl of whom his mother hadn't approved nor deigned to recognise as her daughter-in-law, she had demanded it back. He had refused.

"It's yours, my darling," he'd whispered defiantly. "As my wife you're as worthy of it as any." And he had made fierce, possessive love to her.

Maybe he had forgotten it when he'd said she could keep everything he'd bought her. He was like that, his mind mercurial, important matters cast carelessly aside. Mary wondered as she extracted it from the glittering pile if it had ever crossed his mind at any time since the divorce. The family too had probably forgotten about it or never even bothered about it or even knew of it, shabby-looking thing. Well, it was hers now, to do with as she pleased.

She smiled, recalling her words to Geoffrey – "I shall keep it safe" – all the while thinking, *Who'd ever want to wear such an ugly thing?* Marring every dress she wore, it had lain at the bottom of her jewel case since then. Ugly. It could go with the rest.

Getting up from the dressing-table, she went and took out from her wardrobe the four fur coats and three stoles that reposed under dust sheets, as did several beaded dresses, all unworn since her days of splendid opulence. After these were taken out, what was left was a pitiful sight – two plain outdoor coats and a few day dresses, skirts and blouses, forlorn and sorrowful hanging there on their own. She spread them out on their hangers to make them seem more. They didn't really.

Laying each fur lengthways on her bed, the fine *haute couture* dresses flowing gently on top of them, Mary stood back, surveyed them for a minute. They wouldn't bring much, but every little helped. All done, she went into the bathroom and washed her hands, face, and the top half of her body – a subliminal, almost ritual gesture of cleansing away the past. The past must be the salvation of the future – she hoped.

Drying herself slowly, still in a ritual gesture, she put on her nightdress and in the light of the single table lamp sat down in a wicker bedroom chair near the window to wait for William.

–

"Still up, love?" He looked surprised to see her.

He had come in, his dark overcoat and trilby wet with early spring rain, already taken off in the hall and hung on the coat rack. Bow tie, jacket and waistcoat taken off in the lounge, clad only in shirt and trousers, he entered the bedroom on tiptoe, so as not to waken her, as he thought.

"Has Helen been waking you up?"

"Not at all," she replied. "I was waiting for you, to speak to you."

He was undoing his shirt, slipping it off to reveal his narrow but strong muscled arms and torso beneath the white vest.

"This time of the morning? Can't whatever it is wait until later?"

"I didn't want to wait until later, what with Helen to take care of."

William raised one eyebrow in that quirky way he had. "It must be important."

"It is." She turned her face to the pile of jewellery glittering in the light of the bedside lamp.

His gaze followed hers. "What the devil's that doing there? You said you'd leave it all in the bank and never touch it again unless we were in dire need. We're not in dire need, *yet*."

Placing a small but significant emphasis on that final word, Mary knew instantly to what he alluded. Who could say when Letts would be foreclosed by the bank calling in its loan, he thrown out on to the street? Who could say with certainty whether even someone of his standing would find another post? A year ago she'd have said it would have been no problem at all, that he could take his talent anywhere. Not today. But today she was making certain that Will would never be thrown into any such dire situation. She smiled.

"This is to ensure that will never happen. I've no other use for it."

He hadn't understood, looked at her as though she'd gone mad. "That stuff's valuable. You can't go selling it just in case I end up out of work."

"Listen, Will—"

"You can't!" he burst in, becoming instantly alert. Weariness from his late night had been all too evident, but now it fled. "You mustn't."

"Let me tell you why I want to."

"No, Mary. I know you mean well, but…"

"Will, please, let me *tell* you why," she pleaded again. "Just listen."

William sighed, noticeably summoning up patience. He let himself sink down on the bed, sitting deliberately on the edge in order to miss the garments she had strewn across it. He stared up at her. "All right. Why?"

Mary came and sat next to him, taking one of his long thin hands in hers, noting how elegant those hands were, waiter's hands, capable of turning the serving of even the humblest dish into a work of art.

As restaurant manager, responsible also for staffing, for rotas, and for the training of new staff, he was the most respected of men, often privy to many a confidence of the famous and titled, usually addressed by his first name in friendly terms by wealthy regulars, even by a royal – the Prince of Wales – who occasionally came with an exclusive circle of friends for supper. William told her of an occasion not long after the prince returned from his tour of South Africa, when the prince had chummily taken him by the arm to share a witty aside with him as he would a close friend.

Will had been quietly proud of that. He had come a long way in ten years, could only better himself were he to join some great hotel such as the Ritz or the Dorchester or the Savoy – who had apparently wanted to take over Letts, except that Henry had refused their offer. But he would never desert Henry, to whom he maintained he owed a lot for his rise in status, though she herself felt that Henry Lett owed him much in return, Will having acted as father to Henry's daughter. Soon he would have even more to thank Will for. At the same time hers and Will's future would be assured.

Meanwhile, earning good money while so many were out of work, they lived comfortably, he even running a little Standard car bought cheaply from someone who'd needed the cash. In it they took little trips into the country the rare times when he wasn't on duty, off for a day to Eastbourne, Brighton or Margate so that little Helen could enjoy the sea air.

Other than that, they lived simply. She didn't miss the social round as she had once thought she might. Nor did she have any interest in ever returning to that state. But with the restaurant back on its feet she'd make sure Henry allowed Will some shares in it. It being a family company, he'd be an outsider but Henry couldn't refuse him after what she was about to do. With this jewellery she had the means to make that all come about.

In the dim glow of the table lamp, Mary explained her plan. "I know you said we should keep it for our old age…"

That sounded so odd to her ears that she almost laughed. Will was the last person she had once thought to grow old with. She, with her wonderful lifestyle with Geoffrey, then her oh-so-brief love affair with his brother, to find herself with William Goodridge…

"I'm glad I didn't take your advice to give it all back to Geoffrey. He'd only have spent it all. He did leave it to me. One of his better traits was that he was never mean."

It was like speaking of the dead. She saw nothing of Geoffrey these days so that he might as well have been.

"Now I've found a proper use for it," she went on. "I've made up my mind and I won't allow you to talk me out of it, Will. But I am going to sell the whole lot. Every bit of it. I'll get in touch with some high-class auction house. I don't know how much it will fetch but it should bring in something substantial enough to help Henry pay back what he owes the bank..."

She stopped him as he made to interrupt. "It's not generosity, it's business. I don't want Henry's thanks. What I'd like is for him to make you a shareholder in the company. I know it's a family business but he'll owe us that. He has to pay back what he owes the bank and banks are cold-hearted enough to see a restaurant go to the wall. They don't care who they ruin so long as they get their pound of flesh. They won't wait for him to pay it bit by bit out of profits. With this depression they want their money now or they'll have the restaurant sold from under Henry's feet, lock, stock and barrel to get it."

William sat silent and dumbfounded as Mary continued.

"I've been thinking about things, and I'm sure you didn't just come to see me that day out of the blue and decide to marry me. I thought so at first, but I've had a long time to think about it, and I believe Henry asked you to do it. How do you think I feel, Will, palmed off on to someone else so that he wouldn't have to be embarrassed? I've never blamed you, my dear. But I wish…" She broke off momentarily, on the point of saying "I wish I could love you as I should". Instead she said, "I wish I could make it up to you for what you did."

He came to life. "But I love you, Mary. I've always loved you."

"I know," she replied, miserable with herself for not being able to match that love. "And I want to make that up to you as well. What I want is for you to become someone of note in this rotten world."

"I'm that already. I'm almost at the top of the tree in my profession."

"No you're not. You could go higher. You could have a restaurant of your own one day. Until then, I want to make sure of you being given the proper promotion Henry Lett owes you. You deserve it."

To anyone listening it might have sounded that bitterness rang in her words, but she didn't intend it that way. In fact, the love that she had given to Henry lingered still, often threatened to obliterate that which she had for William. It was this that perhaps made her bitter against herself. Neither man had ever made demands on her, not as Geoffrey had done. She put thoughts of Geoffrey away from her, her heart long since having hardened towards him.

As for Henry and William, she tried to tell herself that she loved both equally, but it wasn't true. Each had tried to do right by her, had treated her gently and with respect, each going about it in his own way. But though she honoured them both, if she had to be candid with herself, she knew which one claimed her heart and which claimed only her affection.

"I want Henry to do well out of this, as much as you," she said.

Eight

Mary's tentative phone call, supplying a description of the jewellery she hoped might attract the man from Sotheby's enough for it to be thought saleable brought only casual interest. Her description as a mere afterthought of the Victorian brooch, however, prompted a suggestion that he come to her home to "take a look at it".

Taking a look at it, turning it this way and that, one would not have thought it to be of any real value but for a gleam of avarice in his eyes.

"Hum! Yes." Mary watched as he scratched his chin, smoothed his trim moustache with a middle finger. "This could be of interest."

Mary felt disappointment. If an ugly old brooch *could* be of interest what hope was there for what she'd imagined to be a fortune in diamonds and pearls? "What about the rest?" she asked.

He eyed the glittering selection tastefully laid out for his scrutiny. "Modern of course. Very good quality. Yes, we can help you there. But this piece must be sold separately. If I may take this away for written appraisal…"

"But how much do you think I'd get for it all?"

"All? Quite a decent price. This piece… ?" He turned the ugly thing over in his fingers once more. "Hard to say what it would fetch in auction. In the region of five thousand." Mary contained a gasp — it was not a time to show undue excitement in case the offer was lowered. "A very rough estimation, you understand. It needs to be seen by the appropriate department. It does depend on the interest of the bidders what it fetches. It might not reach its reserve figure, in which case it would be withdrawn from sale. On the other hand it may well go above, but it's very much a matter of what is being sought, you understand. I shouldn't worry about that if I were you. It will be printed in the catalogue for collectors of such pieces. If you have decided, I will give you a receipt for all this and you'll hear from us shortly."

As he spoke, Mary noticed him studying intently two small pictures, both scenes of Florence, on the wall by the door, one above the other. She hastened to oblige, telling him that her former husband had bought them for her a few years ago, but she kept back the fact that she'd never really liked them, their colour faded and grimy.

"My husband said they were both antiques," she provided instead, without enthusiasm. "But they're so dirty I can't even see who they're by. We were going to have them cleaned, but things went on and we never did." She wasn't going to go into details of her divorce.

"Have you ever had them valued?" the man asked suddenly.

Mary shook her head. Whatever Geoffrey bought, it was always worth money. He never considered anything that wasn't. But there they had sat, she trying to look pleased with them at the time, not wanting to hurt his feelings. Like the brooch.

"May I take these with me as well?" he was asking. "Unless you intend to keep them?"

"Not at all."

They would surely fetch something if they were worthy of his notice. She'd be only too happy to be rid of them. They only hung there to fill a blank place. Nor did she really want anything of Geoffrey's if it could go to helping out with his brother's debts.

The same with a largeish vase on which the man's now acclimatised glance had also descended, having got his eye in, so to speak. This vase she did like. Geoffrey had bought it years ago when he had taken her to Paris. They'd gone to the flea market and, rummaging around, he had come up with the bulbous vase with its swan neck, highly – she would have said garishly – decorated with branches and leaves, fruit and flowers. It was Chinese, quite pretty she thought. She hadn't exactly treasured it, but it went well with her hall wallpaper as it sat in splendour on a lace doily on the small mahogany hall table.

She watched the man pick it up almost reverently and upturn it to study the marks on the base. She heard him murmur a Chinese name and something about royal signature.

"Would you be interested," he asked, "in selling this as well?"

There was a moment of wrench, then she made up her mind. "If it brings in a decent bit of money, otherwise, no."

She saw his lips quirk a little as though finding what she said a joke. Then he became serious. "I think, Mrs Goodridge, that between this, the paintings and the brooch, you may raise quite a decent bit of money."

"But what about my jewellery?"

She could almost imagine him saying, "You can keep that!" as he gave an insignificant shrug. "Oh, yes, your jewellery. Well, it's very good quality. I think we can do quite well with it. So may I give you a receipt for all this, and you can make up your mind after our assessment whether you still wish to sell or not?"

"Fine," she agreed and saw him off the premises.

–

After the next couple of weeks spent in pounding agitation, a letter finally arrived, the reserve price for the brooch a little disappointing after what she had been given to believe, the other pieces around what she had expected. The two paintings they said had been done around 1740 by an Italian artist named Joli. This time the reserve price looked far more promising, as did that of the Chinese vase, tending to take her breath away and brighten her eyes considerably.

"I never dreamed an old vase would be worth that much," she told William. "Nor a couple of dirty, faded old paintings. I've never even heard of the artist."

She wrote in reply that she was willing to go ahead. There had come a point when to even glance at the stuff Geoffrey had let her keep made her bitterness rise like gall. Thank goodness that on the face of it, it promised to be not a bad haul to hand to Henry.

William still had reservations about it all but she wasn't listening. All she could visualise was the gratitude on Henry's face as she handed him the cheque. A drop in the ocean maybe, she didn't know yet, but it had to be of some help. The next problem would be whether Henry took it. She was determined he would for she was doing all this out of her love for him.

–

She and William entered the auction room to the low murmur of voices, further hushed by oak panels, plush furnishings and heavy carpet. Crystal chandeliers and wall lights glowed softly. Old paintings in over-large gilt frames frowned darkly from the walls. Spindly red and gilt chairs were placed in rows, three-quarters of them already occupied.

They found two empty chairs at the rear. Everything smelled of old furniture, musty books and a special indefinable richness. Articles for sale were being placed on side tables. The auctioneer was bending down talking to someone. More people were coming in, the rows filled quickly and people were now standing at the back and in the wide doorway.

"It seems lots have come," Mary whispered, and Will nodded, amused by the simile, the other "lots" befitting auction rooms.

There were many items before hers. With some the bidding was brisk, with others, slow, any item not reaching its reserve price withdrawn, making her feel that the same fate could await her things. Then, piece by piece, her own jewellery found homes, bringing in a tidy sum. Henry would be helped some way to paying off the bank. Now she caught her breath as the turn of the old brooch arrived. All at once she was sitting upright, excitement gripping her as the unencouraging reserve price was reached and passed. But for it being a sort of heirloom she might ignorantly have let the brooch go for a mere song ages ago.

The bidding continued and Mary felt that her ears had begun to ring, her head to spin, her heart to pound with sickening thuds of mounting anticipation.

Everything moved so fast she didn't really hear the final price as the the gavel was finally brought down with a somewhat unassuming click.

"What did it come to?" she whispered in Will's ear. He was looking as white as a sheet. His voice was hoarse.

"Just over eight thousand pounds."

"Good God," she whispered, the whirring in her ears starting again. "For just one piece?"

She felt as though she was no longer in her seat but floating way above it, hardly caring what went on during the rest of the afternoon. At the end of it all, managing to get herself to her feet, she went and signed her assent as requested, the cheque to be forwarded once the auction rooms had taken out their various expenses.

Emerging on to busy New Bond Street, Mary still couldn't believe it. "All that money for one old brooch. Geoffrey's family would have a fit."

William grinned. "Best not tell them, then." He didn't seem in the least troubled that none of the money would benefit him or her, and she felt her respect for him grow. He was such a wonderful man. If she could only love him more than she did. He deserved so much more.

"Best that the family never do find out," Will cautioned again, this time with more seriousness, as they walked on.

The brooch, given a date of somewhere around 1830, had turned out to be of Russian origin, possibly once owned by a noble family. How it had come to the Lett family, Mary didn't know, nor care. She'd got rid of it and that was that. She had money instead which would do far more good.

"Henry will ask questions," she debated, sobering, watching fleets of buses passing by.

"Just don't tell him the whole truth then," William said. But she was not convinced.

"He's bound to be curious as to how I came by so much money. And he must know that Geoffrey gave the things to me. He might wonder where they went to."

"Another thing, Mary," Will said now as they skirted a knot of people about to board a bus. "You ought to hang on to just a little of that money."

"No, I want to give it all to him."

"I'll be surprised if he takes it. He's a proud man."

Mary looked at him sharply. "He's in trouble, Will. He has to take it, for the sake of Letts."

"*We* might need some of that money one day," Will persisted.

"No." Disappointed in him, she put on an angry spurt, weaving in and out of the crowds ahead of him. "The brooch was his mother's in the first place," she said as he caught her up. "He has a right to benefit from it, Will. I know he'll always look after us. Out of gratitude."

But she didn't want Henry's gratitude. What she wanted was his love.

–

There was still the auction for ceramics and paintings to come. A few days later found her and Will in a similar auction room, heart in her mouth as she followed the bidding, this time a little more astutely. Here, too, both the pictures and the vase passed their reserve price and continued upward so far and so fast that she felt sick each time the gavel came, finally reaping an astounding eighteen thousand pounds for one picture, twenty for the other. As if that wasn't enough to give her a heart attack, the final bid for the Ch'ing vase was forty-nine thousand. She'd had no inkling of the fortune she'd been sitting on after Geoffrey left her. Neither had he, probably, or he'd have long ago frittered it away.

Walking home on Will's arm she remained speechless with disbelief at it all. Back at the flat, Jenny, Helen's nurse, brought the baby to greet her mother, and Mary let herself collapse into a chair while William hurried off to make her a cup of very sweet tea. All she could do was ask Jenny to take Helen off with her until she could pull herself together, then they would cuddle and play.

Helen was nearly a year old now, a beautiful child – Henry's child. She loved her so much that her heart began suddenly to ache for him. It should have been all so very different to this. Sipping the tea Will handed to her, she found herself caught up with the thought of how wonderful it would have been if Henry and not Will had been there with her at the auction. Handing back the emptied cup, nodding to his enquiry whether she was feeling better, it struck her how ungrateful she was being in even wishing it.

"I'm glad it's all gone, all that stuff," she said defiantly.

After all the excitement she felt drained, as though something had been taken out of her. She contemplated how Henry was going to take being given all that money. Over a hundred thousand pounds; it would go a long way to settling his debt with the bank. The bank, made happy, would probably let him pay off the balance in easy stages. She just hoped now that he would realise that she had done all this solely out of love and would accept it.

–

Tanned from an Italian holiday, Geoffrey paced the library of Swift House, his face contorted with anger as he now rounded on his brother.

"You must be stark raving bloody mad to have gone through with it! What bloody got into you, Henry, giving away part of your shares to someone outside the family? It's a family business, a private company."

Henry drew in a lungful of cigarette smoke. "I told you at the meeting. You, Maud and Victoria. I had to do something after what Mary did for us. Anyway, all three of you finally agreed to it."

"I was a fool to agree."

"Then why did you?"

"Because you caught me on the hop. I'd hardly got home before the meeting was called. No one told me about it."

"We wired you and waited until you got home."

"Just about," raged Geoffrey. "Maud and Victoria were outraged by what you were asking."

"They agreed in the end," Henry pointed out in a level tone. Geoffrey wasn't going to get him riled.

"Because you practically bent their arms. I wasn't happy about it."

"But you went along with it," Henry reminded him. "You know I had no option but to eat humble pie. The bank was at our throats. We'd have lost everything but for Mary. I had to do something in return."

"You didn't have to go offering shares in the firm to that man she's married to. A thank-you would have sufficed."

"I don't think so." Henry's tone hardened. Geoffrey had no idea of the real reason behind it all. Mary, the mother of his child. His illegimate child needed to be kept a secret for all time. As far as everyone was concerned it was William's child. Only he, William and Mary knew the truth.

"I'm indebted to them both. We should all be. I believe in honouring a debt such as that with whatever means I feel are needed."

"Then you're a bloody fool! You've always been a bloody fool, Henry."

Henry held his glare with his own steady gaze. It was still painful having to accept Mary's money. He felt sick every time he thought about the humiliation of having to accept what could only be described as a hand-out from the very woman who'd given birth to his child, but there'd been no other option. Without her, the family business would have gone under due to his own puffed-up stupidity in trying to expand the restaurant in times like these.

He had already been confronted by the family for his failure, his own sisters quick to reproach him. They were ready enough to enjoy the profits but as soon as things went wrong, the first to complain, offering no help at all. But for Mary's selfless act, they'd all have been finished. It was only right to express his gratitude with more than a mere thank-you after all she'd done for him. But all they saw was him taking money from his own brother's ex-wife. They couldn't see how close they'd all come to losing the family business and, it seemed, neither did Geoffrey.

"So now they have a say in our business — a woman of no account and some paltry employee?"

"She was your wife, Geoffrey," Henry reminded harshly, exhaling a savage cloud of cigarette smoke. "Surely you've more respect for her than saying she's of no account. And Goodridge isn't *some paltry employee*. He's the restaurant manager, the husband of someone who sacrificed all she had—"

"Which I left her with," spat Geoffrey. "Not to bloody well piss up the wall! I bet she knew what she'd get out of it. You don't throw that sort of money around without knowing you're going to get something out of it."

Henry felt himself beginning to lose his temper. "She did it with the best intentions, Geoffrey. After what she's done for us, you should go down on your knees to her. But for her, the wife you bloody divorced for another woman, you'd now be without a bean. The bank would probably be taking everything we've got."

It was a point he had put to him and their sisters at the emergency meeting, drumming it in until they finally had to capitulate.

When he'd first told his sisters what he intended to do, they'd refused to countenance it, their reaction: "What if the restaurant suddenly begins to make more money than ever dreamed of? This person, this employee, will reap a fortune. A fortune! *Our* fortune!"

Speaking as though they were being done out of millions, they each had ten per cent of the company, which wouldn't be that trifling an amount if Letts ever reached the giddy heights of becoming one of London's top three or four restaurants. If it ever happened it probably wouldn't be a private company any longer but be floated on the stock exchange as most sizeable businesses were.

Fighting them around the table had taken it out of him. As principal shareholder, if he couldn't call the tune, who could? His father had left Mother the controlling interest. On her death, he as her eldest son had come into the majority share while Geoffrey, whom she'd never truly forgiven for having married a girl from their very own kitchens against her wishes, received significantly less. He'd never got over it, his pitiful rebellion being to absent himself from the restaurant as much as possible. The remainder had been divided between Maud and Victoria, still keeping the business in the family. So why should making a gift of a few of his own shares to William Goodridge, whose wife had done so much for them, be so important to everyone?

Puffing at his cigarette, Henry watched Geoffrey's pacing. "Ours has been a family concern from the very beginning. It was how Father wanted it."

Devoid of expression, Henry stubbed out the smouldering butt. He felt heartily sick and tired of his brother's carping. "I notice you weren't so hot about it remaining a family concern when you were for us expanding. You were willing enough then to float *this family concern* on the open market – you could hardly wait."

"That was different. A second restaurant would have given us an even better standing in the world."

"Except that it didn't work out."

That was another thing which made him feel sick, the recollection of all that enthusiasm, all the high hopes, all the money ploughed into it, the humiliation in seeing it all come to nothing, them owing thousands into the bargain.

Geoffrey gave him a baleful glare. "And whose fault was that? What matters now is you giving away the family firm."

Henry sighed. They were just going round in circles. "Geoffrey, we've been through all this. If you're so hot under the collar about it, you should have said something at the board meeting instead of coming here moaning about it after it's been done. Had it not been for Mary—"

"I don't want to hear about Mary," burst out Geoffrey. "What matters is the bloody cavalier way you went about it."

"Damn what I did! I'm talking about Mary." Riled at last, it didn't occur to him that their raised voices were being heard all over the house, that the staff were creeping about, ears keen so as to regale one another later with what each had heard, and that upstairs Grace had put little Hugh, with whom she'd been building coloured bricks, away from her, and was hurrying down to the library where the voices were becoming ever more heated.

"Victoria might agree. Maud might too, after you soft-talked them. But I still don't. You think you own the whole bloody firm. I'm seeing our solicitor, seeing if he can do something about it."

"There's nothing you can do, Geoffrey. We owe our financial lives to Mary. You agreed to me doing what I did. Now it's done."

"I'm damned if it is! And she can take back her damned hand-outs."

"If you mean Mary, speak of her by name. It's the least you can do. It was for you as well as for me. For us. You're beholden to her."

"I'm damned if I am. Scheming bitch! I know what she's after."

If anger could be said to be white hot, that was how it came, Henry's eyes blazing. "Take that back, Geoffrey!"

"What? That she's a scheming bitch? She always was. That's how she got me. And if I'm right, she's after you now. Probably wants the big fish. That husband of hers — it's you she's after, you mark my words. Sacrificed all she had? Christ, she could reap a fortune. Dangle a sprat in the water to hook a big fish. I know her sort. I learned about them the hard way!"

"Take that back, Geoffrey," bellowed Henry, "or I swear I'll land you one!"

It was to see these two glaring at each other, on the balls of their feet, fists clenched, that Grace opened the library door. But at her interruption each seemed to freeze, eyes turned to her on the instant while Grace stared from one to the other. Her gaze came to rest on her husband.

"My dear, what's going on?"

For a moment she sounded like their mother, and each moved away from the other with a crestfallen expression, anger dissipating.

Henry was first to recover, adopting a tone of reprimand bom out of sudden embarrassment. "Grace, go back to Hugh. We're talking business."

His expression must have frightened her because she turned and hurried away, closing the door after her. But Geoffrey wasn't done yet, for all his voice had become somewhat subdued.

"You should have spoken to me first before taking her money," he blustered on, though the power had gone out of his attack.

Henry's own voice moderated. "I couldn't reach you."

"You should have waited until I came home."

"The bank wasn't prepared to wait."

"There's such things as cables."

"And where would I have sent it? You'd floated off as usual on some whim – you and Pamela." He had never liked Pamela, had tried to bring himself to, but always failed, the woman sharp and tart with a tendency to look down on people less wealthy – "tradespeople", a term she loved to use for those like himself, her family's wealth – what some called "old money" – inherited down the years. Geoffrey had done well there, though whether she looked on him in that same light, Henry didn't know nor care.

He was beginning to feel riled again, despite a resolve to remain calm, while Geoffrey began to rage once more, "It's my business where I holiday."

"Not when you overlook informing us where you are," he flung back. "You were the same with Mother – getting married without telling her. I can understand her never forgiving you. As a director of this firm, you've a duty to let me know where you are."

"I'm not a bloody prisoner to report to you wherever I am."

Geoffrey's voice, rising, sounded petty. Henry thrust it aside, battling to keep his own voice even.

"It was only because of that Naples earthquake and you deigning to grace us with a cable saying you were unscathed and only slightly shaken up that we knew of your whereabouts. By that time, Mary had stepped in and given me her ultimatum about the shares. Something in return for—"

"Her ultimatum!" Geoffrey cut in. "Using the jewellery I gave her to wiggle back into the family. I can see what she had in mind even if you can't – getting back at me. That's what she's doing. Wangling that husband of hers into the business. Making fools of us all."

"Not at all," Henry defended heatedly. "As far as I'm concerned Mary is still connected to us by her marriage to you. She wanted to use what you left her in order to provide us with a way out of that mess. And that's what she has done."

Geoffrey's eyes had narrowed with suspicion. "Are you sure it's not something more than you thinking her connected to the family by my marriage to her? Though divorcing her did away with that. But I know you fancied her. Does she have something over you? Does she?"

Henry found himself turning abruptly away, fumbling agitatedly for another cigarette. "Don't be so bloody stupid," he burst out as with shaking hands he lit the thing. "She's a married woman."

"Why should that stop you?"

Again a wish to thump his brother. Yet to attempt to would merely lay his own soul bare. How could he reveal the truth? Truths have ways of resurrecting other truths, truths that need to remain buried. Should it get back to Mary that he'd engineered William's marriage to her in order to save his own reputation...

"I couldn't see the place go under," he said instead. "All this fuss over giving someone a few shares as thanks for a good deed!"

Geoffrey gave a derisive snort. "A good deed. Huh!"

Henry turned to face him squarely. "It didn't come out of your pocket, Geoffrey. But for Mary there'd be no restaurant left for anyone."

He'd been dumbfounded when William had come to him to say that with the jewellery Geoffrey left her on their divorce Mary had been able to raise two-thirds of the amount needed to pay off the bank; that the bank would be lenient and let the rest be paid off later. Embarrassed, he'd protested that he couldn't take such a sum from her and insisted that if she'd told him what she was doing he'd have prevented her doing it.

But he knew why she had done it. She still loved him enough to make such a sacrifice. Instead of lightening his heart, he'd been mortified that her marriage to Will had made no difference to her feelings for himself; that Will, generous to a fault, was the loser. He must know, or feel, that he was. An image of her and William together sprang into his head; the man trying to please, to satisfy; the woman smiling but not returning that love as much she might; the man frustrated, trying to cope because his situation told him he must; turning his back, trying to sleep. Which of them lay sleepless and staring into the darkness? Maybe both. "I can't take her money," he'd said lamely.

William's voice had been forceful. "You have to. You can't hurt her twice. She's done this thing for you. Take it. Unless you want to add more to the harm you've already done her."

"It leaves you both with no nest egg for the future," he'd said.

William had become ill at ease. "No need to feel anxious. She wants something in return. For me to be given a few shares in the restaurant."

The relief that flooded over Henry had surprised even him. Mary, at last feeling her feet, had become tough. Indeed, he'd felt a stab of admiration for her. Had he not granted her wish, would she have withdrawn her offer and seen his beloved restaurant, his life, taken from him? He still wondered about that.

Geoffrey's voice brought him back to the present situation. "I'm not happy about all this. Not one bit."

Henry lit up another hasty cigarette to cover the entreaty in his own tone. "Do you think I wanted it this way? Just remember, Geoffrey, it was your ex-wife who saved us."

"With my money," Geoffrey reminded acidly. He was stalking towards the door. There he turned and looked balefully back at his brother. "If you think *I'm* going to thank her, however, you've another think coming, old man. As far as I'm concerned, she's done nothing for me. If you enjoy eating humble pie, that's up to you. But remember, brother, with this selfless little act of hers, she's got you just where she wants you. Though what you two've been up to for her to be so bloody generous, I wouldn't care to guess."

Guess all you like, Henry thought with a caustic sense of the ironic truth behind that departing remark as the door closed sharply leaving him alone in a now silent room.

Stubbing out his barely begun cigarette, he stood gazing at the golden freckling of dust motes caught in the shaft of sunlight from the tall windows, then went and took another cigarette from the ebony box on a small table, entirely forgetting the one he had this minute put out. Throwing himself into the winged leather armchair, he lit up, sending a cloud of blue smoke wafting upwards to mingle with the shaft of dancing dust caught in the August sunlight.

Mary would never hold anything over him — she cared for him. He felt the stirring of longing deep in his stomach. He still loved her but she was beyond him now. He had done that all by himself too.

–

"Sorry, Mary." William's posture exuded apology. "Late night again."

She looked sleepily at him over the top of the counterpane, drawn up to her chin against the freezing chill of December, for all the flat was excessively warm, as ever. He was always complaining of the flat being unbearably warm. She sat up, looked at the bedside clock then back at him.

"One night, Will," she said, unsmiling, "I am going to get your bed sent over to you."

"I said I was sorry," he whispered, moving towards her to drop a kiss on her proffered cheek, still creeping on tiptoe though there was no need. Helen, in her own little room, would not hear him if he were to walk normally on the carpeted bedroom floor. Tiptoeing was a sort of deference he always adopted for coming home at three in the morning.

The kiss accepted, she sat back on her pillow. "You could pop over to let me know you're still around. It's only a couple of minutes across the way. Or telephone to see if Helen is all right. Or me. That takes only a minute." Stripping off his black jacket and waistcoat, he put them carefully on hangers in his wardrobe, undoing his bow tie and unbuttoning his shirt and trouser fly, turning his back on her to clamber out of the rest of his clothes. "Christmas in a week. Not had a minute. People already celebrating."

"Yes, I know that," she conceded lamely.

He got into his pyjamas. "Getting busier each night. Festive season."

"I know that too."

With William moving off into the bathroom, still with exaggerated care, to brush his teeth and have a quick wash, Mary let the palm of her hand move reflectively across her lips to her cheek and the nape of her neck. More than half a year had gone by since Henry had given him those shares. Talk about Greeks bearing gifts! They had in their own way virtually fettered Will to the restaurant, his whole time now given over to it. He spent so much time there it seemed as though it had become his very soul.

Whenever she pouted at his being so seldom at home, he'd laugh off her fear that she was losing his love for her and say, "I love you, Mary, every bit as much as when I first saw you. It's for you, for all three of us that I need to give so much time to the restaurant. It will get better, I swear, then you'll have me all to yourself again. And I'll have you. I can't wait, darling."

Left to care for Helen, for the flat – little of that with a daily coming in – preparing meals for herself and Helen, he most of the time eating at the restaurant, she couldn't help but fret. Often she recalled days when she and Geoffrey hardly saw the inside of their home except to give parties. What parties they'd been. What a marvellous life it all now seemed.

Not that she and Will didn't live well, but the social world she'd once known had gone. With Helen she'd wander along to Oxford Street, Regent Street, Mayfair, Kensington, looking in the shops, seeing the rapid changes in fashion. So much had altered – skirts were now calf-length, frills and feminine curves had returned, hair grown longer and Marcel-waved, make-up less dramatic than once it had been, less harsh, a woman again looking like a woman and not like some immature boy.

Aware of how the fine new styles put to shame what was still being worn by ordinary women, current fashions for most of them an unaffordable luxury, she'd buy herself something in one of the fine shops like Harrods. Often she would come away wondering what had been the point when there was nowhere to wear it these days.

"You shouldn't mope around the place so," William said when she spoke of boredom. "Get a nanny in to look after Helen and go and seek out some of your old friends."

But she had no old friends – not ones she cared to see.

"What about the women in this neighbourhood? They're a nice class of people."

But women in this neighbourhood lived their own lives, had their own social set, went out with their husbands, their children left in the care of a resident nanny or one they'd hired from an agency. She could have done the same had Will kept reasonable hours and had he not been too tired to take her out when he did come home.

"Then join something. There must be ladies' clubs around here," was his argument. "You'll soon find new friends there."

But she wanted *him*, to be introduced to *his* friends the same way that Geoffrey's friends had become hers, until the divorce when they'd all drifted away.

It was no use – so full of his own life, Will was incapable of seeing how isolated she was becoming, the kind of associates he was making not encompassing her. He'd tell her about them when he *was* at home, these last twelve months having become involved more and more in the running of the restaurant.

–

"I seem to be taking over Geoffrey's role these days," he told her. "I'm sure he forgets that as a director he should be seen more often than he is." It was July 1931 and as usual Geoffrey was somewhere in Italy. "It's got so that few ever ask after him, and then only to wonder idly at his not being around."

Rather than condemning Geoffrey for being so remiss, he relished the man's absence, being given a new status with customers turning their attention to him instead. And why not, Mary thought with admiration. Will was a perfect substitute, sociable, charming, a somewhat loose-limbed grace about him that made him appear entirely at ease with himself, they enjoying his dry humour that probably matched their own. They might still look to Henry to unburden their small problems, and Mary well knew the comfort he could dole out, but sharing a good joke was reserved for William Goodridge now, where once it had been reserved for Geoffrey.

It seemed Will was making friends with all sorts, from the Hollywood stars in London en route for Paris – who found Letts an informal but respectable venue in which to cavort until dawn before returning back to their hotels, the Savoy or the Ritz, to sleep it off – to Members of

Parliament frequenting the place to unwind, and rogues with money to go places. Stage people often called him "darling", politicians addressed him as "Goodridge" or "my dear chap" or plain "William", and rogues — of whom Letts saw its share, well-dressed and respectable on the surface — endearingly referred to him as Billy. He saw them all in the one light so long as they behaved while on the premises.

He would speak of them often by their first name — name-dropping as Mary saw it, though she was proud of his new social standing with them all — Noel (Coward), Miss Valois (of ballet company fame), Frederick (Ashton), also of ballet fame, Constance (Lambert) and so on. But even Henry, who knew everyone, never name-dropped. It was at times embarrassing, Mary considered.

Some he had come to know better than others. Sir Oswald Mosley, invariably with a different woman on his arm for all he was married, was a noisy diner holding sway over those with him, usually on some favourite political topic. The orator had taken to William owing to those occasions when he'd cornered him and Will, instead of giving an excuse to be somewhere else, had appeared to take the time to listen to what he had to say. Henry, polite though he was, had his own, strong, views on politics and there Sir Oswald knew he had met his match. William was far more pliable.

"You must come to one of my meetings, old boy. I won't ask as to your politics but I will open your eyes to what's going on in this country."

William's political views this last year or so had, as with so many in despair of the present government with depression hammering at their door, been thrown into some confusion. By his very upbringing he had naturally always leaned towards the party striving for the ordinary man. Now, despite his exalted position as restaurant manager of a high-class establishment crying Tory to him and the present Labour government proving incapable in getting men back to work – his own father, a man of integrity, had been given the push last year – it was still against his nature to see the Tories as his choice. Mosley and what he called his New Party, having lost patience with Labour for rejecting his radical ideas for economic regeneration, were like salvation to William's present confusion.

"Labour was a mess," William told Mary in September. Labour having resigned, the general election loomed. He'd mentioned the expelling of Mosley by Labour, who had then banned all his supporters. Even before the election an already formed coalition National Government looked to win it with flying colours, everyone sick of party muddle. Will had his own thoughts.

"That won't alter things," he went on as, leaving Helen to her own devices, Mary set out his tea. "Taking us off the gold standard and devaluing the pound, putting the Bank of England in a panic." He failed to mention that several other countries had also come off the gold standard. "What we need is a complete change. Look how Sir Oswald dealt with Labour after what they did to him. Split the Labour vote at the Ashton-under-Lyne by-election in April with his New Party so the Tory got in there. It proves his New Party is what we need. He knows where he's going. He's just the man to lead us out of this mess."

"He's the man to lead you up the garden path," Mary countered as she gazed at Helen dawdling over her supper. Two years old in April, the child was not a hearty eater by any means, causing her mother many a fraught hour coaxing her into getting a few spoonfuls down. Now Will had come home, early for once, only to plague her with politics.

In her estimation she wasn't politically minded and felt disloyal to the single-minded women who'd fought to win the right to vote. At this coming election, she, now with a vote, wasn't even certain how to properly exercise it, more shame on her. She'd vote, but for whom? One thing was certain – it wouldn't be Mosley's party. For herself, she didn't trust him.

Or maybe it was that she was sick and tired of hearing about him through Will. She heard about him everywhere else, too. Everyone had heard of him: bom into wealth, married into more wealth, a notorious womaniser, a Tory MP, then a Labour MP, only to walk out on them all to form his New Party. The trouble was that people struggling to make ends meet might be willing to follow him as their golden hope to security, William among them.

"Leave it alone," she advised, taking Helen by the hand to wash her ready for bed, having given up on the half-eaten supper. "I don't trust the man. He seems too much of an upstart turncoat to me."

But Will only snorted. "You ought to take more interest in politics. It can be so absorbing. You could come with me, you know. Then you'd see."

"And what about Helen?"

"Get someone in to look after her. You need a break, love."

But she never went. Had it been a theatre or the cinema she'd have gone willingly, but that was seldom offered – the last time they'd had an evening out together had been to see Gertrude Lawrence and Noel Coward in *Private Lives* at the Phoenix Theatre, a year ago – and she wasn't going to ask now.

Nine

In the weeks coming up to the general election William went to four of Mosley's meetings – another cause to keep him out late. After the first meeting Mary found herself telling him angrily to remember that he had a home. She could forgive him late working hours, but this going off to enjoy himself without a thought for her alone in the flat, Helen asleep, and nothing to do – it was like the days after Geoffrey had left her.

Whether Will made any mention of her anger to Henry or not, to her deep gratitude he called in on her the next three times, saying he guessed that she might need a bit of company. A bit of company! She could have thrown her arms about his neck. But that would have set something off, and complication was something she did not want.

That first time she was indeed edgy, visualising the rekindling of their old affair, but Henry conducted himself as properly as any old friend might. She looked forward to each visit, the sight of him at the door brightening up her dull day. He would take a moment or two to peek at his sleeping daughter, Mary standing quietly behind him, aware of the oddness in knowing that he was Helen's father. Those days were so like a dream, she often forgot for long periods about his relationship to her daughter.

After closing the door softly on the sleeping child, he would come and sit in one of her big leather armchairs with a glass of brandy she'd begun to have ready for him.

"Do you mind if I smoke?" he had asked that first time. She'd shaken her head eagerly, remembering the days when the tang of Virginia tobacco smoke would linger well after he'd left, a fragrant reminder of the joy of their love-making.

After that he'd light up as a matter of course. They'd sit opposite each other, chatting, she about Helen, about her loneliness and feelings of isolation, he about the restaurant, sometimes of his uneventful married life with Grace. After her one trip abroad with him she'd lost all interest in holidays, content only to be with their son. She showed no interest in himself; he'd not had relations with her for so long that it had become a habit.

Mary's heart would go out to him, not entirely self-lessly, longing to give him the comfort he so craved but conscious also of the need she herself had for him still. It was as well to smother it, knowing that at the first semblance of encouragement he'd be in her arms. Then she'd have to face Will later, certain that he would detect by her face what had gone on. Of course he knew of Henry's visits. She was entirely honest about that and he didn't seem put out, rather he saw them as an open cheque to follow his own pursuits.

"It is about time he took you somewhere a little more exciting than that," Henry remarked after she had told him about Will's offer to take her with him to his political meetings.

"He's never here long enough to take me anywhere," she answered, sipping the sherry she had poured for herself. "Helen's no barrier, we can get a nanny in for her. It's just that he never even mentions us going out."

"You've not asked him to give you more of his time?" The way he said it made her suspect that he already knew she hadn't. "When he's always so very busy?" she said sharply, and because it sounded as if she were censuring him in allowing his restaurant manager to work such long hours, even though it was William's choice, she added hurriedly, "He loves his job so much. I'd even say that the place is in his blood."

"It certainly is," Henry replied with a grin, but sobered immediately. "Even so, he should consider you more than he does, at least take you out occasionally. Unless, of course..."

He paused at that, in a guarded manner, and in a more cautious tone added, "*Someone* ought to be taking you out, getting you out of yourself, or you'll be having another nervous breakdown." She couldn't recall having any such breakdown but supposed her depression following her divorce might have made it appear so – or perhaps he was referring to her behaviour following Marianne's death. But Henry was going on, again with exaggerated caution. "I wonder if William would mind were I to take you out one evening. Just to give you a little relief from this flat."

Mary's heart gave a leap of excitement. "I could ask him." She prayed that her joy did not show too much in her eyes. "I'm sure he wouldn't mind."

William didn't mind, or at least appeared too preoccupied with all he was hearing at his political meetings. He seemed almost relieved to have the responsibility of her taken off his shoulders. "Fine, if you want to go."

His ready agreement left her wondering if he loved her at all. When they'd first married he had spoken of his enduring love through all the years he'd not seen her, but lately it seemed to have died. It was her fault for turning from his affections from the beginning, her heart with Henry, until she had finally killed Will's love. She cared for him but it was Henry she still loved. Geoffrey of course was a distant shadow; hard to believe they had ever been married.

Henry took her to Drury Lane to the opening night of Noel Coward's *Cavalcade*, a truly lovely story of English life from 1900, with himself and Mary Clare starring. Afterwards Henry took Mary backstage to add his congratulations to all the others on a fine success: he and Mr Coward were on close speaking terms through the actor often patronising Letts for supper after a performance. Mary had met Mr Coward before when she and Geoffrey had been together, but he didn't appear to recognise her though he greeted her affably when introduced by Henry as a sister-in-law. Taking Henry's hand he promptly led him through the crush of the hot and swarming dressing-room, with Mary following, to where a girl was pouring champagne, bidding Henry to have as much as he wanted for it had been, "A fine first night, old boy, don't you think?"

For the occasion, Mary had poured herself into a pale green cinema satin sheath evening dress she'd bought at Harrods. At the time she'd wondered where on earth she would ever wear it; now, mingling with social wealth, it was like old times. She didn't want it to stop.

She certainly was in no hurry to leave. Will wouldn't be home until the small hours, more likely going off to a club for a drink with the political friends he was beginning to make. He'd come home to tell her all about them and the meeting, boring her to death with his euphoria about all the good things Sir Oswald Mosley was promising to do for the country as he gained power. Mosley was certain of his New Party winning seats enough to convince the next government of his radical but right views, and confident that he would finally make this a country fit for heroes.

Henry's lack of hurry about leaving matched hers. Grace wasn't even at home, spending a week or two entertaining local friends, of whom she had many, at Swift House. Her parents, just the other side of the village, could enjoy seeing their daughter and their grandson. She'd written a couple of times to Henry about it. Other than that, he was a free agent. They had all the time in the world.

The gathering dispersed just before midnight, and she and Henry finally got themselves a taxi for the short journey back. The night was a stormy one with a high, rain-laden wind, but in the taxi it was cosy. With the champagne affecting her, Mary sleepily laid her cheek on Henry's shoulder, feeling his hand gently holding hers. It was lovely being so close to him, the warmth of his hand on hers, the texture of his suit smooth against her cheek, his breath touching her forehead now and again. Almost like being in bed with him.

In the flat, the young woman hired to sit with Helen put on her coat, handed Mary her bill to be paid to the agency later, and departed with a smiling remark: "Your little girl has been a darling, Mrs Goodridge. No trouble at all. I hope you and your husband have had a lovely evening."

"Oh, we have," Mary replied, compressing her lips to suppress a giggle. Closing the door, her suppressed laughter escaped its barrier in a burst of merriment. "Thank you for a lovely evening, *Mr Goodridge*. Would you care for a brandy, *Mr Goodridge?*"

Henry laughed too and, while she poured his brandy, sat himself in the deep leather armchair which he appeared to have made his own. He shifted slightly to one side of it as she handed him his glass, and patted the space he had made, enough for her slim figure to fit into. "Come and sit here. You need to calm down after rushing from the taxi in that wind."

She had indeed arrived at her flat on the second floor out of breath, for all it had been just a few yards to the door with the wind buffeting her.

"Almost as bad as August." She gave another giggle as she stripped off her coat and hat, dropping them in a heap on the carpet. "My, that was a terrible gale we had, with floods and everything." A small hiccup stopped the flow, and she came towards him, still on the verge of giggling. It all seemed very funny, rushing like that from the taxi, nearly losing her hat, racing up the stairs, trying to get her key in the lock, making it after the third attempt, the young woman, Miss Something-or-Other, handing her that time sheet and saying…

"Mr *Goodridge*," she spluttered and threw herself into the narrow space Henry had made for her on the armchair, even so enough for her slim frame to squeeze into. "Mr *Goodrid*…" The rest of it became smothered by Henry's lips on hers.

Suddenly sobered, she put her arms about his neck and drew those lips down even tighter upon hers. For some time they clung together, she feeling the heat rising up in her, the desire for him making her head reel, her whole body cry out for him. It was the champagne. No, it was more than that – it was an ache for love. For so long she had been without love quite voluntarily: her own fault, for only Henry could give her what she truly craved.

Breaking away from her, he put down the brandy glass and, getting up, took her in his arms, carrying her towards the bedroom. She did not protest but let him lay her on the bed and undress her while every fibre of her tightened with an ever-mounting need as he took off her clothes, then his, all the while seeming not to have let go his hold on her. The time to the union of their two bodies seemed to consume them until finally they lay side by side, not moving, each with their own thoughts. Mary felt his arm come around her, heard his voice whisper, "Are you all right?"

She nodded and for a while they lay quietly, then he said, "I must go." Again she nodded. If Will found them like this...

Dressing was automatic, silently done, almost an embarrassment. She followed him into the lounge, distantly heard Helen briefly call out in her sleep as she turned over. The sound brought words to her mouth.

"Will you visit here again?" Somehow it seemed that he wouldn't, for he didn't answer immediately.

When he did, his tone was flat. "Do you want me to?" *Oh, yes!* For a moment she thought she had said that out loud. "Do *you* want to?" she asked instead, inanely, then impulsively, "I'd like you to." Then emotion got the better of her. "Oh, darling! I couldn't bear for you not to."

She was in his arms and they kissed with the desperation of those destined never to meet again. "I will," he whispered. "When William..." He sounded out of breath, it coming in a gush. "When he's out again."

"Yes," she replied and knew they were forming a conspiracy.

–

"There something not quite right there," Mary said.

William had told her how Letts did not seem to be making the profits its busy times warranted. Henry's accountant had said the books appeared in order and he could find nothing to account for the low turnover.

"I don't believe him," Mary said. "Beevish is an old dodderer. He was Henry's father's accountant long before the brothers took over. He must be nearly eighty."

"Seventy-five," William corrected as he put on his bow tie in readiness to leave for his evening on duty, which would probably take him well into the small hours, it being Saturday night.

"Well, he acts as though he's eighty." Mary intended having the last word. Someone was fiddling the books. Someone who knew how useless the old retainer had become. "Henry ought to get rid of him. I bet a younger man would find a discrepancy or two somewhere."

"Henry says he hasn't the heart to dispense with him."

"What about Geoffrey? What does he say about it?"

"I haven't seen him for weeks. Neither has Henry. No good turning to Geoffrey for anything so long as his share of the profits comes rolling in. You should know him, Mary. You were married to him. He doesn't care a fig so long as he knows the money is there to spend."

Since the collapse of Henry's hopes of expanding the business, Geoffrey had acted as though Henry had committed the most heinous of sins in using the cash from the sale of her jewellery to get the business out of trouble, and in showing the gratitude to create William a shareholder. Recently he had all but melted into the background, almost a sleeping partner. With no mother now to lay down the law, he did as he pleased while Henry worked himself like a slave. Not that Letts *obliged* anyone to work like slaves; it seemed to have the power to shackle the hearts of such as Henry and William willingly. It even shackled her, who'd had no dealings with its running in recent years. Now, however, hearing how little profit was coming in despite all Will and Henry's hard work, William remarking that it seemed to him there were more overheads than he thought there should be, Mary was intrigued.

"Has anyone spoken with the office manager?" she asked. When she had worked in the office the then manager's eyes had hardly ever lifted from the accounts. It seemed this one was more engaged telling his employer that places like Letts naturally create a great deal of outgoings and that in his opinion much of it stemmed from the present head chef – who, he continually hinted, was not half as capable of ordering as wisely as Sampson once had. "Not everyone's a Mr Sampson," appeared to be his favourite remark.

"When someone starts laying the blame at someone else's door," Mary observed as Will donned his black waistcoat and jacket, ready to leave, "it's time to take a look at the one laying the blame."

Will gave a short laugh. "Perhaps you should install yourself in the office," he challenged at the door, "a lady Sherlock Holmes. Solve the crime!"

There was mild sarcasm in the tone, probably not intentional, but she rose to it. "You never know, I might do that," she said huffily, presenting her cheek for him to peck.

Closing the door after him, she went to pour herself another cup of tea, Helen still sleeping. Mary stood by the table, sipping her tea, deep in thought. But her thoughts had moved from the situation of the behaviour of finances to those of emotions.

The thoughts assailing her were of the night she and Henry had made love. That night had been repeated the following week, causing her to scoff at her fear, but it had proved to be the last time.

The week after that had seen the general election, a landslide for the National Party, a complete rout for the Labour government, every member of the former Cabinet having lost his seat bar one. But Mosley's New Party had been completely destroyed. Disillusioned, Will stopped attending meetings, which Mosley nevertheless continued to hold, as tenuously as a bulldog unable to let go of the tattered remains of the seat of a pair of trousers long after the wearer had fled.

It all meant, of course, that a crestfallen William stayed home after work, giving Henry no more opportunity to call on her. She ached for Henry's touch, and in desperation allowed Will to make love to her, much to his surprise and joy. But it was hard to respond. Closing her eyes and imagining it to be Henry helped, that alone making her come alive and gasp with short-lived pleasure. If Will knew he would have been so hurt. The last thing she would ever want to do was hurt him. But oh, how her heart cried out for Henry.

Mary put her teacup down sharply as both meditations, financial and emotional, came together in a blinding flash of brainwave. Will's jest was the answer. Were she to coax Henry into having her on the staff, whether she helped in solving the unaccountable loss of money or not, she'd be near him, he sneaking off from the restaurant, she waiting in the darkened office. It brought memories of how she and Geoffrey had made use of that place – but this time there would be no one to walk in on her, for it would be Henry himself making love to her and Will had no cause ever to go up to the office. Henry's wife away or contented in the penthouse with her young son, their hideaway would be perfectly safe. The thought made her insides twinge with anticipation, her need of him an agony.

To her joy he was all for it, aware without saying what her being there implied. A nursemaid was found for Helen, and Mary took up her old job as a comptometer operator, the new office manager with no idea who she was. During the next year his darkened office after everyone had gone became the rendezvous for a brief joyous half-hour whenever Henry could get away from the restaurant.

"If there's any underhandedness going on here," Henry whimsically remarked on one occasion they were together, "it's us."

Mary had laughed, but there was a serious intention to do what she could to uncover any dishonesty. After all, no company survived long once a crook found a foolproof way of milking its finances. If she did uncover a culprit – and there had to be one – Henry would be so proud of her. It was for his sake she was doing this. There was also a matter of personal acclaim in proving her worth, not just as his mistress. In this she felt so much happier.

"You don't seem to mind my being late as much as you used to," Will told her after his customary apology for being late home. "You're looking a lot happier lately. I'm glad."

Indeed she was happy. There were times of course when she wished she was married to Henry, and she would feel that wish weigh heavy on her. But one thing she did know – her affair had taken away the humdrum aspect of marriage to Will and in some odd way had actually improved it.

–

William couldn't help but relish the change in Mary. No longer did she fret over his long hours of work, nor was she as cold towards him as she had been. Whatever had brought about this improvement in her, he thought best not to question it.

Always at the back of his mind was the pact he'd made with Henry Lett all that time ago. Neither he nor Mary ever mentioned it, other than that once when she'd voiced her suspicions. She had never asked outright and he in turn kept well away from the subject, but sometimes he couldn't help wondering what her true feelings on the matter were, for although she had never shown any bitterness towards Henry, he sometimes wondered what really went on deep in her mind.

Less and less was he looking at Helen and seeing only Henry's child. Three years old now, she often felt like his very own – she certainly knew him only as her daddy – until he was brought up sharply by the memory of Henry's startling request. Four years since he had asked Mary to marry him and she'd accepted, but did that love she'd had for Henry still linger? He wasn't prepared to ask.

Once, quite recently, he had made the mistake of enquiring. She had looked at him as though he'd asked her to put her hand into the fire, and had then become upset over something totally unrelated.

But this past twelvemonth she had been so different. He had always been very conscious of the lack of that which usually binds a marriage. It had hurt, but loving her, he had lived in hope of something more than mere affection being awakened in her one day, hopeful that with understanding, patience and tenderness he'd get her to love him and to forget Henry.

In all else she was a good wife. In the circumstances of this marriage he had no right to ask for more. But the change in her over this past year had given him hope. She laughed with him more and seemed much less upset when he was too tired to take her out anywhere.

Perhaps it was being at the restaurant again that had improved her outlook. Women in her position, of course, did not work and he preferred to call it "business", she contracted to winkle out a villain. Once the person was exposed, her job would be done. But the best thing to come of it all was that Mary had become so much more loving towards him.

Ten

"Henry, I've found it!" Mary practically fell into his arms in her eagerness to tell him what she had discovered.

All this weekend she'd been forced to wait, he away at his house in Halstead Green with Grace and Hugh – something to do with the christening of his sister Victoria's new baby girl whom they intended to call Sheila.

It was difficult curbing her excitement at her discovery. She had told Will about it for all she'd been bound by strict confidence. He had warned her to say no more until Henry came back on Monday. But Henry hadn't come back until this evening, by which time she was in such a foment of impatience that it had made her head ache. Now as he came into the empty office she rushed at him.

"Henry, I've found out what's been happening." Henry caught her as she hurried on. "The cash discrepancy. I've traced it to Mr Leeman."

Henry's amused smile disappeared. "You can't be accusing him. He's one of our most trusted people. No, Mary, you must have it wrong. He'd never stoop so low as to fiddle—"

"It has to be him," she cut in, hardly noticing Henry's sharp tone. "Your office manager. He's been forging your signature and using Geoffrey as a sort of cover."

"Geoffrey?"

Henry's tone had become instantly sharp and protective, but Mary ploughed on eagerly.

"I happened to look in that stuck drawer of the old filing cabinet out the back. I forced it open on Friday night after they'd all left. It wasn't stuck because of being broken. There was some cardboard jammed at the back, I think deliberately."

She paused for breath then started again. "I discovered it had been thrown out because the filing clerk complained of it being so stiff to open and that you let them buy a new one. I was told the old one hadn't been in use for at least eighteen months, but that Mr Leeman wouldn't let it be taken away – said he might find some use for it. Well, it seems he did that all right. On Friday I thought of it suddenly, and it was like a miracle—"

"Darling!" He was holding up one hand to stop the excited flow. "What has all this to do with Geoffrey?"

"I'm trying to tell you," she said impatiently. "You know Mr Leeman has to send off regular cheques to Geoffrey after you've signed them? I found some torn up and stuffed into that so-called broken drawer under a load of other old papers. I pieced them together. Each one had a mistake of some sort on it and been cancelled as null and void. Then I found a bit of paper with your signature done over and over again. He has been forging

166

your signature, Henry. He's been sending your brother a rewritten cheque, then making another out for himself, passing it off as expenses, and with the same date trusting it won't be so noticeable. He knows how doddery old Beevish is getting. I don't suppose Mr Beevish keeps as strict accounts as he once did. He should have been retired years ago, but I know you keep him on like some family retainer. And Leeman has taken advantage of his age."

"I'm as much at fault as he is," mused Henry. "I didn't even bother to look into it. I took it for granted Beevish had it all in hand."

"There you are, then," Mary declared. "Leeman probably did it once and, when it wasn't queried, got bolder. That silly old accountant of yours didn't even notice. Leeman's been skimming off a bit here and a bit there for ages. But with Christmas coming up, he got bolder. He's probably been throwing away the deliberately spoiled cheques but forgot those he'd first hidden in case of trouble. I don't know what excuse he'd have given if they had been discovered. He probably had one lined up. You ought to get the police in, Henry. And get them to look into his savings. I bet you'll find it very rosy."

Henry grabbed her to him, held her in tight embrace. "Mary, you're a marvel! I'm so proud of you."

That evening he made love to her on Mr Leeman's own desk, sweeping telephone, blotting pad, ink stand and all else on to the floor, leaving them still lying on the floor when they left.

"That'll give him pause for thought," he laughed as he locked the office door behind them. "Now it's over, our twice a week in this office must come to an end. What I'll do is rent a little room nearby where we can be together in comfort. Now you've so cleverly solved this wretched business, you won't be here any more. I don't want our meetings to end here." He kissed her long and hard. "I want you all the time, Mary…"

"No." She broke away from him, leaving him staring at her. "Somehow *this* never seemed cheap or underhand. But renting a room especially for it would make it feel sordid. I don't want it to feel like that."

He stared at her through the darkness in surprise. "I'd never let you feel like that. I love you, Mary. I couldn't go on without you. Are you trying to tell me you want it to be over?"

"Oh darling, of course not." She too could not bear to think of her days with Henry no longer there to make love to her. "What I'm saying is, you'll be giving Leeman the sack, without references, if he's not sent to jail, which I think he will be. You'll need someone else in charge of this office. Why not me? I've got used to working here again. To think of going back to being just a wife, a housewife… I'd die of boredom. And the misery of being without you. I want to continue working – here. I want to become something. Henry, please let me stay. I could do such a lot of good here. I could even manage the reception desk as well." And why not? Not only was she still pretty but she had gained poise over the years. She'd be an asset. She was aware of her ability to turn heads, radiating a certain something – she wasn't sure what except that it was that something the silent film star Clara Bow, the It Girl, had possessed. All three men in her life had told her that. Using that talent she would attract the customers. Men used to male staff all the time would welcome a pretty face here.

Her mind wandering, Mary became aware that he was laughing. "You can't do everything, my love."

Mary pouted. "I've been in the background for too long, Henry. I want you to show your gratitude for what I've done by letting me be seen in Letts, just as you expressed your gratitude when you made Will a share-holder. Do the same for me. *Then* you can find that room somewhere."

For a moment Henry stared at her, then with the promise sinking in slowly, he relaxed, kissed her again, and whispered, "Mary, my darling girl, whatever you want."

–

Christmas 1933, as with every year since Mary's marriage to Will, was spent with his parents in their flat in Shored-itch. A sort of ritual, all his family in the one small front room, it was all about eating throughout the day, singing around the piano in the evening and playing cards into the small hours, finally leaving for home for a few hours' rest before returning Boxing Day. She and Will never spent Boxing Day there, however, preferring to stay quietly at home.

With no family of her own she was always made warmly welcome. Her poise and accent, refined over the years, was of no consequence to these people who

169

marvelled only over her and Will's obvious well-being while his aunts crooned over the four-year-old Helen as they crooned over all the little ones.

"Oh, look at 'er little dress – all Christmas red. Ain't she just a peach, though? Bet that dress and them shoes cost a bob or two."

His uncles were loudly envious. "Done well fer yerself, Will. Look at them togs. Talk abart the Duke of bloody Monte Carlo!" Slaps on the back to go with it, while other relatives gushed over Mary.

"You look smashin', luv. Where'd you get that luvly suit out of? Wish I could afford one like that."

His dad, a little better off this year, one of the lucky ones to have found work, said to her, "Our Will's done well fer 'imself. Who'd've thought it, him a restaurant manager? Always knew he'd get somewhere. Nice ter know that he's got you be'ind 'im."

She wasn't sure if Will had ever made any mention to his father of the sale of her jewellery helping to get him where he was – though given time, he would have got there under his own steam, she was certain. But she was glad at his father's pride in him.

His mother, as usual, heeded nothing but her table being lightened of as much food as possible by the end of the day, proof of everyone having a good time. "Come on, luv, eat up. Another piece of chicken – more brussel sprouts – a bit more stuffing?"

But it was always noisy and hot and tiring. She had to admit to relief in having Boxing Day with just the three of them, Helen surrounded by her new toys, Will stretched out before the fire, for once not having to work.

New Year's Eve was as different from Christmas as anything could be and something she always looked forward to. This one was as good as any there had been as the minutes ticked by to 1934 with a hundred or more invited friends and celebrities building up to the awaited crescendo, she not the least of them.

During the past year Mary had more than made her mark on Letts. After a few months on the office side of things getting the accounts up to scratch, the cunning Leeman having been given eighteen months for embezzlement, Henry, true to his word, had allowed her to try her hand on the reception desk. She had shone. Everyone who was anyone now knew her as well as they knew William or Henry, or – to a lesser extent of late – Geoffrey. It was as if she had never left the society stage, except that fashions and postures had altered, were less uninhibited, mannerisms smoother, life slower.

This evening on Will's arm she was greeted as readily as though she alone ran the place, certainly as exuberantly as Henry, he with Grace at his side, pale and insipid beside the golden tan of Geoffrey's wife.

Pamela cut a stunning picture. Tall, slim, breathtakingly beautiful: no wonder Geoffrey had fallen for her. There had been times when Mary felt she could never come up to her; when Geoffrey left, all her self-esteem had been stripped from her so that she had felt ugly and disgusting, no better than a discarded piece of cabbage leaf. But she had pulled herself up, helped by the two men that now mattered in her life, Will and Henry, both in their ways important to her well-being.

This evening, in a clinging, backless dinner dress of royal blue, her favourite colour, Mary knew she shone. Petite against Pamela's height she might have been made to feel small, but she possessed far more power by virtue of having had to battle for what she had, and was thus more commanding of notice. Pamela would turn heads by the very casualness of poise born of wealth, but Mary knew she had the edge on her as guests migrated to her rather than Pam. She was known here. Pam, gallivanting about the continent, wasn't. She was every bit as good as Geoffrey's second wife, Mary told herself as she smiled and chatted and held her head high, ignoring the dark image of hate for the woman that would ever lurk beneath the surface of her triumph no matter how proudly she bore herself, manifesting itself in that constant need to say that Geoffrey was welcome to Pamela.

It irked that she'd had to scheme for the position of recognition she now held, people clustering around her. She deserved all this. It irked all the more that she had to keep telling herself so. It irked in repeatedly having to remind herself that she was as good as Pamela, despite the fact that while Geoffrey's wife took all she had for granted, as Mary herself had once done, she'd had to resort to unnatural means, leaving Helen in the care of a nanny in order to reach the position she was for the first time enjoying this New Year's Eve.

She hadn't been able to spend the time she'd have liked with Helen before she'd started at nursery school in the spring; this most precious time for any mother with an only child, for it would never come again. This past year she had learned just how painfully precious it was, at any unpremeditated moment finding her thoughts wandering. Was Helen all right in Jenny's care, was she missing her mother, did she have a stomach-ache or something and she not there to cuddle her? All the admiration, all this being on speaking terms with this famous name, that celebrity, was nothing at those times compared to one hour with her daughter.

Tonight they were all here, those famous names. With 1934 only minutes away, conversation and laughter worked up to a crescendo, coloured streamers, balloons and musical toys at the ready, American twang vying stridently with overcooked English, rapid Italian or smooth French. Shrieks of sudden laughter lifted above the sound of a six-piece band, comprising a trumpet, a clarionette, two saxophones, piano and drums, rendering hits of the last couple of years. Couples did slinky foxtrots to "Love is the Sweetest Thing" and "Stormy Weather", or energetic quicksteps to "Forty-second Street" and "Who's Afraid of the Big Bad Wolf", a nasal hail directed from someone on one side of the thronged restaurant floor – the dining tables having been moved to around the edges to give more room – to someone on the far side. Letts had been modernised in art deco style these three years, the famous pillars lining the main restaurant painted with odd shapes and long-limbed, strained-postured figures and sucking in any echoes. Mirrors and pictures, the lighting, the domed stained-glass ceiling were stark and dramatic, promoting a sense of energy. And energy was what everyone possessed as they hung on the last stroke of midnight to break out into cries of over-zestful joy, as it sounded, to hug each other and kiss whoever was nearest to them, and fling about their coloured streamers as red, white and blue balloons descended from the net secured to the domed ceiling, while the band struck up with "Auld Lang Syne".

None would have believed seeing this glittering throng that out there nearly three million were out of work, though the old year had seen that number beginning to drop as industry started slowly to recover, surely a sign that the worst of the depression was over. Those here as the minutes ticked on into the new year were giving no thought to whether the number of unemployed fell or rose. Dancing, laughing, spilling champagne all over each other, all other thoughts were swept away.

Only Mary, after William had kissed her joyfully, Henry adding his embrace to William's – a little too ardent in front of everyone here – took herself off for a moment to a quiet recess behind the reception desk to think of Helen asleep at home, to think of the future, working here to make something of herself, the new year... the years stretching ahead... and what was it all for? She found her eyes moistening. While she should be happy over her achievement, she didn't feel happy at all. It was all that champagne she had drunk—

"Are you all right, Mary?"

Hastily she scrubbed away the damp rim beneath her eyes with the heel of her hand, and turned as Henry came towards her.

"Are you OK?" he repeated.

"Fine." She managed a smile. "The excitement's got to me, I think."

He came closer, a small wall by the reception desk concealing them from those passing to and fro. Looking around furtively, he pressed her further back into the recess. His kiss was hungry, his hand on her breast hot through the silk crepe. Mary shivered, wanting him, then eased away. "Not here, Henry. We'll be seen."

"In the office," he breathed.

They hadn't made love there since he had begun to rent that room. Comfortably furnished, it still made her feel as though their love-making was designed, not spontaneous. To be made love to in that place where they had first begun to meet seemed just right at this moment.

"I'll go first," she whispered, feeling the excitement mounting. "Leave it five minutes before you follow."

The key in her hand, she hurried along the balcony to the door that led off the small circular upper dance floor, below her the restaurant, now cleared of tables, a sea of moving heads as couples swayed to the lively dance music from the band above. She would hurry along the corridor behind the restaurant and up the stairs to her destination. Her heart was pounding.

"Where are you off to, darling? Surely not the office!"
The door she had reached led only to the office, isolated

175

from the rest of the restaurant. She came to a full stop and looked at Pamela.

"I was in there this afternoon," she excused herself. "I left my lipstick there. I was going to get it."

She saw Pam's eyes flick towards the figure of Henry now leaving the reception area to watch her. The sight of Pam glancing towards him made him turn abruptly away, but not soon enough that she had not seen him staring after Mary. To Mary's eyes, the move was weighted with guilt.

Pam let out a high, penetrating laugh, her white, even teeth and rosy gums appearing and then become hidden again as, still smiling, she caught her lips between those teeth in a speculative gesture, her deep blue eyes narrowing.

"Well, well. You do get around, Mary darling, don't you just?"

"I'm sorry?"

"Oh, no, don't be, darling. You go on to your little office. I'm sure you'll probably be there all on your own, undisturbed, until you find where you left your lipstick. At least I expect so, *now*, don't you?"

Of course she was right. Henry wouldn't dare come to her now, aware of Pam's look and the high laugh that had carried clear across the space above the dancers and the noise.

Their secret was out. Returning to the party, she spent the remaining small hours in torment wondering if Pam would let the cat out of the bag to someone. To Geoffrey?

To Will? Or would she blackmail Henry, just for the sheer hell of it? She wouldn't put anything past Pamela.

–

Pamela's blue eyes sparkled like ice. "It has to be true, Geoffrey. She and your brother are having it off together."

Geoffrey regarded her from his armchair. "You can't be sure of that, you know. It's only what you surmise, so don't go blabbing it about until you're a hundred per cent certain sure, or you'll bum your fingers."

"I'm not going blabbing it about. I've more sense. But you must admit it is intriguing." Enjoying her agitation, Pam paced the massive lounge of their beautiful home on the edge of Epping Forest. "I wouldn't put it past her. I wouldn't put *anything* past that one. She's a scheming little bitch. Why should Henry put her in charge of everything if there wasn't something going on between them? She behaved as if she owned the place, the way she put herself about on New Year's Eve, grinning like a Cheshire cat, batting her eyelids at everyone, everyone flocking around her. By the sound of the laughter, I wouldn't mind betting she was spilling a nice little risque joke or two. Came off the streets in the first place, didn't she?"

Geoffrey was grinning at her. "Not *off* the streets, my love. *From* the streets. She was just a waif and stray in the beginning."

"Yes, and it shows, for all her social climbing. She made sure of that – first you, now Henry. It seems that restaurant manager chap she married isn't quite high enough up the ladder for her. She wants the top rung."

Geoffrey's grin had widened. "Looks like someone's got their claws well and truly into her. You're not letting her get to you, are you, darling?"

"Why on earth should I? Remember, you left her for me."

"Yes, darling, I did."

He got up, came and put his arms about her slim figure. "You know I see more in you than I ever saw in her. I'd been wasting my life until I met you. If I hadn't met you…"

"Poor darling," Pam murmured, tilting back her chin so that he could kiss her neck. "You *had* to marry her, didn't you? Getting herself pregnant." She conveniently forgot the fact that she too had been pregnant when Geoffrey married her. "It shows what a scheming bitch she was from the start. Now you've done with her, she's after Henry. And he's falling for it. He should be warned."

Geoffrey's lips moved down from her neck towards the gentle swelling of her small breasts showing above her negligee. His breath was warm on her skin. "Let's forget her. I'm beginning to feel just a bit randy, sweetheart. Don't let's spoil it."

—

Pamela gazed with distaste through the window at the dull January morning as she dressed slowly. The cold was practically visible, clouds yellow, heavy with snow yet to fall and cover the dismal parkland attached to the house. Not a solitary thing moved out there. The lake was frozen, the stark branches of trees like dead sticks, the grass still white with frost even at midday. Through a gap between the trees, horizon blended with overcast sky in a uniform wash of yellow. Abysmal. Four weeks since New Year's Eve. Four weeks of tedium. Little happening on the social scene, recovering from Christmas and the New Year celebrations. London was a bore. Being closeted here was a bore for all they'd thrown a couple of weekend house parties. But tomorrow they'd be off to Kisbuhel, escaping the slush of a British winter, at the Grand Hotel in the dry air of the Austrian Alps, skiing, spending some of their time at the exclusive Schloss Mittersill, if they were lucky finding the Prince of Wales there, certainly people like Lady Birley and Lady Diana Cooper, everyone in peasant costume – dirndl skirts, embroidered aprons, lederhosen, Tyrolean hats – all having great fun. It would have been more enjoyable were she not aware that Geoffrey's first wife had also been to such places, on his arm, first.

And there was Henry, another fly in the ointment. Returning home around mid-March, bronzed from the neck up by the clear, strong sunshine despite snow-laden peaks, Geoffrey faced his brother's displeasure.

"It all costs money," he reminded them monotonously. But it was hers and Geoffrey's life to do with as they pleased. It was hers and Geoffrey's money paying for these trips, not the restaurant's. And what was the point being a wealthy restauranteur if there was no pleasure got out of it?

At least they'd come back in time for Geoffrey to be with Henry for their end-of-financial-year meeting with their auditor and the new accountant, that fool Percival Beevish finally retired, though the astute young accountant was a pain in the neck with an eye on every last penny, siding with Henry in that ploughing money back into the business was preferable to throwing it to the four winds — alluding to hers and Geoffrey's behaviour, of course.

With the London scene livening up, Pam put aside the business of Mary. That summer in Salzburg, already sizzling hot, she was again having too good a time to concern herself about Mary, and put it back to some later date. Mingling with all the smart people, she and Geoffrey found themselves invited to parties thrown by Max Reinhart in the Rococo Palace of the Prince Archbishop, everyone there: the Mitfords, the Sitwells, William Walton, Lord Berners, Harold Acton. At the Festspielhaus, Mozart operas bored Geoffrey to death, but it was the place where everyone interesting and influential met, and when they finally left for home, Pam felt ready to face dull Britain again, until next year's winter holiday.

Except that coming home via Munich, everywhere Pam looked was marred by the sight of the SS guards of the German chancellor Adolf Hitler. So much ominous news had been filtering out of Germany this year — news of shootings, Jewish persecution, the business of what had been termed the Night of the Long Knives with thousands, including some of Hitler's own so-called close associates, dragged from their homes and executed. All these sinister, black-uniformed guards unnerved her.

"I'd rather stay away from Europe for a while," she told Geoffrey when they arrived home.

But it was hardly better in England with Mosley confident of himself once more, he and his fascist supporters putting people's backs up, lauding the German chancellor's actions in clearing the country of upstart Jews and Communists. There were reports of running battles between Mosley's blackshirts and Communists, fist-fights and stink bombs thrown, fascists and anti-fascists alike arrested by the police, London an upheaval in places.

"Geoffrey, let's get right away from it all," Pam pleaded at the end of September. "We could go on a cruise to somewhere where it's nice and warm and there's no conflict. We could go on the *Queen Mary's* maiden voyage."

Two days earlier the new British liner, the largest in the world, had at last been launched. For so long she had been known only as "number 534" while she lay unfinished at Clydebank with the work held up all the while unemployment was rife, but now the depression had finally lost some of its grip, and Her Majesty Queen Mary had named the great ship after herself. In Pam's mind was the fact that Geoffrey had once taken his ex-wife on a cruise. He'd never yet taken her. She was sure it had been a ship's maiden voyage too. The *Mauretania*?

"Don't you think enough of me, Geoffrey," she demanded, "to at least consider it? There is bound to be a rush to book. You managed to go on a cruise to New York once, didn't you?"

Geoffrey, taking the dig, cuddled her and to make her feel better said he'd look into it very seriously. But a spring and summer of high living had been a drain on his bank balance and there were bills to be settled, servants' wages to be paid and a host of other expenses. Christmas and New Year would take their toll as well. Although it'd be a long time before the *Queen Mary* was fitted out, bookings, even this far ahead, would have to be paid for on the nose for something so popular. First class of course. Plus there would be expenses, hotel bills, and naturally, paying for all the clothes and jewellery Pam would buy – he remembered how Mary had spent and spent. And the way he and Pam lived, it wasn't going to be easy putting by for it all. There was nothing for it but to see Henry about money. He had always paid up in the past. But there's ever that one straw that will break the camel's back.

"I'm sick of you coming asking for hand-outs," he said when Geoffrey visited Swift House. "I give myself the same director's salary as you, yet you are always broke, and we both know why. Why can't you learn to live more modestly? The upkeep of that damned mansion of yours must cost you a fortune in itself. You're never in the country. You pay a bloody great staff to look after it when you're not even there. I'm sorry, Geoffrey, I can't allow you any more advances. You owe the company enough now. And I bet you're in debt to the bank too. I suggest you draw in your horns, because I'm not going to pay your debts for you. I've done that too often. I'm afraid you're going to have to learn to manage from now on. We're not that far out of the depression to start throwing money about. I've not forgotten our last venture when we nearly lost everything."

Geoffrey cut hotly through the flow. "That was your idea, not mine."

"But you went along with it eagerly enough."

"What would you have said if I had objected?"

"That's all water under the bridge now." Anger made Henry reach for a cigarette, a lifeline as always. "Speaking of water, it'll be a good year or more before the *Queen Mary's* fitted out. I suggest you take a chance on booking in six months' time and until then try to recuperate some of your expenses so you can pay with ready cash. That's all I have to say."

Geoffrey was glaring at him across the table. "Is that your last word?"

"You have to understand." Henry blinked appeasement through the blue haze of cigarette smoke, betraying his loathing of treating his brother this way. "The restaurant's not a bottomless well. I have to be careful. Or at least know not to throw money about. So should you."

Geoffrey's eyes narrowed but he said nothing and came abruptly away. Pam would be furious.

Eleven

He should have known something was wrong when Pam and Geoffrey did not appear at Letts' New Year's Eve party this year, offering no good excuse, only saying offhandedly that they were thinking of having a small private party at their own home. Henry guessed immediately what it was over, especially having heard nothing from them since then.

They had gone off on a winter skiing trip to Austria, that he knew. So much for saving to sail on the *Queen Mary*, he'd thought scathingly. They'd be back in two weeks, Geoffrey's butler informed him – it was just a short break. Henry had moderated his unkind cynicism and silently forgave them, Geoffrey no doubt having taken his advice to save for his ocean voyage after all.

True to their word, the pair came home in early February, but still there was no contact. His refusal to finance Geoffrey's cruise probably still rankled, and they wouldn't leave it at that. It would come to a head some-time, he reasoned. So he wasn't surprised when Pam, on her own, came marching into the restaurant one late February morning saying that she wanted a word with him. Not discreetly, not even with a please, but demandingly and in full hearing of all those having coffee. There was no doubt by her manner that she'd been brooding all this time over his own earlier attitude, and like badly fermented wine ready to blow its cork, no sooner had she uttered the normal salutatory opening – that in itself more a command than a greeting – than hers blew.

"Good morning, Henry."

He blinked at the harsh tone, the set expression, but nevertheless smiled. "Why, hello, Pam. What brings you here? Where's Geoffrey?"

"Henry, I want to speak to you."

Henry stalled. "Did you enjoy your holiday? When did you get back?"

Already anticipating that look on her face, he guided her hastily away from the restaurant as he spoke, going up the gilt stairs with her to the less occupied dance floor area where only a few businessmen quietly conversed with each other at the bar or at one or two of the little round tables around the perimeter of the carpeted, oval-shaped upper area.

Gaining the balcony above the main restaurant, he saw it was deserted but for a couple coming through the main glass doors above a flight of eight steps, Mary welcoming them. In a moment they would descend the stairs to be conducted by William down the second more ornate flight to the restaurant itself and shown to a table.

Henry, having managed to get Pam out of hearing and hopefully out of sight before she could say what she had undoubtedly come to say, took his eyes off Mary to ask Pam the obvious: "Is something wrong?"

In answer, she uttered a single word – "Mary." Her tone was deliberately offensive.

Henry reached into his breast pocket for his cigarette case. "What about her?"

"I should have thought that was obvious," she said.

Henry shook his head, extracting a Player's Navy. These days only the strongest kind could satisfy his smoke-congested needs.

"I don't understand. What's obvious?"

"You. And Mary." He made a pretence of a frown of perplexity, but Pam was forging on. "New Year's Eve 1933? Remember?"

Henry shook his head. "What am I supposed to remember from over a year ago?"

"I think you know, Henry, so there's no point my wasting time jogging your memory. I was happy to let things go, what you and she get up to being your business, except I did wonder if her husband was aware of it."

"Now wait a minute, Pam…"

"But when you behave towards Geoffrey as though he's a naughty child you're withholding sweets from, then I begin to ask myself why you should consider yourself so lily white that you can treat others as though they're tarnished through and through. So Geoffrey spends more than he should. At least he's not having an affair behind his wife's back and doing someone else's husband down at the same time."

"Now look here, Pam. I'm not—"

"This is when I feel a few things need sorting out."

She had paused for effect, watched as Henry attempted to cover the uncomfortable moment by lighting up, sucking in a deeper breath than even he normally would and blowing out a thick cloud of smoke. Meeting her eyes through the haze, he said as casually as he could, "I'm sorry, but you're reading more into something than need be."

"Am I?" It was a direct accusation he couldn't combat any further.

He heard himself blustering, "What're you asking of me, then?"

"Geoffrey means to take me off on that cruise, no matter what. But it depends on whether or not he has money enough. I think you hold the key to that, don't you?"

Blackmail. The word hammered through his head. She had the power to tell both Grace and William. William wouldn't be that surprised, he felt. Hurt maybe, but not surprised. He had known when he married her how things had stood between himself and Mary, had consented to step in and prevent the scandal that would have had Grace finding out just how far the affair, brief as it had been, had gone. It was mostly Grace – quiet, modest, loyal, if not passionate – who concerned him. Should any hint of his having a child by Mary ever reach her it would slay her. Slay him too.

He felt his body sag. He sucked in a desperate lungful of cigarette smoke to steady his nerves.

"How much would he need?"

"Four thousand."

Henry gulped. "Four... You're only going on a cruise."

"Expenses. New York. A place like that runs away with money."

"Expenses are up to you, Pam." Smoke drifted from his mouth and nostrils. "Anyway, they'd never come to anything near that much."

"They could come to even more, depending on, well... things."

Henry's lungs seemed to be choking him, as though the smoke still in them had become trapped, making him feel he might vomit any moment. Suddenly his lungs released his breath in an explosion of smoke, and with it the moment of panic. Strength and resolve took its place.

"I refuse to be blackmailed, Pam. That's what you're up to." It wouldn't stop there, once he gave in. How much did she know? Not all that much, he was sure. "You've no proof of anything but what you imagine."

"I don't need proof. I merely need to sow a few seeds of truth in certain ears. It is the truth, Henry. And such a shock for some. It would be for your wife."

He could see Mary looking at them. From where she was she could gauge their facial expressions, their tense stance, and surmise that all wasn't well. Feeling sick again, he stubbed out his cigarette in a chrome ashtray attached to the wall, and immediately reached for another. Keeping his face expressionless he regarded Pam and said slowly, "You're a real prize bitch, Pam. Geoffrey doesn't deserve you. One day you'll do him down too."

He saw the gleam of triumph in her eyes, wide and blue and feigning innocence. "Henry, all I know is that it is really generous of you to consider helping Geoffrey out this way. You have always been a good brother to him. What he would have done without you at times, I'm sure I don't know."

On the point of moving away, she paused. "Thanks so much, Henry darling. I know Geoffrey will be grateful. And if he finds money running out while we're in New York – new jewellery is always needed and decent stuff can cost such a lot – that, and having to mix with nice people on board ship – I know you'll be the first to advance him a little more. Of course, he won't prevail on you too drastically. See you later."

Stealing a glance at Mary, speaking to another couple as Pam, tall and elegant, tripped lightly up the flight of marble stairs, Henry saw her nod to the other woman who hardly bothered to respond as she went past her.

Hardly had Pam departed than Henry was cursing himself for a fool. He should have bluffed it out, he whose business instincts seldom let anything get past him. That's what had kept him going all these years, had made Letts the restaurant it was despite depression, banks' attempts to foreclose on him, Geoffrey's drain on profits in his love of high living. But Geoffrey always had been his Achilles heel one way or another. The shock of Pam's confrontation, her audacity, glimpsing Mary looking at him, he reeling with disbelief that a member of his own family could stoop to blackmail, had all culminated in making him commit himself before pausing to think. Asking how much Geoffrey needed, and calling her a prize bitch – if that had not been playing into her hands, what was? Fool!

Mary, coming down the stairs, her face creased a little by confusion, interrupted his self-anger. Over the years her sweetly animated features had settled to smooth maturity, her poise and elegance despite her small stature causing heads to turn, those steady grey eyes compelling a second glance. His heart leapt with adoration as she came to gaze up into his face.

"What's the matter with Geoffrey's wife? I know we're not exactly close friends, but she cut me dead, both times, coming in and leaving. I haven't offended her, have I?"

For a moment she looked the young girl he'd first set his eyes on and he felt an immediate need to protect her. "It's nothing you've done. You know what she's like, always full of her own importance."

"You both looked so serious. Then Pam walking right by me, I thought there might be some trouble – in the family or something."

"No, nothing." He hastened to sound casual. "Just Geoffrey wanting to spend money before he gets it, and Pam fighting his comer for him."

"Well, I hope you didn't give in to her. Though I know you didn't because she would have given me a smile when she left. By the way, darling, it's Friday. I'll see you as usual?"

There should have been no need for her to ask. Their affair had gradually settled into a pattern of seeing each other every Friday night. In the tiny flat he rented they would make love, feverishly, making up for the days without each other. Afterwards they would go to a theatre or a cinema, eat, then back to the flat to make love again a little less feverishly. They'd leave around half-past midnight, he heading back to his penthouse and Grace who, going to bed at ten thirty, never heard him come in; Mary to her flat, Helen and the nanny she employed, also asleep. Mary always insisted on being there when William came in from his work.

Sometimes he wondered just how much William knew. William knew that he took Mary out on Friday evenings and now and again expressed his gratitude. But for him to find out what really went on didn't bear thinking about.

"It is good of you, Henry, putting yourself out for Mary," he'd say on occasion. "I hope your wife doesn't object, but it gets Mary out of herself."

"No trouble, old man," Henry would reply, guilt rising in a hot wave to his cheeks. "Only too glad. You both work so hard. Least, one can do."

William would nod, but his gratitude often seemed mixed with an odd perspicacity which Henry could not fathom or dare to voice.

The rest of the week he and Mary kept apart. It tore at him not being able to see her, but their weekly meetings, for all they were only once a week, made up for all the time they were apart. For lovers it was an inadequate arrangement but with no other choice, he knew he must content himself and that their affair was all the sweeter for the waiting. They both agreed on that.

At this moment Mary appeared to have been made faintly unsure by what she had witnessed, to his mind reading into it something that might concern them. He hoped not. He hurried to reassure her.

"Of course, darling." He mouthed the word "darling", seeing William coming up the gilt staircase, and was relieved when she moved off, straight-faced, to return to the reception area.

—

"You're quiet, Henry," Mary said as they came away from the cinema. "I've not upset you, have I?"

She must have been tired earlier. She had sighed, when he'd made love to her, said it was becoming rather like tradition to be made love to regularly at seven o'clock on a Friday evening. He had been concerned. He was concerned now, put comforting pressure on the arm tucked through his. "Nothing you could ever do or say would upset me."

"I'm sorry about earlier," she said. "Is that what has made you quiet? Perhaps we shouldn't have gone out."

But she'd wanted to see the film, *The Gay Divorcee*, with Fred Astaire and Ginger Rogers. To stay in would have been even more fraught for him, Pam's threats still with him. It had been an effort to appear at ease and the film had at least provided him with something to talk about, relating how he had once met Astaire, twelve years ago, before Hollywood claimed him. A young man at the time, still smarting with humiliation, coming into the restaurant for supper after a performance of his London stage success *Stop Flirting*, he had angrily let slip to Henry that having admired the white waistcoat of the best-dressed man in town, the Prince of Wales, he'd visited the prince's own outfitters, Hawes and Curtis, to be politely told to follow that royal person's style elsewhere.

Henry's tale had lightened the moment only briefly before the events of this morning came creeping back, giving him little to laugh about or even to inspire conversation. He thought too of William's words when he had offered to treat Mary to an evening at the cinema.

"She certainly needs an outing. And I know she's in safe hands."

Had it been guilt-ridden conscience that left him imagining a slight edge to that remark? William, aware of his past affair with Mary, had agreed to marry her and give his name to their child; it would be foolish not to imagine that he never paused once in a while to wonder if that relationship still smouldered. If he did, he gave no sign, except that at times there would be an edge to his tone, like this evening.

Now this unsavoury business with Pamela. If word of his infidelity were ever to reach Grace… With all this on his mind it was hard to be bright and cheerful. Of course he was going to have to alert Mary to this threat of blackmail. They must both be on their guard now.

Making up his mind he took Mary back to their secret apartment. He would tell her after making love. No point spoiling it with bad news. Love was made a little frantic-ally, with a feeling that it might be their last time together if Pam ever let the cat get out of the bag. But he had no intention of letting that happen. Tomorrow he would give Geoffrey a cheque, see the surprise and delight in his eyes. Surprise, though? He wasn't sure. Would Pam tell him what she had done? If she did, would he be appalled? Perhaps he should enlighten Geoffrey as to the reason for his change of heart. But would he believe him, believe such a foul thing of Pam? Pam would deny it and he'd believe her. Then where would that leave him in Geoffrey's eyes?

A thousand questions marred the usual perfection and joy of his climax with Mary. Nor did he feel as fulfilled as he usually did, though Mary seemed happy, relaxing back, a smile curving her lips from which issued forth a small sigh of contentment. "Mmm."

He lay beside her in the tiny, cosy bed-sitting room, staring at the ceiling, his usual drowsy contentment absent. He could not tell Mary and spoil her happiness, her certainty of that future which he imagined her seeing behind those gently closed eyelids as enfolding she and he forever.

–

Helen was as excited as any child could possibly be. Tables had been laid all the way along the mews making one single surface laden with jellies and cakes and dainty little sandwiches made by the women of the luxury flats all around, or more likely by their staff.

Along both sides of the tables sat the children, in celebration of the silver jubilee of Their Majesties' reign. The girls wore pink and white party frocks, most of them expensively bought for this occasion, their hair curled and beribboned, socks pure white, shoes neat and tidy. The boys were dressed in little blue or grey suits, well pressed short trousers, their socks pulled up straight as drainpipes, not a wrinkle to be seen – and if there was, it would instantly be yanked straight by a parent – shoes polished to a finer-than-fine shine, not a hair of any head out of place, well slicked down by a father's brilliantine.

It was a national holiday, and all across London, across the whole nation, whole streets strung with Union Jacks and red, white and blue bunting displayed similar tables lined with children while mothers looked on, comforting the tearful, curbing the boisterous and waiting on their own and each other's youngsters, every community bent on having the best time ever.

Only in the way they lived did they differ. The children of the upper class, whose parents no doubt had been included on the royal invitation list, were enjoying sedate private parties of their own in the exclusive grounds of their parents' country seats, waited upon by armies of servants. In back streets of every city slum, children wore the best of their hand-me-downs, their fathers having no money for shiny boots, their mothers, in aprons faded by long use, hair just released from curlers, squawking at them to shut their gobs and eat up, food not to be wasted when tomorrow it would only be bread and scrape. In the north, women with arms folded across a shawl about their shoulders gossiped in groups. In villages, fetes were going strong. In the West Country, organised dancing was taking place. In Wales they sang and in Scotland bagpipes were being played – or more likely tortured – by any who saw himself as a musician.

Here in this usually quiet mews snuggled between St James's Street and Pall Mall, those mothers who hadn't lowered themselves to take their children to mingle with the biggest multitude since Armistice Day watching the procession accompanying the King and Queen to St Paul's in the twenty-fifth year of their reign stood a little aloof from each other as though contact would make them less aware of their upper middle-class station in life. Here, under normal circumstances, they seldom bumped into each other, left their homes in taxis or hubby's limousine, returned the same way, had maids to do the shopping, saw more of friends than neighbours, wrapped up in their own little worlds.

Mary recalled the close community of her childhood, the back streets of Soho where prim and seamy rubbed shoulders. She thought of William's people. In Shoreditch they were doing the same as here, only there'd be a piano brought out to entertain everyone, later an onslaught of ribald songs, glasses being filled with beer from barrels from nearby pubs, the smell of fish and chips, saveloys and mustard, pease pudding and faggots, vinegar and pickled gherkins pervading.

Here, there'd be a small glass or two of wine. Nannies would take their charges home, parents would go out to dinner, celebrating in their own way. Mary hoped Will might take her out too for a break, a short stroll to Buckingham Palace where there would probably still be crowds making merry. Maybe on into Hyde Park where around ten o'clock the King would press a button to light a celebration bonfire, a signal for around two thousand other bonfires across the country to be lit. London itself would be as bright as day with every important building floodlit. She didn't want to stay indoors and have it all pass her by.

Perhaps she and Will would go out later, Helen left in the care of Jenny, their nanny. These days Jenny was merely part time, Helen at infant school.

Mary switched her glance to her daughter busy enjoying sandwiches, blancmange, jelly and cake with the rest. A surge of love filled her breast. Forever occupied with the restaurant, she saw so little of her. Soon Helen would be going on to junior school. Her daughter was fast growing away from her. Even so, life was sweet. She thoroughly enjoyed her work. There was money enough to have nice things. She didn't do all the things she had once done, going abroad, going to mad parties, but she was content. Letts gave her a lot of pleasure and some excitement. She had Will who was a caring husband. And she had Henry. How nice it would be if they could be together more... but the waiting for that weekly occasion when they were was a kind of sweet agony that made their meeting all the sweeter. Had they been free to be together all the time, perhaps some of the sweetness would have gone out of it. She was content enough with her lot. If only...

Her eyes strayed again to Helen on that last unfinished thought. If only Helen could know who her real father was. Did it matter? It did, of course. One day she would know. Should anything ever to happen to her natural father, he'd see his daughter would want for nothing, but he'd do it cautiously so that the world would never know of Helen's illegitimacy. If he left a legacy to her and Will, she would know it was really for Helen and pass it on to her. Then Helen would have to know – but life had a way of exposing the truth, sooner or later, in any case. How would Helen feel, the truth kept from her all these years? Would she understand? Would she hate her mother? Would she hate him, her true father? Would she be left to grow up and spend the rest of her life in bitterness, her father not there to explain or defend himself?

Mary shuddered, put these thoughts away from her and turned her mind to this happy occasion, the sun shining, the day beautiful, this sixth of May – not a day for dreary thoughts. She smiled automatically at a stiff-faced woman standing beside her and, their eyes meeting, was surprised to receive a smile in return.

Twelve

"I don't know how he finds the money to gallivant around the globe," Mary said, she and Will and Henry having a quick supper break before returning to their various posts, Henry himself to wait upon the wishes of a party of very special guests occupying one of the restaurant's private rooms.

"I think most of it's his wife's," he said hastily.

"More fool her," said William as he tucked into the pudding one of the waiters had brought them.

"Well, if she's willing," said Henry, giving the waiter a smile of thanks. "It's her business what she does with her own money."

"Granted," said William.

It was the evening after the opening night of Ivor Novello's immense success *Careless Rapture* at Drury Lane. That had been notable for, among a huge gathering of well-known faces, the attendance of the popular film star Marlene Dietrich, crowds going wild to catch a glimpse of her as she arrived. Tonight Novello had organised a select little supper party for six, she among his guests, in one of Letts' private rooms. He'd asked for strict privacy, certain of getting it here rather than at one of the larger hotels where fans hoped to see famous faces sneaking in and out and would congregate to harass their heart-throbs with their excitable adoration.

Not that Letts wasn't accustomed to entertaining the well known, but Dietrich was among one of its more exciting figures, and Henry had asked Will and Mary to have supper with him as an opportunity to discuss what measures they should take to keep the celebrities happily away from the limelight for a few hours.

Work matters settled, the conversation had turned lightly to other matters until, answering Will's casual question as to when his brother would be showing his face here again, Henry had mentioned that he was at present still in Budapest, having spent the latter half of August and the first half of this month there.

"Went by the Orient Express, you know," Henry had said, somewhat coldly, which had drawn the caustic remark from Mary as to how Geoffrey could find the money to travel the world. In early May he had gone on the maiden voyage of the huge Cunard liner, the *Queen Mary*, which must have cost him a fortune, and now only four months later he was enjoying himself in Budapest.

"Well, I think she must be crazy," she added, to William's "granted". Amusement lit her face. "And a bit surprising that she spends her own money for her own holidays. Though I suppose she'd have to chip in with all the places they go off to. His resources aren't exactly infinite, even if he thinks so."

"Each to their own," said Henry. It sounded a little sharp. "Some enjoy saving and going nowhere. Others enjoy spending and going places."

Mary saw Will catch briefly at his lower lip. Perhaps he had taken the remark as a dig at himself. They seldom went out. He was always taken up with his work, and it lay to Henry to give her a break. Will had never been abroad. He saw no need. But sometimes she longed to see Paris again, and New York, and all those other places she could now only dream about. Although Will had savings enough these days to go anywhere modestly priced if he fancied, they didn't even holiday in this country. Neither did Henry, for that matter, but she felt that had they both been free, he'd have taken her places, doing exactly the same as Geoffrey and his wife were doing, enjoying life.

This past eighteen months had been so dull, except when Henry took her out Friday evenings, and those occasions too had become commonplace – theatre, cinema, dinner, cocktails, the glittering surfaces rubbed pale by repetition. Being made love to was still exciting, but soon over. Even the bittersweet tension of counting the days until Friday had dulled. Oh, for one weekend together.

And so the months had slipped by. So far there had been very little of 1936 to rejoice about: in January the death of King George, the country in mourning, the face of the new king forlorn, as though kingship was the last thing Edward wanted. Mary could remember him last year hiring a small private room for dinner with a stunning young American woman with the unusual name of Wallis. He'd looked so happy then.

There had been a few good times, she and Henry still enjoying each other's company if she overlooked the tedium of once-a-week meetings. But he had not lost that brooding silence. He took her to see the Charlie Chaplin film *Modern Times* which at last had made him laugh. But he often didn't look well. Elsewhere there had been little to laugh about as Europe seemed to begin to seethe: the Nazis walking into the Rhineland, all news coming out of Germany not pleasant; Italy's dictator Mussolini over-running Abyssinia; in July civil war breaking out in Spain between the alarming fascists and the Spanish Republican government. It all seemed so threatening. Mary could feel it deep inside her, and had felt there was little to laugh about this year.

Only Geoffrey and Pam seemed still to find life pleasant. But where Geoffrey managed to find all that necessary money from was nothing short of amazing. It had to be Pam's money, and it struck Mary as a little despicable that Geoffrey could take her money that way.

Will had fallen silent after Henry's quip about people who spend nothing and go nowhere, and Mary felt compelled to prick conversation into life again.

"I mean, the days when a woman's money belonged to her husband are gone long ago. The days when a man had sole charge over his wife's money, giving her just a dress allowance—"

"Pam's a natural spendthrift," Henry cut in sharply. "And so's he. It's obvious they couldn't live on his money alone, the way they live. Anyway, it's their business."

The meal over, Henry got up rather abruptly, not lingering for his after-supper cigar though he had smoked cigarettes between courses, even taking a puff while eating.

"I think I'll have my coffee upstairs before going back on duty. Look in to see how Grace is. See you both later."

Giving them a tight smile he left them still sitting at the table in the small side room next to the kitchen that he kept for his own meals. They looked at each other in bewilderment.

"Did I upset him?" asked Will.

His narrow, good-looking face was a picture of bewilderment and Mary gave him a comforting smile. Odd to be so easily upset, so thin-skinned in private, while in public he always appeared at ease with himself. "He's a bit on edge tonight," she advised warmly. Will was such a good man. She felt at times that she didn't deserve him. "Celebrities expecting to be kept out of the public's way this evening, he needing to keep his reputation for prudence; it's a lot of responsibility."

It was the only excuse she could think of, but it was more than his merely being nervously on his toes. Henry didn't seem the man he'd once been. He was growing quieter by the month, though he'd always been thoughtful, and this past year he'd been given to sombre brooding until she jogged him out of it, then breaking into a too vigorous smile with the excuse that he had been thinking about the restaurant. At work he was withdrawn – not with customers but with his staff, she included. Only with William did he ever converse with any ease.

There was at times a harassed look in his eyes. She would ask him when they were out together what was wrong, and he'd become sharp with her, asking why anything should be wrong. It seemed better to keep silent and let him get over it until he relaxed again. Even his love-making was different, restrained.

"You're not tiring of me, are you?" she asked on one occasion. He had become angry and lost his temper, his voice raised.

"Why d'you need to ask that? Have I said I'm tired of you?"

"No," she'd gasped, taken aback by his uncharacteristic attitude.

"Then why ask? What more d'you expect me to do than what I do?"

"It's just that you don't seem yourself any more," she'd ventured. "When we're together you're not like you used to be."

"If you want me behaving like a lovesick eighteen-year-old, I can't. I'm getting a bit too mature to play silly fools. If I don't suit any more, you can always—"

"Henry, don't!" In fear she had thrown herself into his arms, feeling them circle around her body with desperate strength. His show of temper had dissolved, he had apologised and they had made love as in those early days of secret meetings in the darkened empty office.

From then on she had been careful never to refer to his moments of moodiness, though she was at a loss to think why they should be, and what could be worrying him for such a prolonged length of time. Was he in some ill health which he was keeping from everyone? She recalled the odd occasion when he'd pause in walking after spending time sitting down, go very quiet for a second or two, ignoring her concern whether he was all right, then straighten his shoulders to continue walking. At such times, she'd shudder from a vision of really ill health, of the start of some serious illness he wasn't aware of, even of losing him. But she dare not ask lest he flare up.

—

It hurt Henry to speak to her as he did. He would catch himself too late and try to make up for it, but a word once said was not easily forgotten, and it must have lingered in Mary's mind for all his passionate loving of her.

He wanted so much to say "Forgive me," but it would have led to long explanations, and something he'd not intended to say being revealed.

Eighteen months and Pam was still a burden on his back, growing heavier every time she came into the restaurant. He'd hurry away from whatever he was doing, signalling to one of his waiters, or maybe William, to take over from him. He would hurriedly guide Pam away from curious eyes, but he was often certain that they followed him, William's forehead puckering in a frown, Mary's eyebrows raised. Neither asked questions. But one day they would. It would be hard to think up a plausible reason and he merely prayed that he might never have to.

She never came with Geoffrey when he condescended to show his face, always with beaming gratitude towards his brother, as if he had no idea why all these advances were being given so readily to sustain his ever-growing need of money. Finding it so easy to obtain, Geoffrey threw the money about, never bothering to see that he was draining the business dry. He'd wintered in the south of France in a chateau he'd bought – "Just a modest little place," he'd remarked lightly when Henry had queried its cost – and this spring, of course, he and Pam had cruised to the Canary Islands. In August they'd attended the Olympic Games in Berlin despite Pam once remarking that the atmosphere in Germany after Hitler had come to power had bothered her.

It seemed to Henry that Geoffrey spent for the sake of spending, the money coming so easily. It made his flesh crawl to find himself hating his own brother. There seemed no end to it, but in time others would begin to raise their eyebrows, wonder why the place did not sparkle as it once had.

–

It did indeed become noticed.

"I tell you, Mary," said Will one damp October Monday afternoon as he took off his wet raincoat and flapped it about in the hallway, hooked it on the coat rack there and came on into the kitchen, having come home earlier than usual, "there's nothing doing. That place is going to rack and ruin."

It wasn't exactly going to rack and ruin, but to someone previously used to all the bustle of a thriving restaurant, the sense of hush that had descended over Letts these past months was all the more unnerving for being so unusual. Worse, no one really seemed to know why it should be like this.

"Henry's cutting back on everything. The place needs smartening up, redecorating, but he ignores what anyone says. It's utterly dead today."

"Perhaps it's the weather," said Mary without conviction, busy putting away the last of the washed crockery from her lunch. Mrs Saunders, who cleaned the flat three times a week, had gone before lunch, leaving Mary to deal with the washing-up of her own lunch things. "Monday never was a busy day."

"The food's not half what it once was. Chef's been grumbling his head off, given no free rein these days to do his own ordering as he sees fit. He says he feels he's not being trusted any more to know what's needed. After all, every restaurant's reputation rests on its head chef. He says Henry is interfering all the time. He's even threatening to leave. One of the best men we've ever had. He'd have no trouble finding another place. Good hotels and restaurants aren't backward in poaching men of his calibre. Some even start restaurants of their own. He could go anywhere, name his own price, cock a bloody snook at Letts. Henry doesn't know how lucky he is to have him. He needs to tread carefully. And he must know all this penny-pinching is putting customers off, especially our regulars."

He watched Mary pour the soapy water away down the sink and wipe the stainless steel draining board dry until it shone. "I tell you, Mary, it's not the big evening spenders so much as the regulars who matter, the lunchtime lot. Not finding the old variety of choice any more, they're beginning to go elsewhere."

He was right. Letts had always seen politicians flocking in at midday, taking the short taxi ride from Westminster. Journalists too, and publishers, medical men, lawyers, people from every walk of professional life in fact, lingering over after-lunch coffee, brandy, cigars, enjoying a brief light-hearted chat with the likeable Henry Lett, exchanging jokes with his even more amicable brother. But for not much longer if things went on the way they were going.

"Some are even giving a few sly digs, jokingly, but jokes meant as I see it, of going elsewhere if Letts isn't careful. You don't get things like that, even in fun, when they're satisfied."

Mary dried her hands on a sparkling white tea-towel and hung it over a rail beside the small enamel sink.

"I've noticed things too," she admitted now, making her way down the hall to the living-room, he following close behind like a spaniel at its master's heels. She sat down in one of the armchairs to stare beyond the art deco bookcase and the lace-curtained window at the drizzle-dull mews and sombre brick walls of the flats opposite while he selected a pipe from the rack beside the tiled fireplace. The gas fire was on, had probably been on all day. The flat was, as usual, too warm, for it wasn't really cold outside.

"Shall I turn this down?" he asked absently.

"No, leave it. I want it warm for when I get Helen from school."

Helen no longer needed a nanny, though Jenny, who'd once had full charge of her, still came in the evening to be with her while Mary was at the restaurant and put her to bed, staying until Mary came home. Apart from first thing in the morning Mary saw very little of Helen and she seemed to relish a walk to the local junior school to pick her up and bring her home.

William let himself relax in the other armchair. He tamped his pipe from a tobacco pouch and lit it. Nice to be off duty, though it would have been more enjoyable were it not becoming a regular occurrence. Business was slow, and waiters, trying to appear occupied under the gaze of their station head waiters, saw dole queues still too long for comfort. Andre, Letts' wine waiter, spent more time in his cellar checking his stock than serving it, and Henri, their practically irreplaceable head chef, fumed in his kitchen, berating his staff on the tiniest excuse and no doubt thinking seriously about his future here, maybe with offers already singing in his ears.

Even Mary wasn't needed so much these days, telephone bookings having gone down. Friday and Saturday nights were still busy, but not as they'd once been.

William's own job was secure as long as the restaurant stayed open, he knew that, he and Henry Lett having seen a lot of water flow under the bridge together. They had more in common than most people knew about. But what if Letts itself failed?

He picked up the *Daily Telegraph* that lay on the coffee table. "I don't know what's got into Henry. It's not like him, watching the place going down and not turning a hair. At least he doesn't seem to be. He tells me nothing."

Mary nodded, still gazing absently through the window. Letts had been going down little by little for more than eighteen months as far as she could see. At first it had hardly been noticeable; only thinking back had the slow change penetrated. But just lately, these last six months, it had accelerated until no one could help noticing.

It wasn't just the restaurant, either. For her it was other things, small things. Henry's long moments of brooding—they were together, growing more prolonged; his uncalled-for flares of brief temper, hurriedly apologised for, that shouldn't have happened in the first place; the odd way he'd become uncharacteristically careful about what he spent, he who'd always been so generous-hearted, though not foolish with money as she remembered Geoffrey to have been. Henry was by nature a careful though never a stinting man, but his care had never manifested itself as penny-pinching which it seemed to be heading towards.

Last Friday came instantly to mind. They had gone to see *Careless Rapture* at Drury Lane with complimentary tickets given to him by Ivor Novello himself on that evening he'd celebrated the success of his opening night at Letts. For all Henry hadn't had to pay for them, afterwards at the restaurant he'd still been so noticeably sparing in ordering his own meal, saying he wasn't that hungry, that she'd felt it improper to order that much for herself. And hadn't she seen pure relief on his face when handed the bill? That hadn't been the only time. No longer was it the best restaurant, the most sumptuous meal, the finest wine. Not that she expected him to lavish his money on her, but it bore out Will's observations this evening. And it was getting worse. But why?

So much had changed, but it had been a year of change all round. They had a new king, Edward VIII's coronation set for next May. A sad-looking young man these days – she remembered him years ago so happy-go-lucky, every woman's heart-throb, girls falling over themselves to be near him, his vulnerable looks and light voice making each of them want to mother him at least. The responsibilities of kingship, which he noticeably did not relish, seemed to have aged him almost overnight, giving him a drawn look. And there were whispers in closed circles of a secret love, a divorced woman, that might not go down well with the Royal Family or the country. In Mary's head was the memory of the slim, elegant woman with whom the then Prince of Wales had had supper in one of Letts' own private dining-rooms. Knowing the poignancy of forbidden love, Mary knew how he must feel.

Will rustled his newspaper noisily and, folding it in half, leaned across to show the page to her.

"Have you seen this?"

Obligingly she glanced at the section indicated, seeing little of the content in her disinterest except for a picture of masses of people seeming to be fighting. "I've not really had a chance today with Mrs Saunders gossiping on about her family as she worked."

"It's about some trouble in the East End yesterday. I wonder if my parents saw anything of it. It says this had been coming on for weeks."

He scanned and then began to read. "'A hundred thousand people thronged the streets and built barricades in an attempt to prevent a march by seven thousand supporters of fascist Sir Oswald Mosley through London's East End.' It says that lorries were overturned and bricks thrown at the police and through windows, and a Jewish tailor and his son were hurled through plate glass windows by Mosley's blackshirts. Eighty people were injured, including police, and eighty-four arrested. Thank God I didn't carry on with that man's doctrines, especially with what Adolf Hitler is doing in Germany."

The news was full of what was happening to Jewish people in that country; shops being burnt, they being attacked, many being herded into ghettos, their assets frozen and Germans forbidden to associate with them. That such vicious attacks could be happening here made her shudder.

"I don't want to hear about it," she said sharply, but one couldn't put off knowing what was happening all over Europe.

Hitler was not only attacking Jews but last March had entered the Rhineland in defiance of the treaty of Versailles. The people there seemed to welcome him, but it did look rather warlike. Not only that but Mussolini, dictator of Italy, had invaded Abyssinia. Now there was civil war in Spain between the fascists and Government forces, the name "fascist" raising an ominous fear in people's hearts, her own included, that all of Europe seemed to be teetering on the edge of some unacceptable upheaval, especially France with the Rhineland so near to her own border.

A happier event in August bringing a little light relief to all this awful uncertainty had been the Olympic Games, held in Berlin, which took away some of the trepidation. Mary wasn't much interested in the Games and hadn't missed not being there, but of course Geoffrey and his wife had spent the whole time there, living it up.

The puzzling thing was how Geoffrey was still able to spend money so freely when Henry was growing more tight-fisted by the minute, with the restaurant obviously suffering. Where was Geoffrey getting all that money from? Surely not always from his wife. Mary decided she'd tackle Henry on the subject next time they were together. If he was being too generous to his brother while Letts was going downhill, then he was being a fool and needed reminding that one could be too open-handed. And if he could be open-handed with Geoffrey then why not be a little more generous with herself who'd given and still gave him so much more than she gave any other person she knew?

She had no qualms telling him how she felt about it. After all, their special relationship entitled her to speak her mind. If she could share her body with him, it wouldn't hurt him to share a little of his thoughts and concerns with her, rather than just his body.

Thirteen

It seemed all things stable were being swept away.

Last month the beloved Crystal Palace, a symbol of Victorian stability, had burned to the ground in one night. Instead of mourning its disintegration, thousands flocked like hyenas to see the spectacle, mile-long queues of traffic giving fire engines problems in getting through. Five hundred firemen had fought the blaze, London's sky a lurid red.

Now the monarchy, England's own unique heritage, seemed in danger of disappearing forever as Edward VIII's voice, lightweight but laden with grief, came over the airwaves, which Mary, like every person in England with a wireless, had tuned into. "Dickie" was informing his stunned subjects in funereal tones that he found it impossible to carry the heavy burden of responsibility and to discharge his duties as king as he would wish to do without the help and support of the woman he loved.

Mary wept at those final, faintly wavering words: "God bless you all. God Save the King."

"Oh, Will…" Her own words seemed to abuse the silence that hung for a moment on those closing words, even though hers were whispered.

It was a terrible end to a terrible year, threatening to give no hope for the one to come, the pillars not only of British society dashed down but her own. Her tears were not only for a man renouncing his crown for the woman he loved, but more for the break with Henry, their happy Friday nights done with.

Will didn't know that and came to cuddle her to him to comfort her.

—

It had been an entirely wrong thing to do, she knew that now. She should have shut her mouth the moment Henry's grey eyes darkened, but she had gone on, puffed up with her intention of putting him and the world to rights, telling him what he should say the next time Geoffrey came asking for a hand-out.

"That's what they are, darling, blessed hand-outs. How can you allow him to do it? It cheapens him and it cheapens you."

She should have stopped there. They'd spent a nice evening together. She had learned to ignore much of Henry's continued care with his money, telling herself that what mattered most was that at the end of the evening they'd make love. When Henry made love to her she could forgive him anything.

And so it had been that evening last Friday, except that watching him meticulously counting his change at the supper table, as though the waiter serving them had tried to diddle him out of a couple of pennies, had been so humiliating that she'd remained upset all the way back to their flat. How could he show himself up in public so, stinting himself so openly, and her too? And all the while Geoffrey spent and spent and spent, every penny of it his brother's money. Mary's anger had grown so that by the time they reached the flat she could hardly look at Henry as she took off her street clothes.

"Want some tea? Or d'you prefer a proper drink?"

It was something she always asked, but this time her tone had been abrupt. He had looked at her questioningly.

"I'll have a brandy, darling. What's wrong, my sweet? You sound angry."

Unbelievable how a row can come from so small a thing, the counting of change; how words that one had no intention of saying can leap into the mouth; how one small rock slipping deep in the bowels of the earth can devastate a whole city, out of control. That was how it had felt.

She had whirled on him. "I wonder you can bring yourself to *afford* a glass of brandy. Are you sure it won't hurt your pocket?"

A week gone by – she could still see the pain, the bewilderment on his handsome face. But a brick wall couldn't have stopped the resentment this past year or so of penny-pinching had caused her when he could have so easily put an end to it by telling his brother that there would be no more money forthcoming for his incessant spending. Before she knew it all her resentment had come pouring out. He had retaliated by telling her to mind her own business. And so things had escalated until she had screamed at him that he could keep his bloody flat and his bloody love and his bloody tight-fisted ways too, that until he could treat her at least as well as he treated his brother she wanted nothing more to do with him.

She had gathered up her handbag, her coat and her hat and had stormed out, Henry's final furious words following her:

"If that's how you feel about me, Mary, after all this time, then that's it – you and I are finished."

Whatever else he had shouted after her had been cut off by the slam of the door of the flat. All week they had avoided each other – or rather he had avoided her. Her temper had quickly cooled, and she'd have made it up with him, eager to be back on loving terms, but it was too late. For the first time in her life Mary was made suddenly aware of an underlying obdurate side to Henry, of the pride he fostered stopping him making the first approach. It came as a shock, having always seen him as malleable and good-natured, perhaps to a fault in that he gave in to his brother so readily. Certainly she had thought he was loving and kind enough to forgive her anything. But she'd hurt him deeply, even though to her the argument had seemed trivial, and because it had been his love for her that she'd wounded, he'd not get over it that easily. Unless she made the first move, it was over. Yet what if she would only reap rejection? That was what she feared more than anything else, for rejection meant finality while nothing being done at all held a certain comfort that things might come out OK in time. So she did nothing.

The weeks crept on miserably into the New Year. Now it was late spring, and still she had done nothing towards making up with Henry, fearful of making the first move only to find herself turned away. The lovely Friday nights they had shared had faded to a thing of the past. The abdication of King Edward in December had been an excuse to cry for the loss of love, hidden by Will's humorous, innocent sympathy. She was trying to put on as brave a face as her empty heart would allow, but it seemed to her that Will had an inkling of what was going on. That he asked no questions helped emphasise that fact, though how he should know, if he did, was a puzzle. Herny would certainly not have confided in him about his affair with William's own wife for all he confided most other things in him. Not that it mattered a hoot. She felt too miserable to care.

–

Sick at heart Henry fetched out his cheque book, his brother hovering with an expression of humble gratitude.

"I shan't forget this, Henry. I've learned my lesson this time, really I have. It won't happen again."

Henry glanced up, his eyes flinty. "Yes it will. Lately it always does. It's become an illness with you and it's not as if you were a born winner."

But Henry himself was, in a way, holding the key to this ready source of replenishment. Geoffrey had phoned him earlier this evening asking if it was convenient to come and see him. Henry knew all too well what that meant – the man was short of funds again.

Geoffrey always had liked a little flutter. Over the past year, however, this had become serious gambling, sustained by easily obtained money. For him it had become a policy of easy come, easy go. A brief phone call, like this evening, and then he would race up to London in his sports car to present himself at the door with the hopeful expression on his face Henry had come to know well.

"Pamela suggested I come over, said you'd help me out. Sorry, Henry, just a small advance out of my next remuneration, that's all, if that's OK? Pay it back soon, old chap, I promise."

But he must know he was owing on his next remuneration already, in debt to the business by thousands. Thank God Grace wasn't here to ask awkward questions, though Geoffrey always asked if she was there before coming over. Not that that ever stopped him, but if she was, at least Henry would be forewarned and ready to manoeuvre Geoffrey out of the way before she could indulge in awkward small talk after asking if he was well and how Pam was. Away from inquisitive eyes he'd write out the cheque, hating the sickening gratitude with which Geoffrey accepted it, as if he didn't know why his brother was always so generous and patient. It would have been a whole lot easier to bear were Geoffrey's gratitude not the lie it was. A satisfied smirk as he pocketed the cheque would at least have been honest – were there such a thing as honesty in blackmail.

This weekend, with Hugh away at school, Grace was at Swift House taking time to visit her family nearby. She invariably left on a Friday, his chauffeur taking her in the car, and would phone when she was ready for him to send the car back for her. Such weekends had hitherto been wonderful, he and Mary taking advantage of his penthouse for the odd moments together as well as their Friday evenings. Not any more. Yet Pam and Geoffrey remained on his back. Parasites, the pair of them.

It came to him as he watched Geoffrey fold this present cheque to place in his inside jacket pocket that, with he and Mary no longer meeting, Pam's hold over him was considerably diminished. Immediately the thought popped like a bubble. It would still be there so long as there was the fear of Grace being told, even though it was over. Sometimes he wondered why it mattered. She was seldom here and when she was, she took little interest in him. It was the possibility of Mary being hurt that was his deepest fear. Shakily, he reached for a cigarette and lit it, savagely blowing out a cloud of blue smoke.

"Thanks, Henry," Geoffrey was saying, his tone returning to entreaty over Henry's previous remark. "You know, old chap, I do win quite a bit at times. I just had a small run of bad luck on this occasion."

"Small?" Suddenly angered, Henry couldn't help himself. "Fifteen hundred bloody quid in one go – you call that small?"

"I'll pay you back."

"Like hell you will! When have you ever done that?"

"If I wasn't already owing it… These people are on my back and I am a trifle desperate this time. It's quite a tidy sum. Afraid I slipped up, Henry."

There was no need for all this fawning. He meant not one word of it. "So you're in debt elsewhere," he said sharply. "And like last time and the times before that, I'm expected to pay your damned debts. That's taking a damned liberty." Geoffrey was looking offended, but Henry, now worked up, pressed on. "I can't go on financing your gambling debts, Geoffrey. You have to draw a line somewhere."

"I know. But I was told the nag couldn't lose."

"Then you were told wrong."

"I *was* winning. Those first three races went great. Just a bit of bad luck. I got carried away."

Henry's flinty expression hadn't altered. "As always." He sucked in more smoke. "Next time let me have some of what you owe me out of your winnings before it all goes, all right?"

There was no reply but Geoffrey's face spoke for him. Henry's temper was in danger of boiling over. It took all his will to hold it back. He was so sick of it all. It was making him ill. "All right, I've paid it off for you this time, Geoffrey, but that's it. You get into any more debt gambling and you've had it with me. Do you understand? God! Can't you see the way this business is struggling? I suppose not – you hardly ever show your bloody face. But the moment you need money, here you are looking like something one's dragged penniless from the gutter. Stop throwing it away on horses and in casinos and start acting your age. You've got a wife and a son. Try to behave as if you have. I'm telling you now, Geoffrey, you get in debt again, you stay away, you understand? Or God help me, I'll throw you out bodily."

Geoffrey was moving towards the door, backing away from the look on his brother's face. "All right, calm down. I'll get Pam to sort me out. She's a good girl. But thanks for this, old man. I will pay you back. I promise."

Henry knew hell would freeze over before that promise was ever kept. He knew too that he could expect a visit from Pam. She would put his irate feelings into perspective and next time he would continue to pay Geoffrey what he needed. None of it bore thinking about and as the door closed behind Geoffrey he once again cursed the fool he'd been the day he'd fallen into Pam's trap.

–

Her visit came on the Monday. He was upstairs when she called, and he thanked God that Grace had decided to stay at Swift House until mid-week.

All smiles, the affectionate sister-in-law, but refusing a cigarette or a drink, she came straight to the point.

"It was nice of you, Henry, to help Geoffrey out on Saturday. But he was a little upset at the way you treated him. It was hurtful. He tried to explain but then you began threatening him. Why, for God's sake?"

Her assumed innocence made him feel instantly truculent. Something needed to be said, whether he suffered for it or not. Through a protective fog of cigarette smoke, he told her flatly that he wasn't seeing Mary any more and that between the pair of them they'd end up draining the business dry. "If it goes under, there'll be no more money to give you."

A slow smile spread across her face as she sat at ease in one of the leather armchairs of the sitting-room, her slim, well-manicured fingers drumming casually on the chair arm. "Then it's up to you, Henry, to make sure it doesn't."

He was pacing the floor, puffing continuously. "How the hell do I do that?" He saw her look around the room with its collection of fine porcelain, bronze and silver ornaments, its tasteful furnishings, expensive furniture.

"You manage to do well enough yourself with this lot."

"How do you expect me to live? In a hovel? Grace would certainly ask questions then, wouldn't she?"

"It doesn't bother me what the hell Grace asks. You can live in a hovel or here, as you please, so long as you see your brother all right, darling. And by the way, I can't see as you not seeing Mary makes any difference." She got up abruptly. "Well, I haven't time to chat. Just be sure my Geoffrey isn't made to feel his visits aren't welcome. I have his best welfare at heart, you know, like a loving wife should. OK, darling? Kisses, then."

Pursing her lips towards him from a distance, she was gone, leaving him seething and hopeless, wanting desperately for someone to help lighten his load and finding no one. Not even Mary now.

–

Monte Carlo was bathed in sunlight beneath a cloudless, deep blue sky. Geoffrey looked about him. The pavement outside the Cafe de Paris was crowded with the fashionable set taking tea, bright umbrellas tilted against the sun's intense heat, the chink of teacups and the babble of voices filling the still air with a concerted hubbub. Not one empty table to be seen. Geoffrey clicked a thumb and middle finger twice in quick succession at a passing waiter. On his way to serve someone else, the man instantly deviated and came over.

"Isn't there one single damned empty table here?"

"Two people zere, m'seur, leaving zis seconde." The man indicated with a brief nod of his head and continued on his way, winding expertly through the throng, loaded tray held high to miss every head, swaying and tilting with the agility and grace of a ballet dancer, a joy to watch.

"Bloody man!" Geoffrey swore. He felt rattled. He'd just lost somewhat heavily in a brief spell of roulette, certain he had felt a winning streak coming on or he wouldn't have bothered so early in the afternoon. Pam had said he was pushing his luck, he'd got annoyed with her and now she had gone silent on him. When he'd asked if she fancied afternoon tea outside the Cafe de Paris, she had shrugged, tight-lipped, but had followed him just the same. Bloody girl!

"As much as he could do to be civil," he railed to Pam as they sidled between the busy tables towards the indicated couple, now getting up to leave, laughing with each other. "Cocking his bloody head like that. Not even bothering to show us to our table."

"Oh, shut up!" Pam hissed. The couple having moved off, she sat down. "The man was busy. Couldn't you see that? The world doesn't stop for Geoffrey Lett because he's lost a bit on the tables. You'll get it all back by tonight."

"I bloody well hope so." He sat down next to her, squinting against the white glare of the casino opposite that even in September reflected heat back on to the crowded pavement. Simply everyone who was anyone was here or in places like it: the London season over, they had all flocked to the South of France. The English weren't the only ones; American voices filled the air with nasal twangs and Hollywood film stars mingled with the smart set and locals alike, brash and friendly. There were Germans too, wealthy members of the new regime, certain of them-selves, boasting of their Führer, what he'd done for their country. Insufferable. The place was no longer what it once had been.

Glancing away from the bright glare of elegant build-ings, Geoffrey scowled at the as yet uncleared surface of the neat little bow-legged wooden table. "Can't seem to win anything these days. Why doesn't someone come and clear away this bloody mess?"

"Give them a chance. And for God's sake, Geoffrey, do shut up. And anyway, I don't know why you're so churlish.

So you lost a few pounds. There's plenty more where that came from. Just pop off a telegram to Henry."

Geoffrey glowered. "I can't keep on worrying him."

"Yes you can," Pam said confidently and smiled at the approach of a couple with whom they'd become friendly, the Channons – rich, prosperous friends of royalty.

She made room for them as they came to sit, they calling, "Hello there! Had a good morning? We've been swimming. Delightful, sea's as heady as wine. You to the casino later?" To which Pam nodded firmly.

–

Christmas Day this year was spent with just Will, Helen and herself. Henry had asked Will to take over the restaurant for him on Boxing Day while he spent it with his wife's people at Grace's bidding. Geoffrey and Pam were away too. Naturally. So Boxing Day saw her and Helen on their own.

Will's parents had suggested she and Helen go to them but Mary felt, perhaps a little masochistically, that she rather wanted to wallow in her own company and gracefully declined, saying she'd be too tired to go out after preparing for the day before and, anyway, she'd have to be up early next morning, needed at Letts' reception desk.

It was a fib. She went seldom now, only if the place was extra busy, which wasn't often these days. Boxing Day would probably be busy, though nowhere as brisk as it had once been, Henry still appearing to have lost all interest in it. With so many other fine places around, the Dorchester, the Ritz, Claridges and the Savoy among them, attracting visitors from America and the Continent with plush offerings, Letts had become rather left out.

There had been a brief hope of recovery during the weeks leading up to the coronation of George VI in May, but business had dropped off rapidly after that. During the London season, some of the fashionable set still loyal to the old name of Letts had again patronised it for a while, but that spurt of bookings had been brief too, not enough to sustain any momentum with Henry displaying little enthusiasm still. It was mystifying yet Mary felt unable to approach him as she'd once done. He seemed so depressed of late. Whenever Mary had a chance to speak to him she had to be careful what she said, not only to avoid any reference to the old days of their Friday evenings together and the love they'd once shared, but to the predicament of the restaurant itself. Touchy, he read criticism into every word, even Will no succour for him these days. Not only was the restaurant going down and down but he too. Nothing she could do to help him, and she wanted so much to. Sometimes she wanted to run away screaming, anything to relieve the tension that hung over them.

Busy or not, she saw no reason to put in an appearance this Boxing Day. Henry not being there, what was the point? And she had a filthy cold that had arrived a few days before Christmas. It had been a miserable Christmas, she trying to keep away from Helen in case she caught it, trying not to hug her too much when she'd run to her in excitement about the toys that Father Christmas had brought.

Kissing Will goodbye, Helen still tucked up in bed, a place Mary too felt more like retreating to, she went back to huddle before the blazing gas fire and think dismal thoughts. The loss of Henry's companionship on Fridays was still hard to bear. Over a year had gone by and she still yearned for him. Sometimes when she did work she'd catch him looking at her with pain in his eyes and she hoped he didn't detect the pain in hers. Just as well they no longer met – it would have been only a matter of time before others had realised their secret and provoked an awkward situation. But she pined for the past, for their Fridays, even for those clandestine meetings in the office.

–

Mary had long ago ceased to have anything to do with the office side of things. That was in the hands of a very competent young man, loyal as the day was long. In the staff room, where those unable to get home for lunch ate, she would often sit with Mr Collins.

In February 1938, sharing his table, she noticed he seemed bothered. "I'm just wondering just how much longer my job here is going to last," he said when she asked him what was the matter.

"What do you mean?" She took a small sip of her coffee.

Simon Collins was toying with his cheese sandwich. "I'm wondering just how much longer this place'll keep going the way things are."

"Of course it'll keep going. It's been going since the middle of the last century."

"Things just aren't right."

Mary put down her coffee cup. "Things are a bit dull at present, yes. But they've been so before. You don't have to talk of losing your job."

Collins put down his sandwich and looked at her. "Miss Goodridge." He called her "Miss", the recognised title for married women who worked. "I pride myself on being good at my job. I like to think I am. I run that office. I am in charge of accounts, I supervise the filing, the correspondence, the post, and my staff are loyal to me and honest. But now and again there are some figures I do not understand, not discrepancies, but the accounts do not always appear to balance as they should, and it worries me and causes me loss of sleep that a finger of suspicion might become pointed at me. More, I am aware of sums made out to Mr Geoffrey's expense account – for no good reason, as I can see – and at times it seems outgoings far outstrip incomings. Unreasonably so, and that isn't right. And it all has to do with money to Mr Geoffrey. What does Mr Henry want with such sums for his brother?"

He broke off guiltily. "But it's really none of my business. I shouldn't have spoken except that I'm worried this place is going to fall down leaving me with no job."

"No, say what you're thinking," Mary urged, but he shook his head and, picking up his tea and plate of cheese sandwiches, and getting up from the table, he paused to look down at her.

"Shouldn't've said what I did. Breach of confidence. Please excuse me, Miss Goodridge."

Leaving her staring after him, he went to the tea counter and there drained his cup and, picking up his remaining sandwiches, put the plate on the counter and made for the door leading back to the office.

After that he seemed to purposely avoid her, saying he had finished if she came to a table he was sitting at, or using one of the other two if she was already sitting down. It was an attitude that planted suspicion in her mind, despite the fact that she did not know exactly the content of that suspicion except that it somehow smacked of something not quite in order and which somehow involved Geoffrey. It wasn't her place to go poking her nose in, yet it seemed imperative she find out. To delay the matter could spell awful trouble.

All Mary could think of was finding a way to confront Henry himself without seeming too inquisitive. Even that was fraught with problems, but something told her that he needed help. The trouble was, would he welcome help from anyone, especially an outsider as she seemed to be these days?

Fourteen

There was only one way. To bluff, tell Henry to his face that she knew what was going on and hope he might confide in her. They having been so close at one time, he owed her that much. But what if there was nothing to confide? When it came to it, misgivings filled her that not only was she about to stick her nose in where it wasn't wanted but that she could be barking up the wrong tree. Yet he was looking harrassed lately. Something had to be wrong.

She found him eating in the little side room off the kitchen where he usually snatched the occasional meal if the place was busy. Today it wasn't busy. He could have gone up to his own quarters for a more leisurely lunch with his wife. Mary wondered why he hadn't – but she wasn't here to wonder about such idle things.

It struck to her as she came in at his bidding to her tentative tap on the door that he had become instantly tense, a guarded, even defensive look on his face as though he had been expecting someone whom he had no pleasure at seeing. Finding her there, his smile was visibly one of relief.

"Mary! I thought—" He stopped abruptly, then stood up from the table and hurried to pull out the chair opposite him. "Come and sit down. You don't mind me carrying on eating, do you?"

He was being too light-hearted as he went back to his meal; far too devil-may-care compared to the attitude she'd first noticed. Henry had never been devil-may-care, unlike his brother, and she had always felt warm and safe in his presence, had always felt him to be trustworthy and honest even though since the break-up of their affair the tension between them had lingered for all their outward friendliness towards each other. At this moment, however, she was aware only of the furtiveness that this past year or so had come to dominate him, and this present gallant attitude did not sit well with her.

Made immediately uncomfortable by it, she decided to come straight to the point as she sat down on the chair he had pulled out for her.

"I've been talking to Mr Collins in the staff canteen. He seems worried he might lose his job."

Henry regarded her, a strained smile on his lips. He did not look well, hadn't looked well for quite some time. There was nothing specific about him, just an ageing and drawn look, though he was still as handsome as ever he'd been. Her heart still flipped over whenever they met, ached that they were no longer lovers, burned with hope that one day it would again be as it had been.

"Now, why should he think that? He's a good man. I can rely on him one hundred per cent. He knows his job inside out."

"Maybe a little too inside out." The remark flew out before she could stop it and she saw Henry's smile change to a frown making him look even older and more strained.

Of course he should look older. He was nearly forty. But until lately the years had improved him – there had been hardly a line on his face, and a certain composure that helped to heighten still more the confidence he had always instilled in people. These days, however, he had become nervy and agitated, only just managing to contain a sharpness towards others that, surfacing at unguarded moments, took them by surprise and, being unexpected, hurt all the more. Mary herself had more than once this past year felt the sting of his tongue, and for her it did hurt, knowing how gentle he had always been with her.

Now she was deliberately putting herself in the direct path of it. She told herself she must be mad as she faced the frown that was at once querying and censuring her remark. She hurried to give it substance.

"Mr Collins is an astute young man. Very little escapes him in that office. And now he is deeply concerned."

"And he told *you* that." Henry's tone was harsh. "And told you his reasons. I should have expected such an astute young man in a position of confidence to have kept confidences pertaining to my business to himself. He rather disappoints me."

Realising that she was inadvertently becoming the instrument of the poor man's dismissal, Mary hastened to rectify the harm she might have done him. "But you've just admitted that he is a good man."

"I'm beginning to wonder. People have a way of surprising one."

Ideas of tackling Henry on his mysterious overspending dissipated as she hurried to reverse what seemed to her the possibility of the office manager's livelihood being destroyed. "It was just a remark he passed without thinking because he was worried at the amount going out in excess of what's coming in. He was concerned that the place might go down and he be sacked."

"He most certainly will be after this."

"No, Henry, please." His tone frightened her. "It's my fault. I've made more of it than I should. Don't take it out on him. I came to you because I'm worried – for you. Tell me what's wrong. There *is* something wrong, I know."

"There is nothing wrong."

"Don't give me that, Henry. I know you, remember? We weren't lovers for all those years for me not to know you. I have your child to prove it."

She held his gaze as he looked up at her. She saw his eyes narrow, grow hard and accusing. "So you too want to blackmail me."

"Why would I want to do such a thing?" But tiny wheels had begun to spin in her head. "Henry, what did you mean when you said too? What's going on? Is that why so much money is going out? Because you're being blackmailed? I know the money is going out. Mr Collins wouldn't be so worried about the possibility of the restaurant going down and down if it wasn't. I'm surprised your accountant hasn't noted that more money is going out than coming in."

She didn't know that Henry's accountant had already pointed out the fact, Henry fobbing him off that the more exorbitant outlays were Geoffrey's expenses as the company's representative abroad. It not being an accountant's place to forbid overspending, he had merely warned Henry to take more caution.

Geoffrey had also come into Mary's mind. One who spent money like water, always in need of funds. She remembered how he had spent on her when they had been married, boasting that he could always get Henry to advance a bit here, a bit there. Henry had always been there to help him out of a spot and sometimes she had felt Geoffrey had taken a little too much advantage of it. But surely he'd not blackmail his own brother. What reason had he to?

"Who is it doing this, Henry?" She ignored his bluster that no one was on his back. "Why are they doing it? What is it they've got over you?"

The look he gave her in answer to her last question stabbed her like a knife through the heart. In that instant she knew it involved herself as well as him. She racked her brains but could only think that Geoffrey could know nothing of her affair with Henry unless Henry had told him – and she was sure he wouldn't have done that. He had made a point of wanting to keep their relationship secret. But if Geoffrey *had* somehow found out, would he stoop to such an evil thing?

"Has it to do with Geoffrey?" she probed, and again his pale face told more than words could have. She gasped. "It can't be him."

"No, not him." He drew in a deep breath, and his voice when he spoke was husky with despair. "It was bound to come out in time. Ironic though that you and I are no longer having an affair. It seems it makes no difference – the harm is already done. Certain people who mean a great deal to both of us will be told if I refuse to pay her whenever money is asked for."

"*Her?*" Not Geoffrey, then, even though he was the only one ever in constant need of money, asking for it at odd intervals as the need arose. She voiced her query and Henry's gaze rose to meet hers in abject defeat.

"His wife. Geoffrey's wife. Pamela," he said slowly. "Do you remember New Year's Eve 1933? I kissed you at the back of reception. I thought no one could see us. Apparently one pair of eyes did."

Mary had an instant recollection of the way Pamela had accosted her that night as she made for the door leading to the office building. Pamela had not seen them kissing, that recess was invisible to any eyes, but she had seen Mary leave the reception area, her face flushed from that kiss, Henry leaving immediately after as she made for the door to the office to be alone there with him. She should have known; Pam was the obvious blackmailer. She had thought no more about it when nothing had apparently come of it, angry only that Pamela would have been licking her lips and thinking of it as a scream. Henry had kept the reality from her, and all this time had suffered that evil woman's power over him all on his own. Her heart wept for what he must have gone through.

"You mean this has been going on ever since then?" she burst out.

"Not exactly. She bided her time until one flaming row I had with Geoffrey months later over money – the usual thing – him needing to be baled out. She came storming in here in a tearing rage demanding I help him out or she'd tell Grace and your William about us."

Mary recalled that day too, when Pam had cut her dead on leaving.

"That's why I let you go when you walked out on me that Christmas," he was saying. "It took all the resolve I had not to run after you. I thought then it was the wisest time to end it and she'd have no leg to stand on. But I was wrong. She said she could still put the cat among the pigeons and asked did I want that? Of course I didn't. What could I do? She's getting more and more demanding. Geoffrey's got the gambling bug, he's constantly in debt. I wish he'd have one huge win and maybe I'd be let off the hook, but I can't see that happening. Easy come, easy go. The more he wins the more he gambles it away. He knows that every time he runs out of luck, she'll come to me for more. I can see no end to it. Meantime the restaurant…"

The remaining words drifting off into silence, he sat, head bowed. He had not touched his lunch, his wine glass full still. All he'd done was reach for the small box of cigarettes that lay on the table, putting a cigarette in his mouth, applying a light, hardly aware of it.

"I wish she was dead, that would end it," Mary said without thinking.

Henry let out an explosive, smoke-filled laugh, bitter as the smoke itself. "What good would that do? He'd only take up where she left off. But you weren't really thinking of helping her on her way?"

"I wasn't thinking," she burst out, her eyes unexpectedly filling with tears. "But I wish she were."

They sat silent, glum, each wrapped in their own thoughts. Henry stubbed out his cigarette and reached for another one.

Mary was the first to pull herself together, out of desperation making a decision. "I say let her tell them. We've nothing to hide now. She's got no proof. All she can do is make a bit of a nuisance. I don't for an instant think William will believe her." Yet was she a hundred per cent sure of that?

"I think Grace will. Grace is an odd sort of woman—"

"For God's sake, Henry!" Mary burst out, suddenly losing her temper. "You haven't been man and wife since Hugh was born. You've told me that so many times I've lost count. You couldn't drive any larger wedge between you if you tried. Is it going to make all that much difference if she did know about us?"

"It would make a difference to me."

"Then you'll have to learn to grin and bear it."

It was a heartless remark but she realised that his eyes were bleak as they searched hers. "And Helen?" he reminded. "What happens if she ever finds out who her real father is?"

That silenced her. She hadn't thought to consider Helen.

"Yes," he said at her silence. "I keep thinking of how spiteful Pamela can be. What if she took it into her head to dig and delve about us right back into the past? I'm not saying she would, but you never know."

The thought of Will being told that, after all he'd done in marrying her and giving his name to Henry's child, she had gone back to Helen's father in secret, was the cruellest thing that could happen to him. She still had a feeling that he already knew but had remained silent as he watched her leave each Friday evening with Henry the so-called friend-doing-his-good-turn. Not once had Will ever commented on it. Nor in all these years had he ever referred to Henry as being Helen's real father. When he'd proposed marriage to give the baby his name, Henry hadn't been mentioned. He didn't have to be. It was a subject that lay unspoken by them both, better not to be raised.

There never was as good a man as William and the idea of that bitch willing to destroy him by resurrecting that which he'd rather let lie dormant was something Mary was not prepared to allow — yet might just have allowed had it not been for Helen. Now, like Henry, she too found herself tied helplessly hand and foot.

"We must keep it from Helen," she said lamely and read the smile on Henry's lips, sad and hoplessly wise. Helen was young but would she ever come to accept it? One day, maybe. But not yet. Not for a long while.

Leaving Henry to his meal, she made her way through the restaurant, which was unnervingly quiet these days, making her feel a hand of doom in it. Once it had been so lively, echoing the sound of voices and cutlery (the place never had been truly cured of its echo), waiters once dashing back and forth with great energy through the two-way doors to the kitchen where the clash of plates and dishes and the calling of orders filled the steam-laden air. Now it tried only to *look* busy, staff desperately seeking to keep their jobs. Customers spoke in calmer tones with not so many to shout above, instinctively prompted by the more sedate atmosphere to lower their voices so that the tinkling strains of piano music, once hardly heard above the din, was heard distinctly, in its pathetic way serving to emphasise the sparseness of customers.

But she took little notice as she made her way first up the plush and gilded stairway, then past the dance floor and the reception area where she once held sway, up the marble flight to the entrance itself, her mind, as she took in a deep breath of the fresh, chill air of March, more on how she could convince Henry further of the futility of paying for silence.

She would begin tackling Helen, would gently explain that Will wasn't her real father, carefully add the real truth bit by bit. She was determined – but when it came down to racking her brains how to start, she finally knew that she couldn't. As that knowledge of hopelessness had gripped Henry for so long, so it attached itself to her like a parasitic vine. She knew then how he felt, how hard it had been for him even to bear his tormentor's venom. And she'd had the temerity to scoff at his cowardice, dictate to him what he should be doing? She was as much coward as he.

What Mary had said had put thoughts into Henry's head. That she had been prepared to put her marriage on the line had shamed him. True, the thought of Helen had prevented her rushing ahead with her mad idea, but she was right, it couldn't go on forever, and for a time, a short time, he had felt strong and full of determination. But it couldn't last.

Too soon there came the thought of Grace, devastated, in tears, her gentle eyes filled with pain at his deceit. He saw a tacky divorce, the newspaper headlines: "Well-Known Restaurant Owner in Sordid Affair with Ex-Sister-in-Law". He thought of having to look unconcerned as his rich and regular customers followed him with their eyes and leaned across tables at each other: "Been going on for years, I hear. Not a smell of it, until now of course. Sly old fox covered up his goings-on well, didn't he?"

He thought of his daughter. (He didn't think of Hugh, his son only in name at times – Grace's boy, her darling, himself shut out.) He hardly ever saw Helen but to him she was more his daughter than Hugh would ever be his son. Always on his mind, he would glean news of her progress from her mother when he could, wish things had been different, wish he could hear Helen call him "Daddy", sweep her up in his arms without fear of anyone and hold her close. But he was trapped, would continue to pay that bitch Pamela, unable to face the unsavoury consequences if he didn't. Mary didn't understand. So he put away his thoughts of sending his tormentor packing, awaiting the next visit which must come some time soon.

–

As if she sensed something going on, no word came from Pam. April passed, May, June. Still not a peep. She appeared to be keeping well clear of him, and he dared to hope she'd finally realised that the more time went on the less substance her tale possessed, making her look ridiculous. Except that it was a bit too good to be true. Her unaccountable silence was unnerving and where he should have been the most relieved man in the world, he caught himself laying down obstacles unnecessarily.

After all, his fortunes appeared to be turning at last. This first half of 1938 had seen business perk up. But even that worried him, as though in a place of paradise a dark monster lurked ready to leap. It was perhaps that he, being like a tightly coiled spring all this time, found it hard to unwind.

All he could see was that for a business to come so startlingly to life again after having dragged its feet for so long was against all odds in a world that itself was growing more jittery by the day. The threat of war as yet only hovering, it was there on the horizon all the same: Hitler seeing himself as a god in Europe, Mussolini not far behind, the fascist General Franco having gained the upper hand in Spain – even the Vatican in Rome now recognising him as its leader. Japan had overrun China, stories of atrocities coming out of that country; the whole world seemed on the brink of chaos. Yet, in all this, Letts had begun to pick up customers, they suddenly flocking in, being jolly into the small hours, the pace just as it used to be.

They had no reason to be jolly. The government, already recognising the threat from Hitler and Mussolini, was handing out gas masks, a new law making it compulsory for all schools to put their young children through gas mask drill. Young men were joining the Territorial Army and the digging of trenches in London parks was being contemplated. People protesting at the devastation were nevertheless fearful before what seemed like harbingers of doom. There was talk of the young being sent to safer parts of the country in case of air raids on London. Yet places like Letts had become oddly brighter and busier as though everyone with money sought to indulge in a last great spending spree before they were deprived of their wealth by an unseen force.

Geoffrey and Pam too were apparently making the most of things. One reason why Henry hadn't set eyes on them was that they were abroad, in Monte Carlo, had been there for a good couple of months. Geoffrey wrote gaily of the fun they were having and of his marvellous run of good luck in the casino, allowing Henry to breathe sighs of relief.

In July he asked Mary to come back to deal with reception, which she did willingly, her presence perking up the place even more. At thirty-seven she was a beautiful woman with poise and grace and still with the capacity to turn heads. She was good for business. Customers loved her. And so did he; he even harboured wild thoughts of resuming their Friday nights together. William, too wrapped up in the restaurant to take her many places, would see it as a godsend and think of her as being safe in Henry's company.

The restaurant was William's life. Henry often felt he should have made him a partner. Perhaps one day he would. Geoffrey, hardly here enough to be considered any asset, was certainly beyond any position to object. If things went on as they were going, he would think about it.

—

Geoffrey was almost in tears of frustration. "I don't know how it could have happened."

Pam had no sympathy for him as she sat in the lounge of their spacious apartment overlooking the sparkling, almost wine-coloured deep blue of the Mediterranean.

She was seething. "You should have known when to call a halt."

"I do know usually. But until then I wasn't putting a foot wrong. You know that. I haven't put a foot wrong for ages. Being on such a great streak of fortune for so long, one loss just seemed a temporary setback. The second time, I just told myself I'd soon be back on form. After that it really became a matter of recuperating the loss as quickly as I could. But it just went on and I suppose I got desperate."

"That's when you should have come away." Her tone sharp, she wasn't exactly worried for him, mostly angry that he could be so stupid, so weak.

"I know I should have. But when you start losing you keep thinking it must change for you. I'd been on such a winning streak till then, you know."

She stared out at the sea, the busy promenade and beach below it. "I should have been with you, stopped you. You can be such a fool."

"That's not fair, Pam. You've done pretty well out of me. We've not had to go back to London and ask Henry for any money. Life's grand down here, and look at all the jewellery and clothes you've been buying."

"No more than I ought!" She got up angrily to light herself a cigarette. "I hope you don't expect me to lower my lifestyle just because you've lost a few bob."

"Sixty thousand, Pam! Is that what you call a few bob? I've got to get it back, but I'm scared I'll lose even more. And now that I'm owing…"

She turned on him. "You're owing? How come?"

"I had to. I was certain my luck had to be on the turn."

"How much?"

"Another twenty."

"My God, Geoffrey! How could you be so bloody stupid? Why didn't you come to me?"

"Because I didn't think you'd lend it. And I didn't want you angry."

"Angry! I'm sodding furious! You damned fool!"

"Perhaps if you can pay the debt – just for a few days. I'll get it back."

"I haven't *got* twenty thousand."

While he watched, she leaped up to begin pacing the spacious room with its white walls, cool floor tiles, its modem pictures in black frames, its ceramic vases of Mediterranean plants, dark furniture and soft furnishings of plain biscuit-coloured fabric.

"You must have, darling," he urged. "Can't you wire your father?"

"Not on your life, *darling*. Tell my father that my husband has been gambling away our money? You'll have to go and see your brother."

"I can't do that, Pam."

"But I can ask my parents? No. You go and see your brother. He's very loving and generous to you. He'll cough up. He always does."

"Not with sixty thousand he won't. That's too much to ask from him."

"Not sixty, darling," she reminded acidly. "Eighty. Remember the money you owe?"

"God, I can't! Pam – I just can't."

She paused to turn on him, her blue eyes cold and hard. "I tell you, Geoffrey, if you don't, I'm packing. Leaving here. I'll stay with my parents."

He was looking at her in astonishment. "Leaving? Leaving me?"

"Exactly. If you can't support me, I don't need you. I've been willing enough to support you when you've spent more than you receive."

"But most of it goes on you, Pam."

"Plus a good deal of my own money. You know I can quite easily support myself, and if I have to spend my money so someone else can buy me things, I might as well do for myself."

"Don't you love me any more?" It was a feeble cry. His debts forgotten, he was staring at her with fear and disbelief in his eyes. She shrugged her slim shoulders and drew deeply on her cigarette.

"Of course I do. I'm just not prepared to go on financing your wild escapades." She smiled suddenly. "Darling, now we've got that over with, I know you'll go to Henry and sort things out for us."

The fear cleared from his face. "You were blackmailing me!"

"A little."

She moved towards him, came closer until her slim body touched his so that he would feel its seductive warmth through the gauzy cotton of her dress and that of his shirt. "I'm very good at blackmail, didn't you know?"

She saw him smile in his relief, saw him draw his tongue across his lower lip, saw desire for her creep into his grey eyes, the lids lowered so that the long lashes shielded the pupils to give him a certain look that made her shiver deliciously.

Taking her cigarette from her, he put it to his lips and sucked in a small meaningful amount of smoke, once more master of himself. Without taking his eyes off her, he stubbed it out in a pale marble ashtray on a small table beside their two touching bodies. Smoke emanating from his nostrils, he bent and kissed her, one hand on her breast. In this way they moved off to the bedroom, his lips still on hers, his hand still manipulating her breast, causing the lower part of her body to throb as, by the feel of him, so too was his.

Fifteen

In the late evening, with the last glow of a long summer day having only just faded, Letts was already filled nearly to capacity and up on the mezzanine floor the bar was crowded. A five-piece dance band was playing. Couples would go on dancing into the small hours. At the moment, with the music lively, the beat jumping, they were jitterbugging. It had been like this for most of the summer against a growing background of tension, with Britain and France threatening hostilities should Hitler march into Czechoslovakia in the face of their dire warning not to. But few here dwelt on this.

Henry leaned on the balcony balustrade gazing down on the crowded restaurant. Soon he'd go down to move casually between the tables, nodding to faces he knew — and there were a great many of those reappearing of late. They'd nod back to him.

"Hello, Henry, old man! Great to see you! How's tricks?"

"Fine," he would say. "Couldn't be better."

"Had the place done up I see. Looks great, old man. Just like the old days, eh?" He would smile and move on to another familiar face.

Yes, they were all coining back. With no word from Pam or Geoffrey, apart from Geoffrey's one joyful letter, Henry felt he'd been given a new lease of life. He'd had the place redecorated in July, just after Mary's return, and even felt able to afford engaging dance bands with famous names, always an attraction.

He glanced up to where more people were flocking through the glass doors, their coats being checked in by a young girl under the eye of Mary, herself busily engaged with telephone bookings and those being made on the spot. Fully in his view, she was now bending her head over the blue and gold appointment book, one finger running swiftly down the list. He saw her look up at the enquirer, nod confirmation of the couple's table and with a smile beckon a young *commis* to conduct them to it.

Henry watched her turn her attention to the next couple. She worked so smoothly, so efficiently, yet with such friendliness that things at the desk went, as usual, without a hitch, despite the small crowd with more coming in. He felt a surge of love rise up into his breast, memories of their Friday nights flooding back. They must resume those meetings. He ached for her. Next week he would set the ball rolling again, say to William casually that he thought Mary was looking a little down of late and might perhaps do with being taken out of herself for an evening, offering himself as chaperone, of course.

William was sure to agree, always so wrapped up in this place. Next weekend Grace was off to Swift House with Hugh before the lad returned to school for the last term before Christmas. He and Mary would have the penthouse to themselves. Suddenly excited, Henry drew his cigarette case from the inside pocket of his dinner jacket and swiftly lit one.

Downstairs William was standing to one side as he always did, dark eyes like those of a hawk surveying the tables, ever watchful, the hurrying waiters directed by a switch of the gaze, a hardly discernable nod of the head. Good restaurant manager that he was, his directives went unnoticed by diners as if he wasn't there at all, but every waiter was most aware of him and hurried to each command his eyes gave from the restaurant's shadowy perimeter. Very little escaped William's notice. Had those watchful eyes, Henry wondered with a small twinge of guilt, seen him look up at Mary? Had they penetrated his thoughts about her?

He put out his cigarette hardly smoked and hurried down the gilt staircase. If he went to have a brief word with his restaurant manager on the pretext of restaurant matters, he might deduce whether William had in fact read anything amiss in his scrutiny of Mary.

He must have hurried a little too fast, for at the bottom a pain caught his chest, making him catch his breath. This did happen now and again, lately with increasing regularity. But he still hadn't consulted the quack. He thought again of it as he paused and tightened his lips against the sharp pain that sent a slower, heavy ache down his right arm. To cover the pause, he spent the moments casting his gaze around the room and by the time someone hailed him to exchange a friendly quip, he was recovered.

"I thought I'd ask you before speaking to William." To Mary his words would have struck a somewhat banal note had it not been for what had transpired only moments before.

He had caught her on the marble staircase as she came into the building. Tuesday morning it was quiet before the rush of lunch, just a few stragglers taking morning coffee. Helen back at school, Mary had little else to do, so had come in for the morning. She came in whenever she could, a chance to see Henry, if only from afar. He had come up the stairs as she was about to go down to the quiet bar to get herself a quick coffee. It seemed by the pace with which he'd mounted the stairs to meet her that he'd been waiting for her.

For a second or two he had stood out of breath and strangely drawn-faced, his hand on her arm. She'd asked if he was all right. He had nodded tersely – she would have said angrily – and for a moment she thought she might have done something wrong the previous evening. Then he had blurted out, "Mary, I must see you!"

"Well, I'm here," she had said lightly, but he'd gabbled on.

"No, not here. I mean, I must see *you*. Do you understand?"

Seeing her nod, with a backward glance at the quiet restaurant below he had conducted her back up the stairs and into the reception area. There, drawing her into its hidden recess, he had grabbed her to him, his lips closing hungrily over hers.

Dazed, seconds later she was as hungrily returning his kisses, her sighs, muffled by his lips, repeating, "Oh, darling…" over and over again.

She heard naked urgency in his voice as, covering her face with his kisses, he spoke of so wanting to return to their old relationship, of wanting to see her last week, thinking Grace would be away but realising that she, deciding to wait till Hugh was back at school, was going this weekend instead.

"I'll be on my own on Friday. We could go out for the evening, then come back here, upstairs, for coffee." Full of meaning until those last words, "I thought I'd ask you before speaking to William," had broken the spell.

Now she moved away. "Henry, no."

She saw the perplexed look on his face. "Why not?"

"We had a narrow escape last time. We shouldn't tempt fate."

He had told her of Pamela's continuing non-appearance – a sort of weekly report whispered at her across the reception desk as he passed: "Still nothing." His face registered growing relief and the lines of harassment were slowly lifting from his forehead and the corners of his mouth, making him look so much younger again. Mary's relief had matched his own, but that didn't mean they could renew their relationship as though nothing had interfered with it. It was still too early to get complacent.

He was looking at her now with pleading in his eyes. "Is that the only reason, Mary? That we could be tempting fate? Not that you don't love me? I know you still want me as much as I want you. Darling…" He drew her close again. "We have to be together. I need you so much."

"And what about Will? And your wife? Pamela finding out about us and doing what she did was a warning to us. Henry, I can't, not this time."

"It's all right now, darling. She's obviously realised she never did have enough to go on to carry out her threats."

"She seemed to think she had. And you thought she had."

"It was my fault. I gave her the impression I was guilty of something, the way I reacted. She merely read more into what I said than I'd intended."

"But that evening she caught me sneaking off to the office… She'd been watching us. She knew then without you giving yourself away."

"She surmised, that was all. And I panicked. All that money I've given to Geoffrey, all for nothing. I've been such a fool, Mary."

"But she can still spread her damned poison."

"Anyone wicked enough can do that, but if they've no real proof, who would believe them?"

"They would. They'd say there's no smoke without fire. And I wouldn't want to see Will hurt."

But Henry's face was glowing with new confidence. "Mary, it's over. We can forget all about her. We're safe. She can't do a thing, and from now on I'm not paying Geoffrey another brass farthing. We'll put these last couple of years behind us and be back together again. It's been a bloody terrible time for me, and you too. Mary, I can't live without you. I need—"

"No." She broke away as he made to kiss her again.

"Mary…"

"No!" She almost ran from the reception area, pausing only to grab her hat and handbag from beneath the counter. His stupefied gaze following her, she pushed blindly through the glass main door and out into the street.

At the corner she sped on across the road without a pause, heard the screech of a car pulling up sharp, heard the frightened driver's shout, but she didn't even look the man's way as she made for the mews opposite, not stopping until she'd gone the couple of hundred yards to where her flat was.

Will would still be home, on the point of leaving home for Letts' lunch session. He would see her all distraught and ask whatever was the matter. What could she tell him? And he would persist until she finally thought up some lie or other to satisfy him. She stood at the entrance to gather her wits, taking in deep breaths to calm herself. He must not see her like this. But it was hard to control how she was feeling.

She wanted so much to have Henry love her again, to feel his hands on her naked body, have him claim her. But it mustn't happen. It couldn't. With their drifting ever further apart, she had resolutely set her face towards making her marriage with William work. She'd finally made a life with him and Helen, they at last becoming very much a family. Will still worked nearly every hour

God sent, though during the slack time of last year and the first part of this, he'd had more time to give to her and Helen. Together they had taken Helen to museums and just after Christmas to a pantomime at the London Palladium and to the cinema to see Walt Disney's first feature-length cartoon, *Snow White and the Seven Dwarfs*, though Disney's creation of the wicked stepmother had given Helen nightmares for a time so that she and Will had taken turns to go into her bed to soothe them away. The arrival of better weather had found the three of them visiting Regent's Park Zoo and spending another day going up the Thames on a pleasure steamer. With the arrival of summer they had gone rowing on the Serpentine, just like any other ordinary family. Did she really want to spoil all that? Maybe she would never love Will in the same way as she did Henry, but with one lay peace and contentment, if only she let it; the other, anxiety, frustration, and in the end – always in the end – heartbreak. Henry would never willingly allow his marriage to fall apart, that she knew. It was better not to start things up all over again. It was far better to… to what? She didn't know. Only that they could not, must not go back to what had been. It was over. It had to be.

Taking a deep breath to pull herself together, she opened the door and proceeded up to her flat to face Will with a smile.

–

"I can't *help* feeling frightened," Grace said tremulously as Henry told her, a little irritably, over his breakfast eggs and ham, that there was no need to be that terrified. "The newspapers are saying Germany is still ready to march into Czechoslovakia despite all we've told them. France is sending troops to the Maginot Line and cancelling all army leave, and we are mobilising our fleet. Can you wonder we are all feeling frightened? It's not just me, Henry. We are all worried. It *could* lead to war. And Hugh only eleven."

Henry pushed his plate away. "What's Hugh got to do with it?"

"He's only just started his new school. He will feel so alone. And with war coming—"

"We don't know that yet."

She went on as though she hadn't heard him, toying with the boiled egg she had hardly touched. "If his schooling is affected, how will he ever be equipped enough to go on to university?"

Henry got up sharply, dropping his napkin on to the table. "For God's sake, is that all you can ever think about? Hugh? I'm amazed you were ever able to let him out of your sight to go to boarding school. Anyway, it might never come to a war. Chamberlain doesn't want that any more than we do, any of us. He'll do his utmost to ensure against war. So do stop worrying about it."

Stalking towards the door he turned, anxious to calm her nerves for all he had spoken sharply. "What do you intend doing today, dear?"

She still sat at the table as though mesmerised by her hardly touched boiled egg. She shook her head in a dazed sort of way. "It's Sunday. I think I'll go to church and pray for peace – for us all. I might decide to go back with my parents and spend the day with them if you don't mind, Henry."

"No, I don't mind," he muttered. "You might feel better with them."

"I'm sure I will," she agreed wanly. "I'll be back this evening in time for dinner. If I can take the car. Will you be needing it, dear?"

"No," he said shortly and left her to her boiled egg which he knew she would leave uneaten.

Ensconced in the library with his *Times* and his cigarettes – he had already gone through quite a few since getting up this morning – he heard her go upstairs to her rooms, and after a while come down again, saying something to Freeman, their butler, who answered politely. He heard the car come round to the front, its tyres crunching on gravel; heard first one door then the other click closed as Grace and the chauffeur got in, the car starting up with a deep-throated sound, gliding off down the drive. Henry breathed a mt ntal sigh of relief. To be alone, to relax.

Tomorrow morning he would have to drive back to London for the start of a new week. Whether Grace would be with him was up to her. Until then, he would take things easy. This pain in his chest – he ought really to eat more slowly and regularly, unwind a little. Indigestion could be the devil at times. He really ought to pay his doctor a visit. Maybe next week.

He was halfway through another cigarette, the second since coming into the library, when more crunching of gravel under car wheels distracted him from his paper. All thought of peace dissolving, he glanced through the window, half expecting to see the Bentley returning with Grace having changed her mind.

Instead, he saw Geoffrey's Mercedes. For a moment his heart seemed to stop. The only reason for his turning up here would be money, a loan he would promise faithfully, abjectly, to pay back but never would. It was that part which always sickened Henry, that fawning attitude always a front. If only the man could be honest with him.

He already visualised the look on Geoffrey's face as he refused him, for this time he intended to. He would be aghast, disbelief of what he was hearing written all over his face. But there would be no savouring of it, and he was going to have to be strong. He could have shed tears at all the money he'd parted with, had almost broken his back to see the business didn't suffer by selling long-held stocks and shares. But it had suffered just the same.

All those shares in people like Cunard, Courtaulds, Portland Cement, had been bought not long after Mary had saved them from the financial problems following the 1929 crash when others were still off-loading as hope of the shares climbing back to what they'd once been faded. He had congratulated himself at the time and when they had stayed down for ages, had chastised himself for taking such risks. But slowly they had come up. And again he had congratulated himself. Then, with Pam turning up, in desperation to keep Letts from suffering he had sold bit by bit until little was left.

The family trust had remained safe. It was safe still, though it had come damned near to not being so. But paying for Pam's silence hadn't been the worst of it. He had lost heart and that's what had nearly brought Letts to its knees, his lack of interest.

Geoffrey hadn't only taken Henry's money, he'd robbed him of his will and he hated him for that. But most of all he hated Pamela. Geoffrey was a weak, self-indulgent man who thought he could skip over the surface of life hardly pausing to see the ravage he left in his wake. Even blackmail held no deep meaning for him, Henry felt. But Pam was an evil bitch with no heart, or whose heart was a black lump inside her. It was Pam he really hated for it wasn't so easy to hate one's own flesh and blood. Yet because of her, Geoffrey was going to have to suffer too. Henry's only regret as he watched his brother mount the steps to the porticoed entrance in a single confident bound was that it would probably not cause a rift between Geoffrey and his self-seeking wife. Why should it? The two of them were in it together. Well, no more. Everyone has a point when they are at the end of their tether. Today, Geoffrey coming here out of the blue after he had imagined himself out of the wood was that point. Putting *The Times* aside and getting up out of the leather armchair where he had settled himself so comfortably hardly fifteen minutes before, he prepared to meet his brother head on.

He heard the jangle of the doorbell, counted Freeman's steady steps to the door to answer it, heard the exchange of voices, Freeman's measured and polite, Geoffrey's animated and somewhat excitable as it always was, as though he had some enthusiastic piece of information to impart. There came a gentle knock on the library door which opened quietly to his bidding, and Freeman announced: "Mr Geoffrey is here to see you, Mr Henry."

Henry was just taking a deep breath to say, "Thank you, Freeman, send him in," when Geoffrey shouldered past his butler, his face one ingratiating grin.

"Thought I'd just pop over to see you, old man," he said, sitting down in one of the leather armchairs without giving Henry any chance to invite him to.

Henry's face remained stony. He remained standing. "I thought you were in the South of France."

"I was, old man. I was. But with this business of Germany and Italy, I thought it better to come home. Safer here, you know. Funny things going on on the Continent these days. Can't beat being home, times like these."

"So you came to see me? Where's Pam?"

"Oh, she's at home. Said it best I pop in to see you alone, though why is a mystery to me."

Not to me, thought Henry, and aloud said, "So to what do I owe this honour?"

Geoffrey smiled up at him. "Don't be like that, old man. Stiff-necked. I know I've not been around as much as I ought this year. But I know you and that William Goodridge chap, your restaurant manager, between you hold the fort well without my interference. You know I never was much cop at business. I muck things up. Always did. Best to stay out of the way, don't you think?"

He was exuberant. Too exuberant. "So what have you come here for?"

Geoffrey's smile vanished. He became intense, leaning forward. "Don't stand there looking down at me, old man. Sit down."

"I prefer to stand." He reached and took a cigarette from the box on the table next to which he'd been sitting before Geoffrey had arrived. "Geoffrey, I know this isn't a social visit. You never come here uninvited without a reason. You only come here when you want something. So say what it is."

He saw his brother gnaw briefly at his lips, all his pretence of light-heartedness leaving him as Henry had known it would. His lips began to move agitatedly. He even cleared his throat awkwardly, the two-faced bastard, as if he knew nothing of why he could worm money out of his brother whenever he pleased.

"Yes, you're right, Henry. I'm afraid I told a bit of a lie. Pam is still in Monte Carlo. I've got to get back there as soon as I can. The truth is, I've got myself into a bit of debt."

He paused as if expecting Henry to chime in with a reprimand, but when Henry remained silent, he went on.

"You see, I've been playing the casino. Been doing well out of it too. But then, I don't know how, but my luck changed. I mean, when you're on such a winning streak, a little setback is expected before you climb back on to your winning streak. That's what I thought, so I carried on. But I began to lose more and more. I was so certain all that luck would come back. It couldn't just fly out of the window. So I borrowed from a friend. Trouble was I lost that too and he lent me some more. I was sure I'd get it back."

"How much?" Henry couldn't keep the coldness from his tone.

"I really thought I'd get it back, be able to pay him back, but what I owe him has just got more and more and he's turned nasty. I tried to reason with him. I thought he was a friend, but he's threatening to set a few of his 'acquaintances' on me, as he puts it."

"How much?" Henry demanded again.

"Unless I come up with twenty thousand, plus interest – it goes up by the day – I'm in trouble. Bad trouble. I've found out that these *acquaintances* are a syndicate specialising in lending cash. They say they'll lend me more to recuperate but first I must pay back what I owe. If I don't..."

He leaned even further forward in his chair in abject appeal. "You're the only one I can turn to, Henry. I know you'll help me out. I don't want to get myself beaten up. Or worse. Henry, you've got to help me."

Twenty thousand pounds! All Henry could come out with at that moment was to repeat the amount and burst out, "Who d'you think you are – some bloody Rothschild? How in hell's name can you get rid of a sum like that?"

"It's easy enough, gambling."

It might have sounded flippant but Geoffrey's face registered no flippancy, only devastation, and Henry saw all his resolve not to give him another penny flowing away as though someone had opened a valve.

Geoffrey's story had made him blink. He too had come up against crooks. A part of being a restauranteur was to be alive to the various rackets that went on. He was used to sartorial members of the underworld thinly disguised as respectable members of society doing business with each other at his tables, he being slapped jovially on the back, being called friend, with a shady deal or two offered him.

"A few he'd accepted over the years, nothing too drastic. Others he had steered clear of. Geoffrey, aware of such people, should have known what he was getting himself mixed up in. If his story was true. That was a thought – could this tale of his be believed?"

"How could you be so bloody stupid?" he hollered at him.

Geoffrey looked as if he were about to cry. "I know. I should have realised. But I've known this chap for years on and off. I had no inkling. He's well to do, respectable. He knows all the right sorts."

"Of course."

"I never once imagined… He's Italian, but lives permanently in the South of France, has a huge mansion, gives vast parties, all the best people, even royalty go—"

"For Christ's sake, Geoffrey!" Henry's roar cut him off mid-sentence. "I don't want to hear how bloody wonderful this *friend* is — was. How much do you owe together with this interest he's asking?"

Geoffrey's voice sounded sheepish. He sank back in his chair. "Three days have gone by and it's now twenty-one five. Tomorrow it'll be twenty-two and he says he's being lenient by not charging any larger per cent."

Once more he leaned forward. "Henry, I've got to have it. I've got to get out of this. I promise, after I've paid it back, I'll come home. I've learned my lesson. This has terrified me, I can tell you. If you—"

"All right!" Henry stubbed out his cigarette viciously in an already half-overflowing art deco ashtray nearby. Making a rapid calculation, he supposed he'd be able to write out the cheque now and tomorrow get rid of a whole batch of his personal shares. He would not dip into the restaurant any longer. The place wouldn't be able to take it. Nor was that trust to be touched, and anyway he'd have to consult their sisters before he could do that. He'd still have a decent few shares left, depending on what those sold would bring.

Quickly he got his cheque book from the bureau at which his father had so often sat keeping his accounts straight, frugally, astutely amassing a fortune from what his own father had left him, which he'd made from the restaurant his grandfather had begun as a small oyster bar from a stall. Feeling somewhat as though every stroke of the fountain pen was being torn from him, he made out the cheque, signed it and held it out to his brother.

"Twenty thousand. The rest you can find yourself."

Geoffrey was sitting very still. He merely held up one hand and took it rather like an automaton, his handsome face rigid. "I won't have a bean in the world after paying the interest. I was losing around sixty thousand of my own and Pam's money before borrowing in hope of getting it all back." Losing their rigidity, his features began suddenly working. "Henry, old boy, I'm destitute. After I've paid off this loan, I won't even be able to afford to get the two of us home."

Before this last gabble Henry stood gazing at his brother, the pen still in his hand, unable to take in what he was hearing. His mind whirled at the sum confronting him. Eighty thousand pounds. God Almighty! Something snapped in his brain. With a violent wish to kill, he turned and aimed the fountain pen clear across the room with all the strength he had in him. It hit the wall, leaving a trail of ink splattered across the expensive wall-covering as it clattered to the floor.

"Then go to hell! Take the fucking cheque and do what you have to do! I'm not parting with another fucking sou. Damn you and damn her! You and she can do what you bloody like, because I've had enough!"

When he turned, Geoffrey was still sitting there, staring at him. "What am I going to do?"

"I don't care."

"But you've always been ready to help me out of any spot. Why now when I need it more than I've ever done in my life? And my life might even depend on it?"

"Because I'm sick and tired of being blackmailed. I can't even be sure if you're spinning me a tale. You've done that before now. But I tell you this. It's over. You and Pam can tell whoever you like. I don't care any more."

There was a deep pain in his chest making it hard to breathe. It was travelling across his shoulders, down his back, his arm, even up around his jaw. Damned indigestion. Should have been resting after that heavy Sunday breakfast, but instead he was dealing with this. He felt he'd never hated Geoffrey and Pam as much as he did at this moment.

"Blackmail?" Geoffrey was saying. "What blackmail?"

"Don't tell me that," Henry gritted. "You and her had it all nicely sewn up, didn't you? Well, it's over." He screwed his face up with the pain deep in his chest. "You can sing for your supper somewhere else."

He had to get out of the room, get away from that smarmy look of bewildered innocence.

"Why should I blackmail you, Henry? What about, for God's sake?"

"Liar! Bloody liar!"

"I say—" At last Geoffrey rose to his feet, but Henry was railing on.

"You know as much as Pam. Don't tell me she hasn't told you." The pains were making cold sweat break out on his forehead. His cheeks had begun to feel strangely flabby. "One more of your bloody lies, Geoffrey? You and she are in it together."

"In what together?" Geoffrey had come to stand with his face a few inches from his own. "I don't know what you're talking about. And call me a liar again, I'll biff you, Henry, right where you stand."

He got no further. Henry's own fist shot out and caught him clean on the jaw, knocking him off his feet. Not pausing to see if he had knocked him out, Henry turned and made for the door, flinging it open, practically falling into the hall. Collapsing to his knees, arms hugging his chest against the pain there, he felt himself topple slowly forward on to his face.

Sixteen

Henry was in hospital, his wife at his bedside, his sisters popping in from time to time to check on his condition. They would be sad if their brother died, but since their marriages they had not been that close. Of course, if he were to pass on, there would be a will that could disrupt their lives, but they'd pray it wouldn't come to that.

Geoffrey too hung around the hospital but for the most part stayed well away from his brother's private room, consumed by guilt, seeing Henry's heart attack as his fault.

In the background Mary waited discreetly and gleaned what news she could, mostly from William who, virtually running the restaurant single-handed, was being kept up to date with the sick man's progress by his wife.

Sick at heart, Mary spent her time isolated from him on her own and, knowing of his wish that their relationship remain secret, not daring to visit and praying to the God that she, like so many people, seldom thought of except when in need. She even felt, superstitiously, that her lack of communion with Him during easier times could even be being punished, Henry taken from her for all her last-minute prayers.

Pam was another kettle of fish. In the South of France she'd received Henry's cheque with bad grace, cabling her parents to bolster her bank account to pay the interest owing, facing Geoffrey's creditors alone. She had come home to sulk in Epping and have a furious row with Geoffrey - or at least he had had one with her, furious that she could stoop to blackmailing his own brother.

"And how the hell would you have survived if I hadn't?" she shot back at him, striding about the house, he following her wherever she went, intent on having this out with her.

"I wouldn't have been such an fool as to gamble like that," he yelled back. "Him being so generous. I just thought he—"

She turned on him. "You thought! Did you not ever once query *why* he was being so generous – over-generous – with you? Did you not ever stop to *wonder* why he should be that open-handed? Did you not think at times that it was just a little bit unnatural?"

"NO!" was all he said, though he bellowed it out.

"Then you're a simpleton, Geoffrey."

"You should have told me what you were up to. You've been keeping me in the dark and I can't forgive you for that. I always thought we were honest with each other."

"Don't be an idiot, darling. Would you have gone to him so trustingly if you'd known?"

"He accused me of knowing. I was outraged. I was even going to hit him. And all the time…"

"It's done now." Pam shrugged her shoulders. "From now on you will have to learn to draw your horns in, at least until your brother recovers."

"*If* he does," Geoffrey bawled at her. "And if he does, I suppose you'll expect to continue your little racket. Well, I want no part in it. I never dreamt you could be so damned underhanded. I'll never forgive you, Pam."

"Yes you will," she said simply. "You couldn't exist without money."

–

To Mary's intense relief, Grace's also; maybe the vague disappointment of his sisters, kept to themselves, of course; Geoffrey's heartfelt gratitude in no longer having to feel guilt, and Pam's pleasure, Henry began to recover.

He spent weeks in hospital, then convalescing. He should have gone away to sunnier climes to recuperate with winter coming on, but things in Europe remained unstable despite Neville Chamberlain waving his bit of paper at the end of that September signed by himself and the German and Italian dictators, proclaiming Peace In Our Time to the overwhelming relief of the British people. So Henry had spent his convalescence in Eastbourne.

It was there, with the mid-December evening already closing in, that Mary came to see him in answer to a letter he had written her. Making sure his wife and anyone else visiting had left, she crept into the nursing home, telling the sister in charge – who had said that by rights he should now be resting – that she had travelled quite a distance. The nurse relented, saying she would allow her a few brief minutes.

She found him reclining in an easy chair reading a book. Glancing up as she entered a loving smile flooded his face.

"Mary! Darling. You got my letter."

"Don't get up," she urged as he let the book fall to do so. He ignored her concern and came towards her to enfold her in his arms.

"Oh, my darling. I've wanted for so long to see you."

"I didn't dare come before," she gasped out.

"I know," he said as he kissed her, no one here to eavesdrop on them. He looked amazingly well, gladdening her heart.

"Are you all right now?" she asked, breaking away. "No danger?"

"I'm fine now," he said as she remarked on it. "But I've been told I must take life easy – no stress."

At this he gave a bitter laugh as he sat back down in his chair and she dropped on to a hard chair beside him. "That's the biggest laugh. It will all go back to what it was. No difference if I know that bitch."

Mary's eyes widened, discounting his wife. "You mean Pamela?"

For a moment he hesitated, then appeared to come to a decision by the deep sigh he gave. "She came to see me last week. Says nothing has changed. Said she was so glad I'd come through, otherwise Geoffrey would have been lost without his little hand-outs. Hand-outs! Twenty thousand pounds, a hand-out?"

"Good God!"

"Yes. He lost it gambling. But that wasn't all." He quickly related how much Geoffrey had really expected out of him and why, and how he had lost his temper and hit out at Geoffrey, sending him spinning. Then, of course, there had been the heart attack. "Stress. And they say I mustn't be stressed? I told her that if I had died there'd be no more money. She said, 'Yes, there is that.' So calm I could have killed her. I mean, really killed her."

Mary felt the blood flow through her in a hot surge of hatred for those two, and in a rash need to protect Henry, burst out, "You can't start giving in to her all over again. When would it ever stop?"

"I told her that. I said I couldn't go on with it. She was furious, said Grace would hear everything. Your William too." He heaved another sigh. "To tell you the truth I feel I don't care. I'm tired, washed up."

Now Mary felt a different rush of blood, this time of fear, immediately followed by anger, unreasonable after she herself telling him he couldn't go on paying. It was his head on the block if Grace were told, but it would be her marriage as well. Could he who held the key let the door swing wide open and to hell with her well-being, her life? Selfish!

Sharply she pushed away the anger, hearing him say, "It's easy not to care much about things when you don't know when something like a heart attack can happen again. Next time it could be fatal."

This really frightened her. But a stand would finally have to be made. Better to face it and the consequences now than to suffer the stress that this continuous blackmail – one of the most evil of crimes – could cause. In his case it had nearly put an end to his life. She forced herself to be resolute.

"We must be strong. You refused Geoffrey once. That's a start."

"And look where it put me – in hospital."

"But you can't back-pedal now. You can't fall into their hands all over again."

"I'm tired, Mary. Sick of the whole business. But Pamela's right about no more hand-outs for Geoffrey. If I'd died, Grace would have been the one to inherit most of the business, as my wife, and Hugh as my son. Geoffrey wouldn't be left out of course. But I don't think he and Pam would get round Grace as they do me, and she knows it. No, with her it's plain vindictiveness – she enjoyed doing what she did. She'd tell everyone about you and me just for the pleasure of it. I just want to have done with it."

He looked suddenly at Mary, holding her with his gaze.

"That's why I asked you to come – what I wanted to see you about. If I suffer another heart attack, next time could be fatal."

"No!" She couldn't help crying it out, but he held up a hand.

"There's something I need to get sorted out. Forget Pam – though I still live in fear of her one day discovering the truth about Helen, and what I want to say concerns our daughter. Mary, my will is all taken care of. But if Grace does get to hear about you and me, neither she, nor anyone else, not even Geoffrey and Pam, must know Helen is my child. For her sake it goes with me to my grave. Only two others know. My solicitor, who drew up a trust for her and whose profession binds him to secrecy, and William. I have to tell you, Mary, he's known from the time she was born – before, in fact."

Mary gaze remained steady. "I know he does. He's never mentioned it. We've never spoken of it, but I know. I guessed. And he knows that too."

She had always felt a sense of having been cheated, of being a victim of an ongoing subterfuge. "Why didn't you both tell me openly and honestly that he knew? It's always hurt, being apparently kept in the dark, having to pretend he didn't know." Angry tears began to blur her vision. "All this time, Henry. I had a right to be told. I had a right."

"I know. He wanted to tell you, but I thought it better not to. I had no idea you already knew – or had guessed."

"And you put him up to marrying me to get yourself out of a hole."

"I'm sorry, Mary."

"And thought you'd leave me to think it was out of the goodness of his heart."

"It was. He'd been in love with you for years before that."

"And took the opportunity of doing well for himself at the same time. You saw to that, promoting him, *gratefully*." Without warning such a deep bitterness rose within her that it made her draw her breath in sharply. It was as though'd been suppressing it all these years, yet she'd always thought that it had never been there, that she had long since come to terms with that which she had guessed at and suspected to be true.

Henry rose from his chair. "It wasn't like that, Mary. Don't blame him. I put him up to it. He'd lost track of you, but when I... Mary, he loves you. He'd do anything for you. For you he took on another man's child. He asked for nothing. What I gave him, in gratitude, as you've said, he never asked for. You must believe that. He is a good man, Mary."

She sat very quiet, but inside she was a mass of conflicting emotion like a corpse moving and writhing with maggots, being given no rest.

She had been staring down at the soft rug on the floor of this well-set-up private room. Now she looked up to see Henry take a deep breath.

"No matter what you think of us at the moment, I need to talk about Helen." He began speaking swiftly as though fearing to be sidetracked by her obvious distress. "I want to see her future taken care of. I have made a trust for her, as I said. It's all drawn up, in the hands of my solicitor. It will come to her when she's twenty-five. I thought she'd still be too young at twenty-one but later she'd be more astute. I want to see her taken care of when I'm no longer around to look out for her."

Mary brought her mind back to what he had been saying.

"You're not going to die, Henry," she said without energy.

She saw him give an ironic grin. The tone of his own voice was flat, formal. "That's for God to decide. I just want to be prepared, that's all."

A nurse came into the room. "Time for you to go, Mrs Goodridge. Your friend needs his rest."

Yes, thought Mary, *friend*. From now on that was all he must ever be. She loved him still, enough not to continue with any feelings of bitterness. But no more would they be lovers. She was determined on that point. She was the mother of his child and for all these years had been his lover, yet that part was over, though if ever he were in any trouble she'd be the first to go to his aid.

It was as though something had been drained out of her as she left the convalescent home. She could blame neither man for his part in all this, for she was as bad as both of them.

—

"… but from now on, Henry, our marriage will be in name only."

He smothered a bitter grin as Grace stood over him. Their marriage had always been in name only, apart from that one brief fling in the Loire Valley when the hot sunshine had made her give herself to him, from which moments of abandon Hugh had sprang into being.

And now Grace, plump and resolute, stood before him, though her face was as gentle as ever. "I feel sad, Henry, but our marriage must to all outside eyes appear as it has always been. I don't think I could stand an unpleasant divorce. What would my parents, my friends say? I can't tell you how shocked I was by what our sister-in-law – I cannot say her name, will never say her name again – had to tell me. She made her news appear to slip out by sheer accident, but she intended I should hear it, the way she drooled. I refused to give her the satisfaction of knowing how affected I was, but I was sick at heart. I can't bring myself to mention in words what she said had been going on. But I am glad that poisonous viper gained nothing from me to make her smirk. If she expected it she was disappointed. Henry, have you been paying that woman to keep her secret?"

Henry didn't answer. A barrier of silence had grown up between them since his homecoming. He was only too aware that Pam had been hell bent on reaping revenge for his refusal to extend Geoffrey any sum beyond his regular director's remuneration. For months he'd been on a knife's edge, wondering how much Grace knew, if she cared. But she did care. It was in her eyes the rare times they'd met his. She'd look away quickly. She never smiled at him. She, kept out of his way, particularly during the first few weeks after Pam had made her last demand of money from him and had obviously gone straight to her. He hadn't known how much Grace had believed, nor dared he refer to it.

Today it had finally come to a head. Something he'd said had made Grace burst out with what must have been simmering inside her all this time. Poor woman. Stolidly he gazed out through the window at the grounds all green in the bright May sunshine and the trees brimming with blossom and new leaves, just so as not to see the tears glistening in those gentle blue eyes as she went on stoically, "It doesn't matter anyway. Henry, I mean to continue to be your wife. Not for one minute do I imagine you will leave me or you would have done so by now. I believe you too have no wish for divorce, our name dragged through the mire. I can only thank God Hugh has no idea what has gone on – he's too young. It's bad enough knowing the country is on the brink of war without us entering into one. He'll see only two happily married people when he comes home for his summer vacation. He must never know that we are married in name only, as I've already said."

Henry retained his silence. She really did believe her words, that she had brought about a change in their marriage. All that had really changed was that Mary – she and William now practically running the restaurant in his continuing absence taking care of himself – was estranged from him by her own wish. Their relationship would never return to what it had been, that he knew, and he in turn understood and respected that wish. It was that, more than his state of health, which had kept him from visiting London. It was that too which made him sit in, day after day, or stare out at the grounds of his home, smoking incessantly despite his doctor's orders, because he was bored and lonely and missing Mary.

These were strange days. William reported regularly to Henry on how the restaurant was doing, he and Mary still holding the fort remarkably well as a gorgeous summer slowly passed. With Henry's agreement they had opened a roof garden, he organising the funds from his home, to the appreciation of those who came to dance away the warm summer evenings in the open.

—

In the Lett family there had been much discussion about the restaurant's continuance since the deterioration of Henry's health. Needing someone to pick up the reins – temporarily, he'd hoped – he'd spoken to his sisters about who would carry on for the while and had received negative replies. Neither wanted to be saddled with it, their husbands each with their own businesses to concern them. As shareholders they reaped the benefits, but getting their hands dirty, as it were, was a different matter.

Geoffrey had shown himself plainly scared of taking over more or less on his own. "You know me, old man. I could do it with you behind me, us two. But taking it all on my shoulders, on my own…"

Henry had shrugged, defeated by Geoffrey's lack of spunk. Geoffrey was still the handsome and debonair man he'd been in his youth, and just as feckless, just as weak under his devil-may-care exterior. But blood was thicker than water, and Henry had chosen to believe him innocent of Pamela's scheming. She'd led him by the nose and still did. Yet it was very much on her money that they continued their high life though now the country was at war, a lot would change.

It was Mary who had come to the rescue, she and William. They had made a wonderful job of it. He felt proud of them, the place busy as ever it had been, perhaps more so. Many of the old guard still visited but since the outbreak of war the restaurant had been thronged by service uniforms, high and low-ranking officers and their wives or girlfriends turning it into a lively place. Dance bands and cabarets played every Friday and Saturday evening, the old days a thing of the past. Glen Miller music was played now instead of Count Basie, bop instead of jazz, the roar of voices singing "Hang Out the Washing on the Siegfried Line" rather than 'Tipperary". A noisy defiance of Hitler's threats to the British way of life had replaced the sophistication of past years. Money still rolled in as it had always done apart from those one or two blips over the last ten years, his mad scheme to expand nearly doing for him, the crash of 1929 and later his apathy. Well, life went on, but sometimes he no longer felt part of it, Mary going on without him. He just hoped she'd be happy.

–

Mary stood to one side watching the sea of uniforms. It was a strange sort of situation, she in practice, if not in title, taking her husband's place as Letts' restaurant manager, keeping an eye on everything that went on, while Will had virtually taken over from Henry. The two Lett brothers were rarely seen, Henry temporarily retired, as he called it, to his home in Halstead Green, and Geoffrey with only his director's remuneration and his wife's money to keep him. What he got up to these days Mary did not know nor care.

She heard the air raid warning start up, a signal for diners and dance band to retreat to the basement that William had pursuaded Henry to have strengthened, there to continue their evening. Others would leave to go to public shelters. The raid would go on into the night, the music being all but drowned out by what was going on outside over their heads.

Here, as in every city in Britain at present under attack, there was a determination to show Hitler that he would never subdue the British spirit as he had the rest of Europe. In defiance they would roar out "Knees Up Mother Brown", do the Lambeth Walk and the Hokey-Cokey.

She glanced across at William and saw him nod to her to get everyone moving. Going to where the band still played, she announced over the mike that dinner and dancing would continue in the basement for those wishing to stay, and that if they would repair in orderly fashion downstairs, a complimentary glass of champagne would be served to every customer.

Mary thought of Helen as she always did during these nightly air raids. Helen, eleven years of age, was safely in the country, evacuated to the home of an acquaintance of

Henry in Buckinghamshire. Should anything happen to herself or Will during what people were calling the Blitz, what would Helen do? Would Henry take responsibility for her then? There was still that small rankle in his having distanced himself from his part in her child. There was the generous trust he'd made for her, of course, but the giving of money – if one has it – is always far easier than the taking up of responsibility.

Before Helen left home last year, she and Will had meant to explain to her about her true father. But at ten she'd seemed so young, and on top of being sent away, it would have been too much for a child of her age to take. In the end they'd decided to shelve it until things returned to normal and Helen would have them by her side to help cushion any sense of rejection that such news might cause. Mary had watched her child leave with sandwiches for the journey, the little parcel tag tied to her lapel, her large hazel eyes brimming with tears, and had known she'd made the right decision. To have heaped such news on top of the trauma of evacuation would have been more than Helen could have borne. Will had agreed that she'd done the right thing.

"You always do," he'd said, holding her close after Helen had gone.

By now the restaurant was nearly empty. The sirens were dying away. There came the distant sound of anti-aircraft fire. Soon London would erupt with noise: the explosion of falling bombs and the ringing of ambulance and fire engine bells. It was not as frantic here as in the

East End with its docks and warehouses, where buildings still smouldered from last night's raid, but the odd shower of bombs would fall here all the same.

She glanced across the now empty dance floor towards Will and a surge of affection filled her. Natural of him to have stuck by her. Her mind went briefly back to the day he'd told her of Pam's visit, how he had heard her out and then calmly told her she was barking up the wrong tree – that he was already aware of his wife's affair with Henry.

Whether that was true or not she didn't know to this day, but she remembered how she had felt as he said that if she really wanted to go back to Henry, he would never stop her. She had shaken her head so violently, bursting into tears, that he had drawn her close, his arm about her while she had sobbed out her heart on his chest, he gently patting her back to comfort her. When she had recovered enough to tell him that all she wanted was him and intended to stick by him to the end of her days, he'd soothed away her tears and for the first time she had returned his love with all her being.

From the door that led to the basement stairs he signalled to Mary to hurry herself. She looked up at him as though lost in thought.

"Come on!" he urged and saw her nod. But still she held back.

"I'll follow you down," she called across the restaurant to him. "I just want to make sure the main door is locked. We don't want any unsavoury characters wandering in when we're not here."

She laughed. He laughed too. "Don't be too long about it," he called. She looked so beautiful to him, so poised, standing there in that slim, shimmering, deep green evening dress, her hair swept up from her temples, her grey eyes so alive. It was the last sight he ever had of her.

—

Steadying his pint of beer, the man caught William's shoulder as he passed.

"Sorry, mate! Didn't spill any on you, did I?"

"No, that's all right. No harm done."

The collision brought him out of his reverie, seeing young Edwin Lett sitting across the pub table to him. The noise of a lunchtime pub buzzed in his ears as he blinked at the lad.

"Is Helen's mother still alive?" Edwin was asking.

Forcing his mind back to the present, he shook his head, watching the man with the beer find a table just along from the one they were sitting at. "No. A bomb landed across the road to the restaurant during the Blitz. She was hit by flying glass."

He realised he had been telling Edwin quite a bit about Letts, but how much had been in words and how much in his mind, he couldn't say.

"I'm sorry," Edwin was saying. "It must have been awful for you."

"Well, it's a long time ago now. All I wanted to tell you was how it was and how it could be again, if one wanted it to be – the restaurant, I mean."

It struck him that Edwin wasn't exactly showing that much interest in the restaurant, though he was looking thoughtful about something.

"Did you tell Helen about her father after your wife died?" he asked and, resigning himself to putting aside the matter of Letts, William swallowed his disappointment and shook his head in reply.

"It never seemed like the right time. She and I became very close after her mother's death and, once I'd lost Mary, I couldn't face the thought of losing Helen too."

"I see. But was she upset, my uncle dying?"

"A little. He was a friend of the family. But not in the way she would have been if she'd known he was her father. And we support each other – we're like best pals." William couldn't stop the whimsical grin widening his lips. "Until I suppose she meets a nice young man whom she finds herself eager to spend the rest of her life with."

He saw Edwin's eyes light up momentarily and dared feel optimistic – remembered the admiring glances he'd given Helen on the day the will had been read, in fact the way both young people had exchanged silent interest in each other. But this wasn't what he was about at this moment.

"What do you think about the restaurant, then?" he queried. He saw the boy look at him as though his thoughts had been miles away.

"The restaurant?" Edwin blinked. "Oh, you mean about Letts being returned to its old form. Yes, I suppose it could be done."

William warmed instantly to his subject. "You bet it could be done. Think of it, Edwin, filled to capacity, thriving, as great a place as ever it was. But it will take quite a lot of money. And a good deal of enthusiasm. The sort of enthusiasm I've always had for it. I'd be sad to see it all go."

For a moment Edwin said nothing as he sipped at his gin and tonic. Then he said slowly, "I've got money. What my parents left me. Quite a bit. I don't know if it'd be enough to buy Hugh and my uncle's second wife out."

Edwin's eyes had moved towards the pub entrance. They lit up quite suddenly, and following his gaze, William saw his daughter walking in, her expression blank as she glanced around at the sea of faces trying to glimpse one she recognised. Seeing him, her face brightened up and she came over.

"Daddy…"

Seeing Edwin, her grey eyes opened wide. "Hello again. How nice to see you. Have you been here long?"

As she looked at Edwin, William saw a glow in her eyes, and glancing at the young man, noted the self-same glow. He leaned across the table to him, his mind already way ahead of these two young people, as Helen sat. Henry's generous trust for his natural daughter lay just waiting to be used.

"Would you buy them out if you did have enough?" he asked. But Edwin was still gazing at Helen, she gazing back, their regard of each other not diminishing one bit.

Becoming aware that his host was speaking to him, Edwin forced his attention away from the girl and with an effort attempted to concentrate on the older man's question. "Sorry, Mr Goodridge, what was that?" His mind was even now in danger of swinging back to Helen.

"If you had enough to buy them out," William repeated, "would you?"

The eyes of both young people were entwined again, if eyes could be that, but he heard the distracted response, "Yes." Glancing from one to the other, William smiled. The wheel had turned full circle.

As though to prove it, Edwin looked momentarily away from Helen to him. "Mr Goodridge, would you mind if I asked Helen to go to a party with me?" Not waiting for a reply, he turned back to Helen. "Would you?"

Seeing her nod eagerly, her grey eyes bright, William picked up his drink and sipped it reflectively. As though planned by some divine wisdom, Geoffrey's son and Henry's natural daughter would inherit the business of their fathers. It was as it should be. And by the look of these two young people, exactly how it would be – he could bet his last penny on it.

Also by Maggie Ford

A Brighter Tomorrow
A Fall from Grace
A New Dream

The Lett Family Sagas

One of the Family
Affairs of the Heart
Echoes of the Past

Affairs of the Heart

Maggie Ford was born in the East End of London but at the age of six she moved to Essex, where she lived for the rest of her life. After the death of her first husband, when she was only 26, she went to work as a legal secretary until she remarried in 1968. She had a son and two daughters, all married; her second husband died in 1984. She wrote short stories from the early 1970s, also writing under the name Elizabeth Lord, and continued to publish books up to her death at the age of 92 in 2020.

C 03 0330735